BLIND FAITH

What Reviewers Say About *Blind Curves*

"*Blind Curves* is filled with a diverse cast of true-to-life lesbian characters. Shy butches, sexy femmes, closeted movie stars and dykes with disabilities, almost any lesbian can see herself or people she knows in the pages of this book…Fans of lesbian murder mystery will love this book. It's a great summer read and the first in a series. I look forward to more Blind Eye mysteries." — *Lesbian Life*

"The catfight setting for this intricate mystery is the world of lesbian magazine publishing—and because half the writing team (Diane) is the current editor of *Curve*, the plot has a patina of possibility. Some action is set in a park; that the other half of the writing team is a former park ranger adds nicely to the authenticity…With help from their dorky but able-bodied office assistant, the dogged duo clear sundry suspects before the killer—not too obvious, thanks to clever plotting—is fingered." — *Q Syndicate*

"…The authors put their own insider knowledge of the queer publishing world to good use, weaving a tale full of so much detail and believability that it's easy to swallow some of the more outré aspects of the book—like a detective agency which only has disabled PIs. With its expected unexpected twists, vivid characters and healthy dose of humor, *Blind Curves* is a very fun read that will keep you guessing." — *Bay Windows*

Named "Top Ten Lesbian Summer Read" from About.com

"A thrilling new detective series…that takes place in San Francisco, the authors' home, and the descriptions are rich and lively, thus making the city itself an additional character in the novel…This easy to read, down to earth novel is electrifying from the get-go. The pace moves at a quick clip, and the authors clearly explain the complex relationships as they divulge key clues. *Blind Curves* is used metaphorically and literally throughout the book tying together the mystery puzzle neatly in the end…The character development though is what makes this novel stand out and will make the reader crave for more in the series." — *Just About Write*

By the Authors

Blind Curve

Blind Leap

Blind Faith

Blind Faith

by

Diane and Jacob Anderson-Minshall

2008

BLIND FAITH

ISBN 10: 1-60282-041-4
ISBN 13: 978-1-60282-041-8

This Trade Paperback Original Is Published By
Bold Strokes Books, Inc.
P.O. Box 249
Valley Falls, NY 12185

First Edition: December 2008

Credits
Editors: Jennifer Knight and Victoria Oldham
Production Design: Stacia Seaman
Cover Design By Sheri (graphicartist2020@hotmail.com)

Acknowledgments

Whoever first coined the phrase "You can put lipstick on a pig but it's still a pig" probably never gave thought to the magic a great editor can do. As pundits were debating that very phrase every night on the evening news, we were able to escape the heated political battles and immerse ourselves in the alarming world of ex-gay therapy. For a change, to talk with women and men who suffered the indignities of reparative therapy was really an eye-opening event. Our first thanks go to our parental units, who love us for who we are, not who we could be: Marlene Foss and Keith Anderson Sr., Luanne Anderson, Paula Hernandez, and Judy and Wayne Minshall. Our many thanks to Jennifer Knight, our tireless editor, who deals with our TV-centric minds and puts the reins on our penchant for packing in too many storylines and giving characters completely illogical names. Also, thanks go to Len Barot, for believing in us as authors, and to the folks on our BSB team (especially JLee Meyer, Cheryl Craig, Lori Anderson, Connie Ward, Lee Lynch, and so many more that we're forgetting now). Thanks to the fans who've been with us from the beginning (hi, Mom!) and the readers who've discovered us along the way. Props go out, too, to our photographer Kina Williams, the entire *Curve* magazine team, Jake's colleagues at KBOO/Gender Blender and TransNation, Diane's peeps on B6, our tireless supporters at GayWired.com, *Bitch* and *Bay Times*, and, most of all, to you, dear readers, for picking up this book and actually caring enough to read this acknowledgement. We love you most of all.

Dedication

For Del Martin and Phyllis Lyon. May our marriage be as long and happy and loving as yours. We're certainly trying. And to our sibs—Tanya, Keith, Wendy, Michelle, Jennye. You each deserve a book dedication of your own, but who knows if we'll ever get another one, so just to be sure, this book is dedicated to all of you. We can't wait to see what new chapters of your own lives you'll write next.

This book is also in honor of the thousands of LGBT kids and adults forced to try to change who they are in the name of God. If there's one message in this wacky murder mystery, we hope that it's about acceptance and understanding. For every religious zealot that wants you to change, there's another Christian or Muslim or Jew or Buddhist who is preaching tolerance and love. Leave your church and find one that will accept you exactly as you are.

CHAPTER ONE

Mid April

Seventeen-year-old Isabelle Sanchez's body was bent nearly in half. She was doubled over, her long hair draped over the silver trash can she was clutching with both hands. As another wave of nausea crashed down on her, heaves rippled through her and bile burned the back of her throat.

Although Isabelle was no longer focusing on the big screen at the front of the room, the cinematic images flickering across it sent flashes of light into the darkness around her. She heard a woman moan and shivered. Goose pimples speckled what Dom had once called her *dulce de leche* skin. Isabelle thought about Dominique, the way the girl's dark eyes captivated her when they were together. Even though it was just a memory, she could practically smell Dom's musky scent and her body responded, dampening the delicate pink panties she was now forced to wear under the unsightly knee-length skirt. These garments were not her choice. She preferred cotton boy-cut briefs, but like a lot of things these days, she didn't have much choice in the matter.

She glanced up at the screen where two women were having sex—their naked bodies crashing against each other, eyes closed and heads thrown back as they took turns making each other orgasm. Damn it. She was now nauseous *and* horny. What the fuck was wrong with her? She didn't even like porn.

The image in front of her blurred, the room spun and Isabelle puked. She wiped her mouth with the tissues provided. This was apparently all part of the treatment. They wanted her to throw up. Why wasn't the fucking therapy working? She'd been stuck here in this kiddie prison for months on end. Long enough to figure out that the pill she took after lunch, the one the counselor insisted she take exactly ten minutes before going into the viewing room, was what really made her sick. It was meant to. This therapy was supposed to keep her from getting hot for other girls. But it hadn't changed a fucking thing. She'd gotten to the point where she *wanted* the treatment to work. She couldn't take it for much longer.

Dom had abandoned her five months ago, vanishing from Pioneer back in November, and if she couldn't be with Dom, Isabelle didn't care if she *was* a dyke anymore. She didn't want some other girl. Without Dom nothing mattered. They might as well make her a breeder. At least her father would be happy. A few weeks ago, Pioneer Institute added electroshock to her treatment. Isabelle hoped it would work—and *soon*. No wonder Dom ran away. But why hadn't she taken Isabelle with her? Why had Dom abandoned her?

The film reached the end of spool and the screen went blank, shining more light into the room. One of the counselors would come soon to usher Isabelle back to the dorms where she could rest until the full effects of the drug wore off. She hoped her escort was Miss Dix today. She was the coolest Pioneer peep hands down. There was something in Aimee Dix's eyes that made Isabelle feel like the woman cared. Maybe she even felt bad for the kids whose parents sent them to Pioneer.

Isabelle would never forget the day she was dragged in, literally kicking and screaming. As soon as they'd driven through the gates and she saw the razor wire curling above the fence, she'd known she didn't want to be here. When the family attorney pulled her out of the car, she'd kicked him in the shins a couple of times. She could feel the corners of her lips curl into a faint smile just thinking about it. Her Doc Martens must have left serious bruises. Served that fucker right, tricking her into coming here. He'd told her he was paid by her parents. They wanted her at Pioneer. Did that mean *papi* actually wanted her back? Isabelle conjured up an image of her father, House Representative Javier Sanchez, standing in front of a podium with his second wife, Bridget by his side. He was always campaigning, a fake smile on his face while meaningless politico-speech streamed out of his mouth. He'd probably left Isabelle's mother for political reasons, replacing her with that power-hungry Republican bitch when Isabelle was ten. One of his campaign advisors probably had statistics showing a WASPy wife would bring more votes. Javier was light skinned and non-threatening. Like Isabelle, her mother had darker roots, the kind that didn't bleach away. She would always blame Bridget for her mother's death just months later, and for the loss of her mother's extended *familia.* Isabelle hadn't seen them for so long they probably wouldn't know her.

Two years ago, when she was fifteen, she came out to her father and he exploded, threatening to lock her in her room until she'd gotten over the crazy notion that she was a pervert. The next day, while he and Bridget were away, Isabelle bolted, leaving their Texas home and drifting westward. She ended up in LA where she'd lived on the streets, adopted by a gang of Chicana trans girls who turned tricks and injected silicone at pumping parties in the San Fernando Valley. They taught her not just how to survive on the street but how to walk in heels, milk men for money, and work every single one of her Goddess-given assets. Somehow giving strangers blowjobs was worth the freedom it afforded her and the T-girls told her it was easier for lesbians to do sex work since they weren't looking for love from every dude on the street. Isabelle could see that, though she doubted turning tricks was fun for any woman. But Isabelle had gotten picked up in a sting and charged with prostitution six months ago. It turned out the john she'd been busted with was some kind of quasi-famous reality TV star, and the story was quickly plastered on tabloids across the country. Isabelle thought the media leak was probably engineered by the guy's publicist after discovering that Isabelle wasn't one of the bionic girls that usually frequented the strip where they were busted. *Big Brother* sex scandal indeed.

Isabelle could imagine Representative Sanchez's face going crimson with rage and embarrassment when he realized the working girl splayed across the covers of those sleazy papers he so derided was his daughter. If the press had made the connection it would have *ruined* him. And she'd probably be dead now instead of just locked up until someone could cure her lesbianism and turn her straight. Luckily for her, she hadn't used her real name when she was arrested and she didn't have any identification documents on her. She didn't call her father for help, not even after she'd been in jail for a week. She knew he wouldn't come. He could have found her at any point, if he'd wanted. But he and the stepmonster didn't care if she'd *died* on the streets. It would have been politically expedient, in fact, if she had.

So it had taken her completely by surprise when their lawyer, Mr. Ibsen, suddenly showed up and bailed her out. She was even more surprised to learn that *papi* had sent him to bring her home. Then the rat bastard brought her to the Pioneer Institute instead and here she was puking through porn, moping quietly over Dominique, and realizing she wouldn't get out of here unless the goddamn therapy worked soon.

Clatter in the hallway yanked Isabelle back to the present. What was taking so long? Miss Dix should have been here by now. The clamor outside the treatment room was getting louder. Someone was shouting. Isabelle stood up cautiously, checking her balance. The effects of the medication seemed to be wearing off. She moved to the door and gradually turned the knob. It was unlocked so she inched it open. Immediately, a rumbling shook the floor beneath her like a herd of cattle was stampeding down the hallway.

Isabelle flung open the door, dipped her head around the jamb, and found herself looking down the barrel of a gun. A group of men rushed toward her at full speed, dressed head to toe in black riot gear marked SWAT, heavy artillery at the ready. Ever hopeful, Isabelle wondered if they were shutting this godforsaken place down.

"Get back! Get back!" an officer barked, motioning her back into the dark viewing room. Sweet Virgin Mary. Isabelle complied, shutting the door and instinctually crossing herself. Holy Mother of God, what was happening? She crossed her fingers and prayed she was being rescued.

Aneko Takahashi's hand shook, causing the barrel of the nine-millimeter Beretta to stutter across the man's cheek, leaving a crimson dimple. *Good.* She hoped it stung. He deserved it. Time seemed to be passing in slow motion, as though she were in a dream. She watched a bead of sweat slide from the man's hairpiece, roll slowly down his temple and under the arm of ebony glasses with lenses so thick they made his eyes bulge like a goldfish's. The droplet settled near his right earlobe where it irrigated a thicket of bushy, oily sideburns. She was certain that trickle of perspiration meant something significant. Could it be a physiological indication of dishonesty? Aneko wished she could hook the bastard up to a lie detector machine before reiterating her questions.

"Where is my sister? Where is Saya?" she demanded, shouting the mantra she'd repeated a dozen times already. This time she pronounced her words slowly, rolling each consonant around in her mouth and pressing the gun deeper into Dr. Barnabas Gage's flesh to underscore the urgency of her question.

"I've already told you, Miss Takahashi," he said in a slow, patronizing drawl that sounded like it belonged on the Mississippi gulf coast rather than in Northern California. "Your sister ran away with another student. I know nothing more than that."

Aneko's every instinct told her Dr. Barnabas Gage was lying. She was absolutely convinced that something disturbing lurked beneath the cultured veneer of the Pioneer Institute and its creepy administrator. Although she could only speculate on the details, she feared the school was responsible for Saya's disappearance. Perhaps Dr. Barnabas had imprisoned Saya in a religious torture chamber, or convinced Aneko's parents to send Saya elsewhere, to some place even worse than this one.

As she ticked through potential scenarios, Aneko held herself back from imaging the worst. She refused to consider that Saya might be dead.

While she wanted to blame the man in front of her for her sister's absence, she worried that maybe this was all *her* fault. After all, it was she who'd abandoned Saya, leaving her to face their family alone. Aneko couldn't have known Saya would follow in her footsteps, coming out as a lesbian and having the same audacity to tell their parents. Coming out was never easy. Coming out in restrictive Asian American families could be fraught with even more complexity. Aneko had ripped their family apart by bringing her lesbianism into the public sphere. She'd been banished for disgracing their name and the psychological baggage around her traumatic coming out had bogged her down for years.

In that time, Saya had fallen by the wayside, left with no support and the knowledge that sharing her identity with her closest kin could cost her everything. Yet she'd fallen in love with another girl and announced the fact to their parents. Saya had always been the brave one. Aneko felt guilty about not being there when Saya needed her. She hoped to God that she was not too late. If she failed to locate Saya she would never forgive herself. Never.

"For the last time," she shouted, cocking the gun so the meaty, sweaty doctor could hear his minutes ticking away. "Where is my sister?"

Dr. Barnabas seemed suddenly blithe, the pall of his skin brightening. He looked almost hopeful. What had changed? Was he finally ready to reveal the truth? Aneko had been trying to get this guy to tell her where her sister was for two months. He was more and more edgy at each meeting, like a nervous finch about to crash into a sliding glass door. This time he seemed close to cracking, but perhaps that was just wishful thinking. His nervousness had suddenly gone and she saw a taunt in his eyes: *I know something you don't know*.

There was a lot that Aneko didn't know. She hadn't even known Saya had been banished to the Pioneer Institute until Velvet Erickson showed up at her door. The reporter was investigating the institute for a *San Francisco Chronicle* article. She'd told Aneko about reports of several missing kids. The families had been uncooperative and by the time she reached Aneko, Velvet was fresh out of leads and seemed to be losing interest in the story. Saya's trail had gone cold, and Velvet had hinted that Barnabas Gage was a major roadblock in the investigation and seemed to know more than he was saying. Aneko was determined not to leave before she discovered exactly what it was Dr. Barnabas was hiding.

She had to make him tell her. The cold steel of the gun barrel against his temple wasn't the incentive she'd hoped for. Clearly, Dr. Barnabas did not believe she could kill him. He was probably correct in his judgment; her conscience offered an environment rather hostile to homicidal impulses. Still, Dr. Barnabas had underestimated her. She might not be capable of murder, but she was *quite* willing to do him great harm. Aneko slid the barrel away from his temple and took aim at his right knee. She flipped the safety off with her thumb, the way the trainer at the gun range had shown her. Settling into her shooting stance, she braced herself for the gun's recoil. Her index finger curled around the crescent moon.

It took a surprising amount of force to pull the metal back far enough to fire the weapon. She applied more pressure and was rewarded with movement in the trigger. It inched slowly backward just as she heard a din in the vestibule outside, the march of feet rapidly approaching. The door to Dr. Barnabas's office was rammed with such force the floorboards shook. Wood splintered and screws turned projectile as the door was ripped off its hinges.

A gruff voice shouted, "Drop the weapon!" and an avalanche of armed men descended, their weapons aimed at her head.

"Drop the weapon, Aneko." She recognized the voice of Dakota Manning, the female police officer who'd spoken with her about her sister's missing person case. Dakota had been frank with her, explaining that Fremont's police department did not have the resources to devote manpower to every reported runaway or missing person. But she'd at least created a file and posted Saya's information in the National Crime Information Center's vast database.

Dakota repeated her demand forcefully, and her voice seemed to cut through the fog Aneko was in. As she got her bearings, it dawned on her exactly what she was doing: threatening a man's life, at gunpoint, in broad daylight. Cops swarmed toward her. If this didn't cost Aneko her life, it would surely cost everything else that mattered: her job, perhaps even her freedom. She'd never live this kind of thing down. Losing her job, going to prison, the shame of it would be too much to bear. Her life was over. Perhaps it was better to die here, in this room. Aneko could suddenly understand why people chose so-called "suicide by cop." She wouldn't even have to do anything. If she didn't put the gun down they would shoot to kill. She would not have to live through a trial and witness her parents telling reporters what a disappointment she'd always been.

"Aneko, *please* don't do this," Dakota pleaded as though reading her thoughts. "Think about your sister. You'd never see her again. Think about what a terrible burden it would be to her if you died here. Saya would blame herself, Aneko. Do you want that?"

She would *never* see Saya again. She couldn't do that, could she? Dakota was right. She had to live. She had to find her sister. This was about *Saya*.

Although her grip on the gun had begun to falter, Aneko found her voice again. "He's hiding information. He knows more about my sister's disappearance, I can feel it. Maybe he's done something terrible to her. Why else won't he tell me what he knows?"

"Aneko. This does nothing for your cause. If Dr. Gage is involved in Saya's disappearance, he will have to face the consequences." She took a step closer. "Saya *needs* you. She needs you to help find her. Drop the weapon. *Please.*"

Aneko relented. "Promise? You have to promise to find my sister."

She set the gun down on the desk in front of her, her shoulders slumping in acquiescence. SWAT members immediately rushed her, pressing her face down on the floor while yanking her arms back and cuffing them behind her. As she was led to one of the many police units parked in Pioneer's front parking lot, she stole a glance at Dr. Barnabas. This time the smug bastard actually smirked.

❖

As Aneko Takahashi was led away the adrenaline rush from the hostage situation drained, leaving Dakota crashing as though she was coming off a sugar high. She felt the tiredness seep into her bones and settle there, the way it seemed to do more and more often when she witnessed a travesty of justice. *Why did it have to come to this?*

Aneko turned her head and Dakota expected their eyes to meet. Ready to silently convey pity through that connection, she was surprised when it never happened. Aneko wasn't looking at her. Dakota followed the young woman's piercing stare and saw the smirk that distorted Dr. Barnabas Gage's face. *That bastard.* Dakota was positive the son of a bitch knew more than he'd admit about Aneko's missing sister and the other runaway girl, Dominique Marxley.

Dr. Gage wanted so desperately to be a celebrity psychologist on par with Dr. Phil that he insisted on the moniker "Dr. Barnabas," even though he wasn't a doctor of any sort. He did hold a PhD, but in theology, not psychology. Dakota knew a few other noteworthy tidbits about the illustrious Dr. Barnabas, having taken the call last fall when Pioneer reported two of its students had run away. She'd been suspicious from the start when she heard the girls had already been missing for three days before the school bothered to report their absences.

Sure, it was true that adults had to be gone for seventy-two hours before they could be considered missing, but with minors the rules were different, and for good reason. Every hour they were missing was an opportunity for them to get farther away or fall victim to a predator.

And even though the police didn't have the man-hours to track down every teenage runaway, time was still of the essence. The sooner they entered the kids' stats in the National Crime Information Center, or NCIC, the better the chance that they would be located alive.

Although she could not prove it, Dakota was certain that Barnabas Gage had delayed making the missing persons' report on purpose. She wasn't sure what his motive could be. Maybe he just didn't want to admit to the parents that, despite the school's hi-tech security systems and razor sharp fencing, Pioneer could not keep, cure, or even contain it's LGBT students.

She remembered the first time she drove through Pioneer's gates. With its razor wire and grim buildings, it looked more like a high security prison than a residential program for troubled teens. The institute was located on the industrial row of Fremont's Peralta Boulevard where it would have blended into the other featureless buildings if not for the fence and oppressive gates. These were fashioned from thick metal bars spaced so close together Dakota's fist would not have fit between them. Each was topped with spikes so medieval looking they seemed best suited for displaying the heads of one's enemies.

She'd pressed the crackling intercom box and asked for entry. There was no verbal response. Movement caught her eye and Dakota spotted the security camera. She showed it her badge and made a number of euphemistic hand gestures. In response, the hulking gate creaked open and she darted through.

The building was a fortress. Inside the rectangle of walls stood a lawn-covered courtyard and sturdy palm trees. This anomalous retreat provided the idyllic photographs Pioneer used to advertise its adolescent penitentiary. Dakota was generally opposed to the whole concept of ex-gay ministries. No matter how many smiling, converted straights they trotted out for their marketing campaigns, she thought the inference that reparative therapy could change someone's sexual orientation was utterly preposterous. With the research supporting her view, she didn't know how these shady programs continued to operate. They should be illegal. They held children against their will and forced them to undergo therapies that were like military torture techniques, not psychological counseling.

The good doctor himself was a lot like the school, a false front with an artificially saccharine demeanor. From his clammy handshake to his "aw shucks" vernacular, every part of Barnabas Gage was insincere. When he spoke in Biblical riddles, he seemed even more unpleasant, almost sinister.

"I'm afraid, Miss Manning, that they were likely caught in the magnetic pull of the Devil," he'd informed her that day, using the first of many non-sequiturs to avoid giving any real information on the two runaways.

"So you think the girls took off because of the Antichrist? I'm not sure I can put that in my report," she said with just enough sarcasm. If he called her "Miss Manning" one more time she'd strangle him.

"Well, Miss—that is, *Officer* Manning," he stammered, drawing out the word "officer" like it was blasphemy. "We find that the souls most in need of ministering fight it the hardest."

His bullshit got on her nerves. He wasn't helpful in determining how the kids had gotten out of the secured facilities, claiming their escape had occurred in the middle of the night while everyone else was sleeping. Just as the best way to find a murderer was by learning all one could about the victim, recovering a missing teen often depended on examining her habits and family history. So she asked to speak with the other students. Barnabas Gage then became entirely uncooperative and called the school's attorney. It was the first she'd ever heard of a high school with a lawyer on retainer.

If she'd been allowed to speak with Saya's friends, Dakota might have learned sooner that Aneko existed. Older siblings living on their own were often the first destination for runaways. Aneko would have been the logical person for Saya to call for help. The fact that she hadn't attempted to contact her sister didn't bode well.

Dakota couldn't blame Aneko for coming unglued after months of silence about her baby sister and she obviously blamed Gage for that the lack of progress, maybe rightly so. Perhaps if Pioneer had reported the break out when it happened, or if he'd been more forthcoming or allowed the police to debrief the other students—maybe then they could have picked up the kids' trail in time.

At least he'd been straightforward about one thing: he said it would be "most unlikely" for the teens to head home. Neither of the runaways came from a supportive environment.

Dakota's own parents hadn't taken too kindly to her coming out as lesbian, but at least they hadn't sent her to a place like Pioneer. If they had, she was certain it would've been the last they'd see of her. Of course that would probably have been cutting off her nose to spite her face. She was glad that she hadn't given up on her family. Eventually they'd grown into the kind of parents worthy of the dedication and loyalty she'd shown them. Still, it was the hubris of youth to think parental betrayal was unforgivable, so Dakota didn't expect the kids to have headed back to Mommy and Daddy. Still, people were drawn to the familiar, especially when running scared and looking for security.

"What will become of Miss Takahashi?" Barnabas Gage asked, pulling Dakota back to the present and her eyes to his face. There she found a look of concern that seemed heartfelt enough at first glance. But there was something under the surface that made Dakota shiver. She remembered a detail she'd heard about sociopaths, how they learned to model the emotions expected of them. That's what Gage's concern felt like to Dakota. Pure facsimile.

"She's being taken down to the station, where she'll be booked. She'll probably get a lawyer and if the DA and the lawyer can come up with a plea agreement there won't be a trial."

"Oh, yes. Well, it really shouldn't come to that. Can't we just forget about all of this?"

"She held a gun to your head and threatened to kill you, Mr. Gage." Dakota thought she saw him wince at the salutation. He'd made it clear in their previous meeting that he preferred "Doctor," but while it was her professional responsibility to remain polite, it didn't mean she had to do cater to his egotism.

"That young lady was just upset about her sister. I'd hate to see her punished. It seems like your department hasn't been much help to her, but now that she understands the situation, I'm sure Miss Takahashi won't be back."

"*Mr*. Gage, the police can't drop this just because you don't want to press charges." If Dakota hadn't been watching for his reaction, she might have missed the tightening of his jaw that told her he wasn't used to being told *no*.

"Why not?" he demanded. "I'm sure Miss Takahashi is contrite and I'm willing to forgive her."

Although his arrogance irritated her, Dakota wished—in this case—that it were that simple. Aneko had a right to be upset with the lack of cooperation from Gage, but that didn't justify her actions and she hadn't gotten him to admit *anything*. And that made it all the worse that her life might be ruined over this incident. So Dakota wished it could all be forgiven and forgotten. But the law was the law, and she was sworn to uphold it. And despite Dr. Barnabas's bloated assessment of his own importance, his forgiveness meant little. The chief had committed multiple officers and deployed SWAT in order to resolve the situation. No one was walking away.

"I hardly imagine they'll be satisfied with anything short of a conviction," Dakota said. "Especially given all the media coverage this case will generate. With a dozen law enforcement officers on scene, bearing witness, the district attorney's office won't even *need* you as a complainant. They can call any one of us."

Gage didn't speak. His eyes were hooded like a habitual user's. Wondering what he was plotting, Dakota said, "If you feel Aneko Takahashi shouldn't be punished, you could speak with the DA. Maybe you can help reduce her sentence."

He responded with an affable smile that seemed genuine. When he grabbed her left hand, Dakota fought the urge to fling him to the ground in one of the defensive tactics the department practiced regularly. He was damn fortunate not to have gone after her right, which was resting on the butt of her service pistol. As she left, a Latina teenager peered out from behind a door. "Hi. Can I ask you something?"

Dakota glanced over her shoulder to check they were alone before answering, "Sure. What is it?"

"That Japanese woman, what did she do?"

Dakota considered her options. She wasn't supposed to reveal the details of an arrest, and usually suspects were only that; individuals *suspected of* committing a crime. But, as she'd just pointed out to Gage, they'd caught Aneko with her hand in the cookie jar. There was no question as to her guilt and the story was sure to make every news outlet in town.

Dakota kept her answer vague. "She threatened someone."

"Wait." The girl's eyes darted nervously up and down the hall. She lowered her voice. "Is she Saya's sister?"

Dakota nodded. "Do you know Saya?"

"Have you found her and Dom?" The girl's voice cracked as though she were about to cry. "Dominique Marxley?"

Dakota shook her head. "No, I'm sorry. Were you two close?"

Before the girl could answer, there was a noise down the hall and she ducked out of sight, closing the door quickly.

"Hello, officer. May I help you?" The approaching woman asked.

"No, thank you. I'm just on my way out."

She offered a hand. "I'm Aimee Dix, one of Pioneer's counselors. We owe you a great debt Officer…?"

"Manning. Dakota Manning." Dakota took the blonde's delicate hand in her own and shook it. "No need to thank me."

"Oh, don't be so modest. You saved Dr. Barnabas's life. He's such a good man, I don't know what we would do without him."

Dakota searched Aimee Dix's face for a hint of sarcasm but didn't find any. *Could she be serious?* "I was just doing my job, ma'am."

"Call me Aimee. Do you mind if I walk you out?"

"Of course not."

They began walking side by side, and for a moment the only sound was the rhythmic noise of Dakota's leather duty belt shifting around her hips with each step.

Aimee broke the silence. "You said you were just doing your job. Are you a hostage negotiator?"

Dakota chuckled. "No. Just a cop."

"But I understand you're the one who managed to talk that young woman down."

"True, but I had the advantage of having spoken with her before."

"Really?" Aimee stopped walking. Her wide eyes searched Dakota's face. "You *knew* her? Then do you know what drove her to such desperate measures?"

"I only know her in regards to a case I worked involving one of the girls who ran away from this place last November, Saya Takahashi. Did you know her, or the other girl, Dominique Marxley?"

"Yes." Aimee looked down and started walking again. In a barely audible whisper, she added, "So they've never been found."

"Do you know something about this?" Dakota demanded. "If you do, it's your civic duty to come forward."

They reached the front door. Aimee stood there shaking her head. "I don't know what you mean."

"Dr. Barnabas waited *three* days before reporting the runaways," Dakota said. "And clearly Saya's sister thinks he knows something."

"That was Saya's sister?" Aimee's brow crinkled. Dakota wasn't sure if the counselor was frowning at her for doubting the saintly Dr. Barnabas, or if she was considering the possibility that things were not what they seemed. "It's too bad she threw away her life for nothing."

Dakota could not agree more. On the way to the station house, she replayed the conversation with Aimee Dix in her head. Could the counselor really be so naïve about her boss? Dakota wasn't so sure. Aimee had hovered at the front door as though there was an invisible barrier there she could not cross. What made Aimee nervous and how could Dakota get the woman to open up more?

Dakota was lost in her thoughts as she parked her car and made her way past colleagues who wanted to know about the hostage situation. She wasn't looking forward to the stack of paperwork generated by the Pioneer Institute drama. She hadn't been at it long when an unfamiliar man passed her desk on the way to the interrogation room. Dakota immediately pegged him as a high priced lawyer. It wasn't just the crisp three-piece suit, or the Italian leather shoes, or the diamond on his tie clip. He smelled of new cars and old money. Her desk was close enough to the interrogation room that when the door opened, she heard him demand, "Don't say another word."

A detective gruffly announced, "Your lawyer's here."

"I didn't call a lawyer." Aneko Takahashi's surprise and confusion were obvious. "I've never met this man."

How odd. Intrigued, Dakota listened as the attorney explained, "I've been hired by Pioneer Institute to represent you."

What the hell? What kind of game was Dr. Barnabas playing? Outside of domestic disputes, Dakota had *never* seen a case where the victim hired a lawyer to defend the perpetrator. She wanted to hear more, but the lawyer stepped farther into the room and the door closed behind him, sealing him and Aneko in client-attorney privacy. They were still cloistered there a half hour later when Dakota finished her incident reports. She was on the way out of the station house when she collided with an assistant district attorney. Was it possible Aneko was already talking about a plea bargain, even before she'd been arraigned? High priced lawyers really did buy their clients speedier justice.

Dakota was intrigued and suddenly determined to get to the bottom of this. She rushed into her captain's office, closed the door behind her, and began laying out her case.

After several minutes of not-so-friendly debate regarding Pioneer's motives for silencing the runaway's sister, the captain said, "Drop it."

"But, Captain, they're clearly hiding something. That's why they don't want this scrutiny."

"Listen up, Manning, I'm only going to tell you this once before I put you on administrative leave. We've got three Norteño shootings on Jackson and bodies are piling up in this gang war. I need you on that case, the one with corpses, not traipsing around looking for runaways who don't want to be found."

The captain was resolute. Though his words weren't menacing, when he cut a bottom line statement, Dakota knew it was time to move on. That didn't mean, however, that she'd drop it. Pioneer and that creep, Barnabas Gage, were up to something and Dakota wanted someone to get to the bottom of it, even if it wasn't her.

Where, she pondered, did she put that PI's business card?

CHAPTER TWO

Aneko was horrified by what she'd done. She could hardly believe that she, mild mannered Aneko Takahashi, had threatened a man at gunpoint. That uncharacteristic act had led her here to police headquarters where she was locked in an interrogation room, seated across from a very angry looking detective.

It seemed like a very vivid dream, as though she were watching herself on screen. She had been so far removed from the situation she hadn't felt fear until Dakota Manning spoke to her, returning her to her senses. She'd been surprised to find the gun in her hand and wondered if she'd been subconsciously planning for this day when she purchased the weapon three months earlier.

She should have waited longer. She should have planned it better. Instead, she had ruined the only chance she had of finding her little sister. She had failed Saya. Again. After all the nights practicing at the gun range, working to get past her discomfort wielding a weapon, she hadn't been able to pull the trigger. She'd been so close. How had she failed?

Dr. Barnabas had told her nothing. The bastard had sensed her hesitation like a dog senses fear, and he'd used it against her. The realization had hit her while the red-faced detective questioned her. He was threatening her with life in prison. Aneko would gladly have traded her freedom for information that might lead to Saya, but she was no closer to the truth. The detective didn't believe Barnabas Gage knew anything. He even suggested it would suit her if Saya was out of the way and that maybe she'd done something to her. Now she was staring at a lawyer who had just told her not to say another word.

Aneko shook her head. "I didn't ask for a lawyer." Why bother? Everyone *knew* she was guilty. With all those police officers as witnesses, she couldn't imagine pretending she was innocent. She had held Dr. Barnabas at gunpoint. She had threatened to kill him. There was no point denying it.

"I don't know this man," she told the detective. Was this guy even a lawyer or had the police sent him in to get her to admit something on tape? Or was he impersonating a lawyer to get close to her and...what? Kill her? Was she really paranoid enough to believe someone had hired this stranger to harm her? What if she'd been wrong about everything? What if she'd had some kind of psychotic break and had just imagined her confrontation at Pioneer?

Platinum cufflinks flashed under the flickering fluorescent lights as the man extended a manicured hand to shake hers. Aneko instinctively raised her left hand. It didn't get far before reaching the end of its leash. She was shackled to the table with a handcuff. She blanched and awkwardly shook his hand with her non-dominant right.

"Aneko Takahashi," she said. 'Who are you?"

"Michael Carrington of Carrington, Williams and Petereli. I'm here to represent you."

"Who sent you? What do you want?"

"We provide legal counsel for the Pioneer Institute."

"Pioneer Institute?" Aneko jumped to her feet, or attempted to. The cuffed hand prevented her from rising to her full height, which was still a foot shorter than the lawyer. She hated the way white men looked down on her. It always felt patronizing. She wondered if Asian American men felt the same way.

"My client, Dr. Barnabas, feels terrible about what happened this morning."

At her nemesis's name, Aneko stopped listening. She tried to look through the mirrored observation window and catch the eye of a detective. She mouthed, "Help me!" Her pleas went unheeded. "Are you trying to get me to deal with the devil?" she asked the lawyer.

"Not at all, Miss Takahashi." He spoke in a voice that probably soothed most people. It was his job to sound reassuring and infallible. "I understand you've had the privilege of meeting Dr. Barnabas" He didn't wait for her to reply. "My client is not a callous man. He understands that you're overwrought about your sister leaving and never contacting you. If it were up to him the charges would simply be dismissed and everyone could put the incident behind them."

Aneko didn't trust him. What was Dr. Barnabas's game? What did he hope to achieve by sending his lawyer to speak with her? Was this some kind of threat? "Why would he want that?" she asked.

"Dr. Barnabas does not wish to be the cause of further suffering. He has forgiven you your trespasses and believes the incident should now be between you and God. Unfortunately," he sighed for effect, "the state does not see it that way. Therefore, Dr. Barnabas has directed me to provide you with the best possible legal defense."

The entire time he was speaking, Aneko could barely stifle a litany of snide responses. She did not believe for one minute that Dr. Barnabas was genuinely regretful or had forgiven her for the humiliation she'd put him through. Was Barnabas setting her up for a fall? Aneko couldn't think of anything to say. "I have already taken the liberty of requesting the DA's office to meet us here with an offer," Carrington said bluntly. "I'm certain that we can resolve this unpleasantness quickly and allow everyone to get on with their lives."

"Wait. Are you trying to say you think you can keep me from going to prison?" Aneko found it unlikely.

"Yes, I have the utmost confidence."

"And what do I have to do in return?"

"You will be expected to follow a few stipulations before I can officially represent you."

Of course. Stipulations. Aneko didn't like the sound of that. "What kind of stipulations?"

He opened his briefcase, pulled out a typed document and slid it across the table. There were three pages, stapled together in the corner. The legalese was so thick it took Aneko fifteen minutes to wade through. She could feel Carrington's eyes boring through her and she was sure he noticed when the color left her cheeks. Her initial horror was quickly replaced by anger. "You can't possibly expect me to sign this."

"Pioneer Institute has made the generous offer of providing free legal counsel. In return, they expect a few concessions."

"Concessions?" Aneko's voice broke as she struggled to control the ball of rage burning in her chest. But she didn't want to be the good little demure Asian girl. Not now. She wanted to be the dragon lady, she wanted to be a sword-wielding warrior princess. "Agreeing never to search for my little sister again is not a *concession*! Agreeing not to speak with law enforcement or the media regarding Saya's disappearance is *not* a concession. Signing a non-disclosure agreement is not a concession. How can you expect me to sign this?"

If she were going to sell her soul it wouldn't be to keep herself out of prison. It would be to ensure Saya was alive, safe, and happy.

Pioneer's legal counsel responded to her outburst with narrowed eyes and a chill in his voice. "Miss Takahashi, you seem to be forgetting that Pioneer's good graces are the only thing standing between you and an eight by ten prison cell. Let me explain your options. A dozen officers witnessed you engage in false imprisonment, battery, and assault with a deadly weapon. That means, even without Dr. Barnabas's testimony, they've got you dead to rights. The little stunt you pulled probably cost the city twenty or thirty thousand dollars."

Aneko felt her eyes open wide. Could it really be that much?

"No doubt it's going to make the lead on tonight's news and there will be a great deal of pressure on the DA for swift and decisive justice. The longer you put off arranging a plea the less likely they'll be to accept one."

"I could plead innocent."

He scoffed. "And you will certainly fail. No jury in their right minds would find you anything but guilty. You'll be sent to Coachella where, if you're lucky, you'll end up as someone's prison bitch and you'll only be assaulted by one violent felon at a time."

Aneko knew his conjecture was unlikely but it still bothered her.

"Those concessions you refused to accept? A lot of good that will do you behind bars. No one will listen to your paranoid fantasies and you won't be there when your sister finally does come home. She'll be forty-something by the time you get out and I'm sure you'll have plenty of time to catch up. Unless she doesn't want an ex-con hanging around her kids."

Aneko flinched. His words stung her as sharply as if she'd been slapped. She considered what it would be like to miss all of the important moments in her sister's life: her commitment ceremony, the birth of her children. What would it be like to be a stranger to her niece and nephew? To miss out on their childhoods? Showing up in their lives twenty years from now…

"You probably shouldn't worry about that, though," Carrington continued. "A little thing like you'll be shanked the first week out. You won't ever see Saya again. You won't be there for her when she needs your help."

Aneko started crying. The lawyer had her ticket. He was quite skilled at calling out all her hot button issues, her fears of prison, of being unable to help Saya, let alone never seeing her little sister again. She'd heard enough. "What do you want from me?"

Despite her growing concern about Pioneer and Dr. Barnabas's role in Saya's disappearance, she refused to believe Saya was dead and beyond her reach. Carrington was right, Aneko couldn't bear if she died or was locked away when Saya was found. Without her, Saya would be alone in the world, sixteen without any family.

"Sign here." He handed his pen to Aneko, who signed and dated the document where he instructed.

The pen shook in her hand. Aneko was an honest person. Adding her signature and initials to a legal document was a serious vow, and she didn't know how she was going to commit to something she could never really, truly, promise.

Then she was struck with the solution. The wording prohibited Aneko Takahashi from searching for her sister Saya Takahashi. It did not prohibit others from looking on her behalf. And it did not prohibit her from searching for the other girl who had disappeared from Pioneer with Saya. Locating Dominique Marxley would surely lead her to Saya. Finally a ray of sun in a gloomy day.

Fighting the smile she felt sneaking from behind the clouds, Aneko confidently initialed the spot indicated. The roller coaster of the day's emotions was nearing its end. She felt her resolve returning and hope glimmer. She was going to find Saya. Nothing but death itself would keep her from that quest and she was willing to risk everything for it. If Pioneer was willing to help her escape a prison sentence, more power to them. She was certain it meant Dr. Barnabas was indeed nefarious. He had something to hide, something that was so important to keep from the light of day that he couldn't tolerate the scrutiny of an investigation and a trial. Aneko was more determined than ever to uncover his secrets.

She had to admit Pioneer's lawyer was *good*. Not morally speaking, of course, but excellent at doing his job. It was almost frightening.

Although she could not see her watch below the handcuff, she reckoned their subsequent meeting with the assistant district attorney lasted no more than a half an hour. During that time Carrington argued convincingly that Aneko was a fine, upstanding woman whose angst over a missing sister had caused her to temporarily lose her grip on reality. With her own lifestyle at odds with Pioneer's mission, it was not surprising that she'd blamed the school for her sister's disappearance.

Aneko found it disturbing that the attorney knew so much about her: that she was a lesbian and estranged from her family, that she lived in Daly City and was involved with the local Asian American community, where she volunteered teaching English as a Second Language, that she spoke five languages and worked as a translator and had even, on occasion, assisted local law enforcement when they required translation services. He also mentioned that Aneko held several degrees, including one from Stanford, and that she'd never had so much as a parking ticket.

She wondered how Carrington, Williams and Petereli had been able to compile such detailed information on her during the brief interlude between her arrest and Mr. Carrington's arrival. Had the law offices researched her background prior to the Pioneer incident? If so, why? Clearly they would not have undertaken the task unless directed to by their client. Had Dr. Barnabas told them to investigate her background?

The ADA seemed to know Carrington well and did not seem particularly hostile toward the attorney or his arguments. Aneko caught herself imagining the two were conspiring. She shook the thought from her mind, telling herself her theory was ridiculous. Just because Mr. Carrington's defense revolved partly around Aneko's disintegrating mental state did not mean she needed to oblige them by *actually* spiraling into paranoia.

Still, the ADA seemed to concede quickly to a plea bargain that involved no incarceration, only three hundred hours of community service and five years probation. Aneko had to relinquish her gun permit and undergo psychological counseling. She could feel her face burning in embarrassment. The reserved and levelheaded members of her community did not believe in psychological counseling. Now, she was facing court mandated evaluation and treatment. *It's better than prison*, she quickly reminded herself.

After the agreement had been reached, she was released into Mr. Carrington's custody. He accompanied her to the courthouse, where she stood in front of the judge and entered a no contest plea. The ADA read aloud the terms of their agreement and the judge accepted it without blinking.

Exiting the courtroom with Mr. Carrington by her side, Aneko felt again like she was caught up in a vivid dream. She could hardly believe that she was free to go. She knew the American justice system was inherently flawed, but she'd never expected its defects to work in her favor. Being a member of a model minority certainly had its advantages. As selfish as it was, she had never been happier to have the color skin and gender she'd been born with. She was quite sure that if she'd been a young African American man she would not have left Pioneer Institute alive, let alone escaped incarceration.

As they stepped into cool evening air, they were immediately mobbed by a media frenzy, light bulbs flashing in her eyes, microphones shoved at her face, questions shouted at her from all angles. "Are you the woman who held an entire school hostage? What were your demands?"

"Aneko, over here!" shouted a familiar voice. Velvet Erickson tried to push her way between two television cameramen. "Did Barnabas Gage tell you anything new?"

Before she could respond to the onslaught, Mr. Carrington grabbed her arm and twisted it, yanking her toward him. She felt his hot breath on her cheek as he growled, "No press. Remember our arrangement."

Aneko nodded and avoided Velvet's eyes. She kept her gaze on the ground as Mr. Carrington dragged her through the crowd. He offered to drive her home but Aneko refused. She would take public transportation instead. She wanted to get as far away from him as she could. He wasn't so easily deterred, though. As she walked to the nearest BART station, he followed her in his BMW. He didn't even try to hide the fact he was trailing her.

She hoped that he didn't follow her onto the train as well. He probably wanted her to see him, so she'd know he was watching and wouldn't run off to speak with the media. He needn't have bothered. She had no intention of speaking with the press, not even Velvet Erickson. Aneko had her sights set on a different person altogether. She needed Yoshi Yakamota, the PI Velvet had recommended. As soon as she'd learned that the Blind Eye Detectives Agency was run by a Japanese American woman, and a lesbian no less, Aneko knew where she would turn if she failed in her own investigation.

Chapter Three

Yoshi heard a crash from her father's room and rushed toward the sound. "Tucker? What was that?"

"Uh…I'm so sorry, Yoshi. Don't come in, okay?"

"Why not? What have you done? What don't you want me to see?"

"No, I just don't want you to hurt your feet."

"What did you do? What have you broken now?"

Why couldn't that girl learn to be careful? Despite her ability to organize the house in a way that facilitated Yoshi's independence, Tucker Shade was so clumsy anyone would think *she* was the one with sight issues the way she knocked things around. It was as if she wasn't in touch with her own body, as though she did not know long her arms were or the dimensions of the space she inhabited. Several teacups and a vase had already borne the brunt of those miscalculations. Still, Yoshi was almost beginning to enjoy the company, and she relied on Tucker more than she cared to admit. That did not prevent her from longing for the day she could have her house, and solitude, returned.

"I don't know what happened."

The sound of Tucker's choked voice quelled some of Yoshi's anger. She fervently hoped the younger woman did not burst into the tears that her quavering voice seemed to threaten. Yoshi did not want to be in the position of comforting her. What would she do if Tucker threw herself into her arms? Yoshi put a stop to that line of thought before it lured her into dangerous waters.

"I was just dancing around with my iPod on," Tucker continued. "And then I guess I knocked it off the shelf."

"What did you break?"

"One of the cat statues. I'm sorry."

Not one of her father's *Maneki Neko*! Yoshi felt like she'd been punched in the stomach. She grabbed onto the door jamb. Hiroki Yakamota had treasured his lucky cat figures. They were one of the few things he held onto that tied back to their ancestors. As he lay in that hospital bed, barely able to breathe, dying from a vicious stabbing, he had used his failing strength to pull her close and whisper in her ear, begging her for a final promise—she must never get rid of the matching cat statues.

The porcelain figures depicted Japanese Bobtail cats, each with a paw upright in the traditional Japanese sign of beckoning or welcoming. The two cats were mirror images of each other. The smiling cat raising its left paw was said to attract wealth, while the glaring cat raising its right paw symbolized the feline ability to see in the dark and was said to protect from evil. It was supposed to protect the owner from unseen dangers and defend her home and all those who lived in it.

"Which one did you break?" Yoshi asked.

"The one without the smile."

Damn. Yoshi had never known her father to be superstitious and did not know if he believed the lucky cat figures really brought the good fortune and protection they were fabled to bring, or whether the pieces held sentimental value. Still, she had honored his wish, keeping the two cats where he'd displayed them, in the southeastern corner of his room. Now one was gone. The pair was torn asunder. Without the fabled protection, would her home suffer? She felt an eerie coldness on the back of her neck, as though a cool breeze had tousled her hair and dried the perspiration from her skin.

"Yoshi? Yoshi, are you okay? You look like you just saw a ghost."

"They were my father's." It was all Yoshi could say.

She barely registered that Tucker had leapt over the scattered shards on the floor. Before she could react, Tucker had one hand around her waist. With the other she lifted Yoshi's arm and draped it around her neck. They had never been so physically close. Yoshi flinched away from the contact as though she'd been burned.

If Tucker felt the tension in her body, it did not deter her. She walked into the living room, pulling Yoshi with her. She was surprisingly strong, lifting Yoshi's hundred and fifteen pound frame so her feet were barely touching the floor. "We're at the sofa," she said. "I'm going to put you down, okay?"

Yoshi nodded. The bob of her head caused her face to brush against Tucker's. When their skin touched, electricity flowed between them. Fine hairs on Yoshi's cheek stood on end as though she'd laid hands on one of those silver balls at the Exploratorium science museum. She was sure her face flushed in response and she prayed that Tucker would not notice. What was wrong with her? Perhaps she was coming down with something.

Tucker lowered her to the quilted ecru divan and released her. As she pulled away, Yoshi had a strange sensation, as though tape was being ripped from her skin and tiny pieces of her soul were torn away with it. The parting was almost painful. Yoshi was certain now that she must be getting ill. She felt faint.

"I want you to lay down for a moment," Tucker's soft voice commanded.

"All right." Yoshi acquiesced.

"Don't worry. I'll clean everything up, I'll buy a replacement, I'll do whatever it takes, okay?"

Yoshi nodded. She closed her eyes and lay back on the divan. She listened to Tucker's footsteps as the younger woman walked into the kitchen. A cabinet door opened and Yoshi imagined that Tucker was collecting the dustbin and small hand broom. When she passed by on her way to the guest bedroom, Yoshi heard something bouncing against Tucker's thigh. The garbage bin from under the sink.

Tucker's footsteps continued to the back room and then she set down the garbage can and dustbin. Yoshi could hear the sound of ceramic shards swept up and dropped into the garbage.

Suddenly she heard Tucker exclaim. With Tucker's voice muffled by the walls, Yoshi thought she heard, "What the *hell*?" She wondered what Tucker had really said.

"Did you cut yourself?" Yoshi asked when she heard Tucker's footfalls echo down the hall.

"Did you know about this?" Tucker demanded, waving something near Yoshi's face that fanned a cool breeze.

Yoshi smelt musty papers that reminded her of the vintage stores and antiques shops she had frequented with Velvet years ago. She crinkled her forehead, trying to imagine what Tucker might have in hand. "What *is* it?" She asked.

"Letters. There were *letters* in that cat."

Yoshi sat up so fast if made her head float away from her body. Gravity yanked it back. "Excuse me? Which letters?"

"There's a stack of letters, tied together a ribbon. I guess they must've been inside that lucky cat statue." Tucker placed them in Yoshi's hands.

Yoshi's fingers confirmed what Tucker had said. It was a bundle of perhaps a dozen letter sized envelopes bound together. She could smell age and ink and something else—the faint scent of a familiar perfume.

"Whom are they addressed to?" Yoshi asked.

"I don' know. It's Greek to me." Tucker laughed. When Yoshi didn't respond, Tucker added, "Sorry, bad joke. It's in Japanese, I think."

Could these letters belong to her father once upon a time? Yoshi pondered. "Would you mind fetching a pen and paper?"

"Sure. Be right back." She heard Tucker dart away before returning a moment later to thrust a pen and spiral notebook in Yoshi's hands.

Yoshi swept her finger tips across the page, verifying that it was a clean piece. Then, trying to keep her penmanship level, she carefully drew the Japanese letters that made up Hiroki Yakamota's name. "Does it look like this?"

She handed the letters and notepad to Tucker.

"Yeah! That is it. Does that say your dad's name?" Yoshi heard Tucker's fingers run along the page, as though she were tracing the lettering. "It's beautiful," Tucker whispered.

Who had written letters to her father? Yoshi wondered. It was not as though her father had dated or had lady friends after her mother passed away. Yet these letters were obviously important enough for her father to keep. Did he want her to have them? If so, why had he hidden them?

Suddenly, it was like the letters had conjured Hiroki Yakamota from the dead. She could almost feel him standing in the room with them, and she was certain there was something he wanted to say. But he couldn't speak. She was sure he would be signaling her somehow, trying to explain through gestures what he meant. But she could not see the expressions on his face or decipher the motion of his hands any more than she could read the words from these letters now.

Although her senses had heightened and she had gained new skills since her eyesight dimmed, sometimes she still felt so *disabled* by her blindness.

"What is the return address?"

Tucker shuffled through the envelopes and then replied, "Uh, there isn't one. Not that I could read it anyway."

"Will you open them?" Yoshi asked. *Just in case.*

She listened as Tucker carefully removed each letter from its envelope and spread it open.

"Okay?" Tucker said when she was done.

"Is there *anything* written in English?"

"No, I'm sorry."

"All right." Yoshi sighed. "I will simply have to locate someone who reads Japanese."

"Is this the date?" Tucker asked. "These three letters up near the top?"

"Yes, probably." Yoshi did not know how that would help.

"Maybe I could at least decipher the dates. That way you'd know *when* they were written."

"That is a nice idea, Tucker, but I don't own a Japanese key board."

"Oh." Tucker sounded deflated, and then changed her tone. "I could try it the other way around, entering English dates into a translation site and comparing the results."

Yoshi smiled at Tucker's tenacity. "If you would like to try, that would be very nice. Remember that in Japanese the year comes first, then month and then day."

❖

Yoshi Yakamota was not easily swayed. The P.I. had long since learned that people were fallible, that truth was subjective and that even the best-intentioned client could be deceitful. But she had to admit Aneko Takahashi's plight had moved her more than anything had since, well, perhaps since Velvet herself was indicted for murder. A gay elder sister, a missing queer teen, and an ex-gay cult—it all had the makings of a lesbian mystery novel. For Yoshi, assisting a beautifully spirited Asian American lesbian in need was a reason enough to consider the job.

With the PowerBraille Display Unit, the gadget her staff gave her last Christmas, Yoshi could finally do her own Internet and database searches. The PowerBraille system translated what was on the computer screen into Braille she could read with her fingers. So, even though she'd normally assign the task to Tucker, Yoshi had been thrilled to do it herself. Independence really wasn't overrated.

She had been able to verify that Saya Takahashi and Dominique Marxley's names, dates of birth, and descriptions were entered into NCIC. This would enable law enforcement officers to identify the girls as runaways if they were picked up for something else. Yoshi also emailed photos of the missing teens to police departments in cities where they may have traveled. Although she focused primarily on California municipalities, Yoshi distributed the pictures to localities as far away as New York City and Key West.

After several fruitless days, the case had driven Yoshi to the Pioneer Institute to come face to face with Aneko's nemesis, the supposedly affable Southern gentleman known as Dr. Barnabas—preferring to be called by his first name like pop psychologist Dr. Phil. Her background check revealed that Dr. Barnabas was neither a medical doctor nor a psychologist, but he did have a PhD in spiritual studies from some religious-based school.

"As I told you Miss…it is Miss, isn't it?" The good doctor was droll and borderline offensive. No, not even borderline. Every word out of his mouth prickled her, raising her ire another ten percent. She was certain he thought the options for women were either Miss or Mrs. No *Ms.* for Dr. Barnabas.

"Yoshi will do just fine," she said flatly.

"Oh sure, you modern gals. Tell me, have *you* accepted Jesus as your personal savior?"

The question caught Yoshi off guard. It took her a second to overcome her surprise. "That's really none of your business, Mr. Gage, and I implore you to answer my question regarding Saya Takahashi."

"Very well." He sighed. "As I said Miss Yoshi, I don't know where

Saya is. She ran away with that other girl and we haven't seen her since. We're not a prison or agents of the state. If our clients choose to leave the program, we simply do not have the resources to chase them down. That remains up to our clients' legal guardians. Are Mr. and Mrs. Takahashi aware that you're here?"

"As *I* explained, Mr. Gage, I am not at liberty to reveal the name of *my* client. But let me assure you that my client's interest in locating those missing girls will not be easily deterred. As their agent, neither will I." Yoshi was peeved. Barnabas was stonewalling, playing little word games to stall her from obtaining any real answers.

"Let me guess: Aneko Takahashi?" His tone was sharp; she sensed the flash in his eyes. The idea that Aneko had hired a private investigator enraged the man. She could hear it in his voice. He had spit *Aneko* as though it were an epitaph. Dr. Barnabas quickly recovered his composure. "That poor confused woman. Definitely a case of spiritual crisis. It's such a shame to see someone turn their back on Our Savior. I'm sure her parents regret never intervening on her behalf. She could use our spiritual therapy as much as Saya."

Dr. Barnabas had passed his anger to Yoshi. She was livid. But she was as well trained in covering her anger with politeness as the Pioneer director. After another fifteen minutes of annoyingly endless back and forth, she hit on a point that seemed to infuriate Barnabas.

"While we certainly wish you well in locating these delinquent girls, we cannot violate our clients' confidentiality, endanger our program, or submit our already fragile students to the allegations of a disturbed woman or the political machinations of our enemies—those who will do anything to further the gay agenda. I'm quite willing to release the personal belongings of the girls who ran away, but I must follow proper procedure."

Yoshi was pretty certain Dr. Barnabas would not be a stickler for regulations if they didn't run counter to his private agenda.

"I'm prohibited from releasing personal items to anyone aside from the student's legal guardians. Still, I'm not unsympathetic to your cause," Dr. Barnabas said. "So here's what I'm going to do. If you can provide a signed statement relinquishing their children's belongings to you, I'll release the items in question."

Although it sounded like she had won a concession, Yoshi did not believe Dr. Barnabas would give up so easily. He must think he was sending her on a fool's errand, the kind of impossible mission of Scarborough Fair. Why was he so confident she would be unable to get signed releases from the missing girls' parents? Before Yoshi was able to decipher the enigma, Dr. Barnabas terminated their meeting.

"Now, I am afraid that I must ask you to leave. I am a very busy man and have much better things to do then to sit around talking about lost causes."

Dr. Barnabas pressed Yoshi's purse and cane into her hands and escorted her to the door with a hand on her bicep. Through the thin fabric of her satin blouse, Yoshi could tell that his hands were clammy but smooth. This was not a man who worked with his hands for a living or a hobby. Judging from his cold and brusque demeanor, Dr. Barnabas was also a man with secrets.

Yoshi intended to reveal those secrets. And she yearned to debase the arrogant man. She vowed to return with the exact item he was so certain she could not obtain—permission for her to gain possession of Saya and Dominique's abandoned belongings.

❖

Nathalia Marxley sounded exactly as Yoshi had imagined, a nasal-voiced, slight woman who was probably more comfortable on New York's Upper East Side than quiet and woodsy Mill Valley, California. She had the manner and cadence of a woman who was used to people being awed by her grace and beauty. From what she had already learned about Dominique, whose friends called her Dom because she was a butchy tomboy who never lived up to her parents affluent upper class standards, Yoshi was certain that Nathalia was a formidable influence in the girl's life and a demanding, if not overbearing, arbiter of Dominique's social failures.

"If I could learn a bit more about your daughter I'm certain I could find her and the other missing girl." Yoshi tried to appeal to Nathalia's motherly instincts but when the wealthy woman did not respond she tried a new tactic. "I am sure you do not want it publicized that Dominique is living on the streets somewhere."

Nathalia was silent. Yoshi was about to speak again when the woman's scent—a mixture of rose, sandalwood, pepper, and merlot—wafted toward her. Nathalia had moved, Yoshi realized, and was dabbing her eyes. Before Yoshi could console her, Nathalia spoke in a quiet, defiant manner.

"I appreciate your concern, but Dominique is dead to me. I don't want or expect her back in my life. Wherever she is, she's on her own now. I have no interest in tracking her down."

Yoshi was stunned into her own silence.

"I know that sounds cruel," Nathalia continued. "But her antics have caused me a great deal of grief over the years. She's been kicked out of three different boarding schools."

"I understand," Yoshi began, although she did not. How could a mother turn her back on her own daughter? "The teenage struggle to differentiate with their parents can lead to many acts of rebellion—but surely once that stage has passed—"

"Are you a *lesbian*?" Nathalia demanded unexpectedly.

"I cannot see how my sexual orientation is any business of yours," Yoshi responded.

"I will take that as a yes," Nathalia said with a sneer obvious in her tone. "Correct me if I am mistaken, but my understanding is that *you people* believe orientation is fixed."

"That is the conclusion that scientific researchers have made, yes."

"Well, you cannot have it both ways. Either my daughter's penchant for messing around with other girls and hanging out at queer bars will not change when she gets older, *or* she was degrading herself with this debauched lifestyle out of teenage rebellion—in which case a place like Pioneer might have turned her around."

"Teenage rebellion is hardly limited to gays and lesbians. You know, many lesbians settle into couples and live lives not so different from their heterosexual counterparts."

Yoshi could feel Nathalia's eyes boring into her and wondered what the woman hoped to convey with the stare.

"I'm afraid my daughter was not cut from the Marxley cloth. I've come accept that she's not going to be a part of our legacy. Pioneer was her final opportunity to redeem herself, we were quite clear on that. If she threw that away..." Nathalia did not complete her sentence. Yoshi thought the woman had shrugged. "Now, if you'll excuse me, I have appointments I must keep."

Her clothing rustled as Nathalia stood. Yoshi took the cue, following her toward the entryway and exiting through the already opened door. As she stepped away from the Marxley house, she wondered what Dominique's childhood might have been like with such a cold and controlling mother. Shuttled from boarding school to boarding school, expelled from each for simply being herself, trying to come out in a world of elitism and affluence and indifference.

More determined than ever to find Dominique and Saya, Yoshi hoped that the latter's parents were more concerned for their daughter's welfare, and more helpful in locating the missing girls than Nathalia Marxley.

❖

Aneko Takahashi's parents lived at the end of Sea View Drive, on a property so large the nearest neighbors were a half block away. Yoshi remembered the neighborhood as an upscale one offering unimpeded views of the Pacific Ocean. Hedges and rows of Douglas fir and redwood trees spared the sprawling houses from noisy neighbors.

The homes were perched on a cliff hundreds of feet above pounding surf, and Yoshi recalled a particularly rough El Nino winter, when torrential rains undercut the cliff, ripped houses apart and sent them crumbling piece by piece into the waves below. She hoped the Takahashi residence was set well back from the cliff face and not at risk of tumbling over the edge.

She could not see, but her cab driver, although his services had not been requested, was quite willing to describe the view. "Never been out here before. Guess rich folks don't take a lot of cabs." He spoke with an accent that had an Americanized Jamaican lilt. "Wait, this your house?"

"No, far from it." She chuckled.

Yoshi grew up in the vibrant Japantown and her life with a middle class cop father was far from that of the Takahashi family's. Hiroko Yakamota had been many things, but affluent was not one of them. Still, he had raised his daughter to value the life she had and she was not intimidated by wealth.

"Whoa," the cabbie said. "Thought the road ended here, but there's a private drive. That where we going?"

"Yes." Yoshi felt fairly certain of her answer.

"There's a call box. Who should I say—"

"Yoshi Yakamota. They should be expecting me."

With a buzz and click the lock released and the gate creaked slowly open. From the sound of it, Yoshi imagined a heavy metal barrier. As they drove down the paved driveway the cabbie whistled. "Bet that yacht cost more 'n my house. My God, that's an Aston Martin. *And* a Bentley?" He let out a long, low breath of air. "Man, these people are fucking *loaded*."

When he let Yoshi out she asked him to describe the approach to the home, so she knew whether to expect marble steps or a winding walk guarded by elegant topiary. By the time a soft-spoken Hispanic woman opened the heavy wrought iron door, Yoshi had braced herself for the worst. The Takahashi's maid led her to a sitting room and brought her iced tea, which Yoshi sipped until she heard dainty steps enter the room.

"Miss Yakamota?" The woman's voice was as wispy as her walk, and Yoshi imagined its owner moving with the grace of a dancer. "I'm Mrs. Takahashi. Thank you for calling ahead."

"Of course. As I mentioned on the phone, I run the private investigation firm, Blind Eye Detective Agency," Yoshi said, as a reminder.

"Yes. You were a little vague about your intentions. How may I be of assistance?" Her query was formal but not standoffish.

Yoshi quietly explained the situation while Mrs. Takahashi occasionally murmured her understanding. She had barely concluded when a man stormed into the room, demanding, "What is going on here?"

Yoshi's heart sank. She had not expected Mr. Takahashi to be home from work so early. She had hoped to preempt his arrival, but her miscalculation may have doomed her visit to failure before she had made her first request. In traditional Japanese homes men were the head of the family and women were expected to defer to them. By speaking with the wife instead of directing her questions to Mr. Takahashi, Yoshi could have been seen as disrespectful. Unwilling to simply give up and go home, she rose from her seat and bowed.

"Mr. Takahashi-san, it is a great honor to make your acquaintance.

I am Yoshi Yakamota. You may have known my father, Hiroki. He was the first Japanese American detective at SFPD. I am—" Before she could finish her introduction, he cut her off.

"I am familiar with Hiroki Yakamota. He was a fine man. His accomplishments brought honor to our community."

Was it her imagination, or was Mr. Takahashi inferring that her endeavors were less than admirable?

He spoke to his wife in Japanese. "You did not tell me we were expecting company." Turning his attention to Yoshi, he said brusquely, "Miss Yakamota—it is still 'Miss,' is it not? I apologize if my wife led you to believe we might have need of your services. We do not."

"I understand, sir, but if you would allow me to explain. I am not asking you to hire me. I am here on behalf of a client." Yoshi pointedly remained vague. It would not serve her to reveal Aneko's involvement at this point. In fact, she preferred the Takahashis remained unaware that Blind Eye was even searching for their missing daughter. After all, if they had wanted Saya found, they would have hired a private detective months ago, someone who could be discreet while ensuring Saya's return, even if by force.

"You are not here about Saya?" Mrs. Takahashi sounded surprised.

"No ma'am," Yoshi replied politely, hopefully scoring a few points. "I am here in regards to another missing girl who disappeared from Pioneer Institute at the same time as your daughter. Did you know Dominique Marxley?"

"No." Mr. Takahashi's gruffness had not diminished. "We have not made Miss Marxley's acquaintance. I am sorry we could not be of assistance."

It was clear that he intended his statement to spark her departure. Ignoring etiquette, Yoshi asked, "Do you know where Saya is?"

The silence was long enough for the couple to have communicated by sign but Yoshi had not overheard the sound of moving hands and she suspected, instead, that their communication traveled via eye contact. She was surprised when it was Mrs. Takahashi who spoke next.

"I hope you will not find me inhospitable," she said, speaking quietly and concisely as though words were in short supply and she was conserving them by carefully considering each one she used. "I am afraid we must ask you to leave."

"My wife will see you to the door. Good day, Miss Yakamota." Mr. Takahashi dismissed both women at once.

"Of course." Yoshi nodded.

She heard Mr. Takahashi's footfalls fade as he exited the room, leaving her alone with his wife.

"I am sorry," Mrs. Takahashi whispered softly. She led Yoshi silently down the foyer to the front entry way. As she closed the door behind her and walked Yoshi down the steps, she leaned in so closely that Yoshi could smell her gardenia and rose lotion. "Please find my daughter. I miss her very much. I do not care what she is."

Yoshi was stunned. Before she could reply, Mrs. Takahashi disappeared as quietly as she had spoken. *I do not care what she is.* On the surface, the meaning seemed clear, but Yoshi intended to dispatch Tucker to determine exactly what Saya was, beyond a troubled lesbian teen, and why the doctor caring for her didn't want her found.

CHAPTER FOUR

Tucker got out of Bud's baby blue Impala and darted through traffic to cross Westmoor Avenue. Bud would park on the other side of the school, go into the office, and see if he could find out anything about Saya Takahashi from the school administration. Tucker was supposed to infiltrate Westmoor High and speak to the students.

The school grounds were deserted. Tucker glanced at the Fossil watch Velvet had given her for Christmas. Velvet was lucky the watch with its ebony wood links was so studly or Tucker would never remember to wear it. But the rectangular face only had four numbers on the dial and Tucker had to practically count her fingers to figure out the time. Maybe her old plastic digital watch hadn't been so bad after all, despite the grimace it evoked whenever Velvet saw it.

It was close to lunch. So where were the kids? Was it a closed campus? Tucker was already worried about her ability to get into the school. Since the Virginia Tech tragedy, California schools had implemented extreme security measures. She looked down at her jeans and T-shirt, hoping she would fit in. She had read on Westmoor's website that they had a strict dress code, and she'd been terrified about what that meant until Aneko assured her there wasn't a required school uniform. Tucker couldn't imagine having to wear a skirt to school everyday.

She had graduated from a rural magnet school in Idaho, which drew students from a thirty-mile radius and still managed to attract no more than three hundred at a time. Twice as many people attended Westmoor High. The numbers were so mind boggling she had no sense of the enormity until she stepped through Westmoor's doors and was swept off her feet. A crush of bodies plowed into Tucker's chest and knocked the wind out of her. A cacophony of noises assaulted her ears.

Before she could regain her senses, she found herself carried along with a hoard of students stampeding toward the cafeteria. They pushed her down the hall, through a room labeled Snack Bar and into the cafeteria. There the hoard suddenly became a neatly organized line, and Tucker was able to escape their magnetic grasp. Completely disoriented, she stumbled into a young woman and almost sent the girl's tray flying.

"I'm so sorry," Tucker apologized.

"Can I help you?" The girl gave Tucker a quizzical look. "You look lost."

Was it that obvious? Tucker blushed. She stuck out like a sore thumb, but it wasn't her clothing. She was the only white kid amidst a predominantly Asian American student body. There were a handful of African American and Latina kids, too, but no one with Tucker's Nordic coloring. It made sense, of course. After all, Daly City had the highest Asian population of any American city outside of Honolulu. But for some reason Tucker hadn't thought about those statistics extending to the student population as well.

"I'm new here," she stammered. "I'm Tucker. Tucker Shade."

"Kahlea Lu." The girl shook Tucker's hand. Her long black hair was pulled back in a single braid. She wore stone-washed jeans, a red blouse, and white jacket. When she moved her arm it tinkled like a bell. A collection of silver bracelets encircled her wrist. "Well, that's the line for the cafeteria. It's pretty good. They serve udon and teriyaki bowls, Indian curries, and Vietnamese sandwiches, Or you can get Mexican if you prefer. You pay with your credit card or, if you're on one of the meal plans, they just swipe your student ID."

Tucker had neither credit card nor student ID and she'd never been very good at lying. "I'm not really hungry. I think I'll just hang out on the quad."

"*In*. We say 'in' the quad. You can walk with me, if you'd like."

Tucker blushed again. She nodded and followed the girl, who cut through the crowded hallway like Moses parting the Red Sea. When they passed a teacher, Tucker kept her head down and hoped she blended in despite her blondish brown hair. Once outside Kahlea sat down on the cement steps. Tucker sat down next to her and looked up at the blue sky.

"So, what are you *really* doing here?" Kahlea asked.

"I told you, I *go* here—to school."

Kahlea shook her head. "I don't think so. Placement at Westmoor is *very* competitive."

"And what?" Tucker was offended. "You can tell by just looking at me that I'm too stupid to go here?" What the hell? Was she being the target of some kind of backward racial profiling? Tucker knew Asian Americans were known for their smarts but stereotypes weren't always true. Why was this girl being so rude?

Kahlea smirked, as though Tucker had made a joke. "I don't know you well enough to say that. It's just that there is a waiting list to get into Westmoor, and I know some of the kids who have been waiting for a spot all year. Plus, I can tell by the way you're acting." Kahlea swallowed another bite. "You don't have a student ID, and you don't want the teachers to see you. So why are you *really* here?"

Damn. Tucker's first undercover assignment and five minutes in she'd already been made. At this rate she was never going to become the kind of PI Yoshi Yakamota would respect. Should she come clean and hope for sympathy or try another angle? *Practice makes perfect.* "You're right. I'm sorry about that. I don't go here. I'm just trying to find a friend of mine." Tucker pulled a photo from her back pocket and held it out to Kahlea. It was a school picture of Saya from her sophomore year.

"Saya Takahashi. Did you know her?"

Kahlea took the five-by-seven. "How do *you* know her?"

"I met her at Pioneer Institute. It's this conservative school in Freemont where parents send 'problem kids.'" Tucker made quote marks with her fingers. "You know, kids who aren't turning out the way they're supposed to because they dress weird or like girls instead of boys."

"You aren't dressed weird."

Tucker smiled. "Thanks. But I don't like boys."

Kahlea crinkled her nose. "That's gross," she said but did not move away. She shrugged. "It's your life. So, if Saya was at this Pioneer place, why are you looking for her here?"

"She escaped. Like six months ago and I haven't heard from her since. I just turned eighteen and my parents couldn't keep me there anymore, so I'm out and I'm trying to find her, you know, just to be sure she's okay. She used to go to school here, so I thought maybe one of her friends might know where she is. Do you know who she hung out with? She mentioned Lisbeth, Johnny, and Thanh Ha." Tucker used the names they'd gotten from Aneko, even though she didn't know if they were current friends or not.

Aneko had really been on top of things. She'd brought a file box full of stuff she thought Blind Eye might find useful, including every letter Saya had sent her since Aneko left their family home five years earlier. The three names Tucker used had all come from the most recent letters—before Saya had been sent to Pioneer.

Kahlea handed back the photo. "I don't know any Lisbeths, but Johnny and Thanh Ha are right over there." She waved vaguely in the direction of a hundred students.

Like that was really useful. Tucker rolled her eyes. How was she supposed to know which kids she was looking for? She stood up, brushed off her pants, and started to say, "Thanks anyway," when Kahlea got up too.

"I'll introduce you," she said. "Just let me bus my tray."

Kahlea presented Tucker to the three students who had been friends with Saya, but it turned out that they weren't very helpful. Either they knew little about Saya's disappearance, or they were lying to protect her. If it was the latter, they had greater skills of deception than Tucker. When she asked the last time they'd seen Saya, they avoided her eyes in favor of each other's. Tucker wasn't sure if they were mentally conferring to pin down a date or trying to synchronize fabricated stories.

"It must have been that last day she was at school, before her parents sent her to Pioneer." The Vietnamese girl, Thanh Ha answered. "You know, no one even told us what had happened. It was like she just disappeared."

"How did you figure it out?" Tucker asked.

"It was Lawrence," Johnny said. "He got a weird text message about checking out Angry Girl blog."

"Angryhapagirl," Lawrence corrected. "It was a blogspot posting from Saya. I mean, she didn't say it was her, but we could tell. It talked about being sent to a fundamentalist Christian program for gays and the kind of crazy assed rules they had. Her parents said there was something psychologically wrong with her and they must have raised her wrong because she'd followed in her sister's footsteps instead of staying on the path God wanted her on."

"Wow, that sucks. Can you give me that address so I can see it for myself?"

Thanh Ha shook her head. "Can't. It's gone."

"Yeah," Johnny said. "It was really creepy. First there were postings that sounded just like Saya, then all of a sudden they changed. It was like she'd been brainwashed and really believed that stuff."

"That wasn't her," Lawrence insisted. "They must've figured out she'd been online and made her write a retraction, you know, saying she'd been wrong, that she'd just been upset and blown everything out of proportion."

"Two days later," Thanh Ha added, "The whole blog was gone. It had been wiped clean off the server."

"Really? Damn." Tucker wondered who had the ability to erase the entire thing.

"I've got a printout." Lawrence retrieved a rumpled collection of papers from a weathered leather messenger bag and, with a nervous glance over his shoulder, thrust them toward Tucker. "Promise you'll return them to me?"

Tucker raised her fingers in the Boy Scout oath and quickly skimmed the papers.

"Here's the shit they spew," Saya wrote. "'Pioneer Institute encourages each client by reaffirming identification with the appropriate gender expressions. Pioneer helps their clients pursue integrity in both the actions they take and the way they present themselves to the world.'"

The rhetoric sounded almost like the way politicians talked. Reading between the lines, Tucker interpreted the sentiment to mean girls should dress and act in the feminine way they were expected to. Likewise for boys.

"'Therefore,'" the quoted material continued, "'any belongings, appearances, clothing, actions, or humor that might connect a client to an inappropriately gendered past are excluded from the program. These hindrances are called False Images. FI behavior may include mannish attire on women, jewelry on men, and *campy* gay or lesbian behavior and speech.'"

Following the quotation, the blog author expressed the opinion, "Lame, huh?"

Tucker had to agree with her. It was lame. More than that, it reminded Tucker of her own teen years and the pressures she'd endured that were aimed at realigning her 'inappropriate' gender behaviors. She thought of how funny it was in retrospect. Most of the farmwomen she knew were far more butch than some of the lesbians she'd come to know in San Francisco. Take Velvet or Yoshi, for example.

"I can't believe her parents sent her to that place," Lawrence interrupted her thoughts. His delicate hands were clenched into fists at his sides. "It's like they thought they could just strain the gay out of her. But she was never going to live up to their expectations. Those bastards drove her away." His voice cracked and Tucker saw his eyes glisten with tears.

Thanh Ha squeezed his hand . "How can anyone do that to their kids?"

Tucker shook her head. She didn't know why parents did the things they did to their kids. Maybe they felt entitled or something.

"We were so relieved when she got away from that place." Johnny said.

"How'd you discover *that*?" Tucker asked.

Johnny shrugged. "I don't know. Just heard it through the grapevine. I kind of expected her to show up around here."

"Saya's too smart for that," Thanh Ha said. "She knew if she came back here she'd get caught and sent back to that prison. I bet she went somewhere her parents' can't get to her, like New York City. I bet we hear from her in a few months and she'll be doing great."

Tucker wondered if Thanh Ha really believed what she was saying, or if it was just something the teenager really wanted to believe. *Was it possible to convince yourself that something you knew was true really wasn't? Could you blindly believe something simply because you wanted to?* She shivered as though a sudden solar eclipse had thrown the world into darkness. For a moment Tucker was certain she was as guilty of mislaid faith as these kids, the folks who ran ex-gay programs, or the parents who sent their children to such places. The feeling passed quickly and she was left pondering what her own blind faith concealed from her. The truth seemed shrouded in shadow. She forced her attention back to the task at hand addressing one of the remaining mysteries. "Do any of you know someone named Lisbeth that Saya might have been friends with?"

While Johnny and Thanh Ha shook their heads, Lawrence just stared at the ground, his cheeks flushed. Tucker felt bad for him. She knew from experience what it was like to be a shy teenager uncomfortable in social situations.

"So Lisbeth wasn't her girlfriend or something?" she asked.

"She didn't have a girlfriend." Thanh Ha answered.

"But she is gay, right?" Tucker clarified. Wouldn't it be ironic if the girl's parents had just assumed she was a lesbian when she really wasn't?

"Yeah," Johnny affirmed Saya's queerness. "She made the mistake of coming out to her folks. That's how this all started." He suddenly grabbed Thanh Ha's arm. "Oh, my God. We have to go!"

"They've got a no-tolerance policy for tardiness," Thanh Ha explained.

Tucker glanced up, half expecting a high school Gestapo to be bearing down on them. No one was there. The courtyard had nearly emptied. It must be near the end of Westmoor's half hour lunch period. She thanked Saya's friends and scurried through the school toward the rear exit. It wouldn't do to be caught by a hall monitor after the bell rang. Best case scenario she'd end up in the principal's office. Worst case, they'd call the cops. She was almost to the parking lot when someone grabbed her shoulder.

Tucker swung around. She was surprised to find Lawrence standing there. "Was there something you forgot to tell me?"

His voice was so low she barely heard it. "I miss her."

Tucker wondered if the reverse were true. If Lawrence and Saya had been close, why hadn't the girl mentioned him in her letters to Aneko? Hoping for a lead, she asked, "Did Saya come to you after she ran away?"

Lawrence shook his head. "Not this time. I don't understand it. She knows I'd do anything for her, but she didn't call me."

Not this time? She'd been so stupid. Most runaways were serial runners. In fact, Aneko had told Blind Eye that Saya had shown up on her doorstep before, after running away. But Tucker had just assumed that incident was the only one. With Aneko estranged from her family, perhaps she didn't know that Saya had run away other times.

"The other time she ran away, can you tell me about that?"

"Why?" He lowered his plush eyelashes. "I'm just trying to find her," she said, trying for empathy. "She left Pioneer with another girl, so maybe that girl's friends helped them."

The idea seemed to lift his spirits. "When she ran away before she sent me a text, telling me where to meet her. She stayed at my place but after that she hid in the pool house in Johnny's back yard. I don't think they ever go back there, so it was safe."

"Thanks, Lawrence. That really helps. Do you think Johnny or Thanh Ha could have helped her this time without you knowing it?"

"No. No way."

Tucker accepted his evaluation. "What about her other friend? This Lisbeth?"

He kicked at a pebble. "That's what I wanted to tell you. I just couldn't say anything in front of those guys. I mean, they're my friends and everything but I just don't know. We never thought they could handle it."

The bell rang.

Lawrence jumped. He looked back at the school with horror. "I'm late. I gotta go."

Not yet. "Handle *what*?" Tucker demanded.

He lowered his voice. "*I'm* Lisbeth." Then he turned on his heel and darted away like a whitetail, leaving Tucker staring after him with her mouth hanging open.

CHAPTER FIVE

Pioneer Institute counselor Aimee Dix finished setting up her tent and surveyed the campsites. Crystal Lake was shaped like an ankh, with land tying two water blades to a longer expanse of water that stretched to the south. Aimee and the other counselor, Carl Lee James, had set up camp between the blades. The boys' camp occupied the east shore, and across the crystal clear, blue green water lay the girl's camp on the western edge of the rocky shore.

Two days earlier the campers had been dropped off on the side of Highway 1 bordering Marin County's Point Reyes National Seashore. From there, it had been a strenuous hike to pick their way cross-country through the dense coyote brush to the lake. Although she and Carl Lee carried GPS units and various maps, they'd placed the students in charge of navigation, allowing them to use only their compasses to plot their course while avoiding man-made trails.

Although Pioneer students did not realize it, the most difficult portion of the trek was behind them. The second half of the trip always sounded more demanding, because they had to hand in their compasses and navigate using only the skills and information acquired during the course. Students who had paid attention would remember that the plant communities that dominated the shaded north slopes of mountains were different from those on the southern hills, which received more of the sun's rays. With that information they could determine compass directions with little more than a representative leaf or flower gathered from the hillside. During their tough few days on the trail they developed leadership skills while learning about geography, geology, astronomy, and ecology.

Usually this was Aimee's favorite week of the year. Spring Survival Camp was a great way to reward the kids who'd achieved some success in their struggles to overcome sexual dysphoria. The experience built trust between fellow students and counselors and improved self-esteem. Carl Lee was remarkably helpful in teaching survival skills to the group so far, but something about him gave Aimee the creeps. He was a last minute substitution for Coach Rex Rawlings, who'd canceled because of a family emergency. Carl Lee had stepped up, and Aimee knew she should be grateful, but she wouldn't be happy until they completed the outdoor education event, hiked into Bolinas, and drove back to Pioneer Institute. She tried to soothe her nerves by reminding herself that there were only a few more days to go. Tomorrow, they would leave Crystal Lake in the morning, first heading south to Bass Lake, and then paralleling the coast until they reached Bolinas. She watched Isabelle Sanchez standing next to her tent while Carl Lee finished tacking in the last of her tent stakes. When had Isabelle become so helpless? Aimee felt a wave of melancholy splash her. Sometimes Pioneer's successes did not make her feel as happy as they should.

She was thrilled that Isabelle had begun to emulate more appropriate gender behavior and deepen her spiritual connection with God. During group therapy last week they'd had a breakthrough when Isabelle finally acknowledged that her home environment had inadvertently primed her for pre-homosexuality. Admission was the first step. The aversion therapy had then begun to work, helping Isabelle fight the urges that stemmed from being raised by a cold and distant mother. This recent progress was astounding, given the many months she'd spent at Pioneer, seemingly stuck in her psychologically stunted sexual obsession with women. But the progress seemed to come hand in hand with a sense of her own fallibility and Isabelle was deferring more and more to the boys and male counselors. As a devout Christian who considered herself both psychologically healthy and strongly independent, Aimee did not believe women had to lose their personal strength to gain their femininity.

Aimee still believed in her work at Pioneer. The students who came to the institute were suffering immensely and Aimee understood that much of their anguish resulted from abnormal sexual impulses and replicating inappropriate gender behaviors. She honestly believed that their only hope of true love and happiness lay in heterosexual relationships.

Despite her beliefs, she was not entirely pleased by the changes in Isabelle Sanchez . She hated to see the spark fading from the intelligent girl's bright eyes.

❖

After dinner, the students gathered around a fire pit in the neutral zone where Miss Dix and Carl Lee had pitched their tents. The sun had gone down behind the trees and it wouldn't be long until the camps were engulfed in darkness.

Isabelle had no idea what the teachers were thinking, sending her into the wilderness. She'd been working so hard to be feminine but a camp out almost required masculinity. It was fine for the boys to be lugging about heavy backpacks and wearing ugly hiking boots. But, she'd just spent the last six months hearing that girls weren't supposed to do either of those things. Her flesh-colored nail polish was chipped, her hair was already matted, and God only knew how she looked without makeup. Dammit, why was this still so hard?

Still, there was something exhilarating about being able to wear trousers for this trip. She had missed the freedom of pants even though in the last month she'd come to tolerate skirts and blouses. The sweatshirt she'd pulled on to fight the evening chill did nothing to flatter her figure and it dawned on her that some of the teachings had gotten through to her. She finally understood that she had to *look* like a girl in order to feel like one. And boys would respond to that, too. Not out here in the boonies, of course, where she was wearing this weird butch outfit and no makeup, but when she got out she was all prepared to attract a real man.

Maybe it didn't even matter if she didn't like them at first. Maybe eventually she'd learn to. The sound of curfew interrupted her reverie and she marched back to the girls' camp, her mind racing with dreams of life after Pioneer. Even if she didn't feel one hundred percent on the right path, she was trying flipping hard and nobody ever had to know what she really felt inside. She missed her chicas in LA though. The poor T-girls who'd taken her in. God only knew what their mothers had done to them.

Isabelle always got a little claustrophobic in small spaces, so she unzipped the front tent flap once she was settled, and poked her head out. She'd been counting stars in the sky for a while when she heard another zipper and saw Erica crawl out of her tent. She disappeared into the darkness, probably to pee. Ick. It was barbaric, girls pissing in the woods like bears. Oops, that was another unladylike thing to think. Girls having to relieve themselves in the woods—that was a much better way to phrase it.

She resumed her stargazing. It was kind of nice to see so many of them. Living in the city, even the 'burbs, you could forget stars were out there. Another noise interrupted her trance and Sarah hurried away from the tents into the darkness.

Isabelle remembered when she and Dominique had slipped away sometimes, ducking into shadows for a quick kiss, finding fleeting moments when they could touch, hungrily running their hands over each other's bodies. It made her almost sick to think of it now, to imagine her hands on another girl. She was no longer looking for maternal love in the arms of another female. Pioneer had helped her fight those sinful urges. In return, she'd pledged to follow Pioneer's honor code, which made it her duty to alert staff when a fellow student broke one of the rules.

Her classmates might be angry with her, but Isabelle knew she'd be doing them a favor. Their immortal souls were at stake. Lives on this earth were short blinks of the eye compared to the life of the soul. Mortal urges could not be allowed to destroy the hope of spiritual redemption. And she knew how hard it was to fight temptation. Even now, thinking about Dom and knowing how nauseatingly wrong it was, Isabelle still felt love there. She knew she was sick but she would keep praying, and that's what Erica and Sarah should be doing too, not sneaking off in the night.

Isabelle slid out into the cool air and crept past the fire pit where a handful of coals still glowed. She plucked at the front of Miss Dix's tent.

"Miss Dix?" she whispered. "Are you still awake?"

"Isabelle?" Like the other counselors, Miss Dix never called her

"Izzy," and lately the nickname had started to feel foreign to Isabelle, too. "Is everything okay?"

"Sorry to bother you, but I'm worried about Sarah and Erica. They went to the bathroom and haven't come back."

"How long has it been?"

"I think maybe twenty minutes," Isabelle guessed.

"You did the right thing coming to me." Miss Dix bent down and pulled a flashlight from the tent. "I'll walk you back to the camp and then go look for them."

❖

Matt Lovelorn was walking back to the boys' camp after taking a piss when he saw a light flashing through the trees on the other side of the lake, over by the girls' camp. *What the hell?* Before they'd left the school, Carl Lee had gone through all the students' gear making sure none of them had prohibited items like flashlights. So it couldn't be one of the kids walking around over there.

Matt felt the hairs on the back of his neck rise. What if a stranger was sneaking around? He broke into a run, dashing toward the girls' camp. *Erica.* He could hardly bear being apart from her every night when they had to go to their separate sleeping quarters. He thought of her soft skin and full lips and the way her hands felt on his body. He couldn't let anyone hurt her. He'd *never* felt this way about a girl. As long as he could remember he'd found himself attracted to other boys. He'd hated that impulse, the way his heart would skip a beat when a cute boy noticed him, or the way his dick hardened when he soaped off in the gym showers next to other football players.

He refused to be gay. He was a star quarterback damn it. He hated queers and he'd beaten up more than a few pussy boys. He was tough and hard and never cried. He was no sissy. But he couldn't stop thinking about having sex with other guys, and then came that Saturday in that park bathroom. Thinking about it still made him want to puke.

That's what he'd done afterward. He'd tried to wash the taste away and wipe his memory by drowning himself in alcohol. That just made him sicker. So, he'd finally got up the courage to turn to Father Tom, the priest who ran the Christian teen center. He'd revealed his secret and begged for help.

After several weeks of spiritual counseling, the feelings didn't change and Matt had even found himself fantasizing about Father Tom seducing him. In the end, with Father Tom's support, he told his parents and begged them to send him to Pioneer Institute.

Matt was thrilled that they'd agreed. He wanted to be cured. Sure, there were still things that pissed him off about Pioneer. They wouldn't let him work out or even do sit ups and it was costing him muscle mass. Dr. Barnabas said the only reason for a man to have a washboard stomach was if he wanted to attract another man. But Matt didn't care about all that, because the therapy was *working*. He was in love with Erica Bingham and she was in love with him. And for once in his life, his body was doing exactly what he wanted it to, responding to a girl's touch.

Matt followed the edge of the lake, so he didn't have to worry about getting lost. He couldn't see more than an arm's length in front of him, but there wasn't as much to trip over. The area was clear of the downed logs and brush they'd humped through all day. Miss Dix didn't shut up the whole time they hiked. She'd rattle off little tidbits about rocks and trees and other crap he'd never find useful. Thank God for Carl Lee. That dude was cool and he taught them real survival skills, like how to start a fire without matches.

"Matt," someone hissed in the darkness. He turned toward the voice and found one of the girls' tents there. The front door was zippered down and a head was sticking out the end. Still he couldn't tell who it was. He stepped closer until he could make out Isabelle.

"Hey Isabelle." He whispered. "Someone out there. I saw their flashlight."

"Yeah. It's Aimee. She's looking for Sarah and Erica."

"*Erica*? Erica's not here?"

"No." Isabelle lowered her voice like girls do when they've got some juicy gossip. "She and Sarah have been gone for like thirty minutes."

"Where did they go? What do you think they're doing?"

Isabelle laughed. "What do *you* think?" She made gagging noises at him.

He did not understand.

"Sex," she said, making him mad. How dare she think dirty thoughts about his Erica.

"Erica would *never* do that."

"Oh, no, of course not," Isabelle scoffed. "None of us would *ever*. That's why we're at Pioneer."

"You don't know her. She wouldn't do that."

"Okay, so what's she doing sneaking off in the dark with Sarah?"

"I don't know but Erica's not that way."

"Right. Whatever. What do you care, anyway?"

Matt didn't answer. Fuck her. He knew Erica. They were in love. She'd never cheat on him, especially not with some girl. Not when what they had together could make them normal. There was probably an innocent reason why she'd gone into the woods with Sarah. Still, he was worried. What could be taking so long? Was someone hurt? He rushed off into the darkness wishing he could just call Erica's name. That would help him find her. But there was a counselor out there looking for the girls and Matt didn't want them to get in trouble. He couldn't bear to see Erica punished. If he could only find her first, he could warn her about Miss Dix skulking around.

When he saw the bouncing yellow light, he ducked behind a tree and hid. They walked in a line, Sarah first then Erica then Miss Dix. He couldn't see the two girls' faces, but their heads were bowed as if in prayer. Neither spoke in defense as Miss Dix berated them.

"I hope you realize how serious an infraction this is. I'm not just referring to the serious spiritual consequences of your actions, or the punishment you'll receive when we return to Pioneer. How am I ever supposed to trust you again? You've done yourself a great disservice here, girls."

When he heard the words Matt felt like someone had pried apart his rib cage and pulled out his heart. How could he be so blind? Isabelle was right. Sarah and Erica had been together after all. How could Erica do that to him? He thought they were in love.

Chapter Six

Several Days Later

Few things were as beautiful as the San Francisco Bay coastline. Velvet Erickson remembered the first time she'd glimpsed the myriad of white vessels that crowded the bay on weekends, sailing in tandem like synchronized swimmers gliding atop water so glasslike it was haunting. She loved the water, from the brackish bay to the cerulean ocean waves, and she loved being in and on it even more. But after her childhood friend Jeff had met his end in San Francisco Bay, Velvet could hardly bear to be in the same city, much less on the water where he had died. It had been almost six months and Velvet still didn't have her sea legs back, but she was starting to feel a little like her old self and ready to brave the Marin coastline.

It had not hurt that her return to the water's edge was necessitated by her first big fashion shoot since regaining the helm of *Womyn* magazine. If there was one thing that could hold her attention and keep her from slipping into a deep depression, it was her desire to revive the foundering publication. She felt destined to make *Womyn* the magazine she'd first dreamed of when she and Rosemary Finney founded it years ago. She wanted to change it from the petty, competitive, un-feminist vehicle it had become before Rosemary's death.

It was Velvet's overpowering desire to forge new ground in lesbian publishing that had led her to this moment, doing something radical and dangerous, something she was certain no magazine editor had done on a fashion shoot before; she'd brought along the competition, Marion Serif, editor of *Bent* magazine.

"Velvet, this is truly a magnificent boat," Marion Serif announced, referring to the relatively petite yacht Velvet had borrowed from one of *Womyn*'s board members.

"It is, isn't it? Now aren't you glad I convinced you to come along?"

"Yes, actually, I am. Now are you ready to disclose why you invited me?" This was no social excursion and Marion knew it.

Velvet adored her old friend, but they were now direct competitors on the newsstands and in the hearts of the nations lesbian readers. She chose her words with care. "Marion, I want to usher in a new era for lesbian publishing. An era in which we can do things differently. You and I don't need to be competitors. We can be allies."

The look on Marion's face was not what Velvet had hoped for. It was a mixture of consternation and pity, as though she suspected her good friend had gone off her rocker. Velvet was hardly naïve. She'd been at the top of this feeding chain once before and she intended to be there again, but she didn't want to reach that pinnacle by backstabbing friends or stealing advertising clients–, corporate espionage practices that were de rigueur during the reign of her predecessor at *Womyn*. Instead, Velvet wanted to broaden the entire category of lesbian publishing and make a place at the table for many publications, not just one or two.

She was just about to explain this aim to Marion when *Womyn*'s art director Bonnie came topside, accompanied by a handful of very sexy women wearing very skimpy clothing. Few lesbians could fail to appreciate women in itty-bitty bikinis, especially when they were paired with butches in board shorts and briefs.

"Velvet, we've got to start shooting soon," Bonnie said. "The girls are freezing in these outfits. It's hardly Cabo, you know. And we're tired of waiting in makeup."

Bonnie was an odd bird, witty and handsome in an old-school butch way. Shy at first, she was often dismissed as stuck up and some people never moved past these misguided first impressions. When Velvet returned to *Womyn* to steer the magazine into the future, she recruited Bonnie to join her. Putting a woman in charge of art direction, especially one who never wore makeup and preferred Wellies to Manolos, was tantamount to heresy in the publishing industry, but Bonnie's creative eye made her the perfect candidate for the job.

It was late in the year to be shooting for their June issue and photographing bikinis, but there was reason to Velvet's madness. She had landed a last minute interview with Dani, the cute, soft-butch, firefighter turned reality TV star, who had become an overnight sensation by beating out twelve lipstick lesbians for one woman's attention. Velvet and Bonnie had decided to photograph Dani topless in swim trunks and surrounded by a bevy of lipstick lesbians, most of whom represented LA's burlesque dance troupe, The Pin Up Girls. They were dressed in Christian Louboutin's Pigalle pumps and tiny Zoë bikinis in a rainbow pattern that was sure to stand out on the cover of *Womyn*'s gay pride issue. It was an expensive, complex shoot, but Velvet was sure it would make the magazine sell like hotcakes. If only she could find the right beach for her shoot.

Since Velvet had last been on this stretch of water, tides and storms had completely rearranged the landscape, tearing the beaches asunder. They'd already spent the morning cruising along the Marin Coast, around the Point Reyes National Seashore. The photographer had shot all she could aboard the yacht and they desperately needed those beach shots. Ever the budget-minded editor, Velvet had not forked over the money required for a public permit, so her team was searching for something rather secluded.

She pushed her binoculars aside, grabbed her iPhone and pulled up MapQuest. A moment later, she pointed to a satellite image on the screen and told the captain, "We're here. I want to go around that little channel to that beach right there."

As they approached the spot she'd indicated, Velvet could tell right away that the little beach was going to be the perfect location for their shoot. With the rocks on one side and the water on the other, it was picturesque, secluded, and getting the perfect amount of sunlight. The girls would be comfortable, the park rangers weren't going to find them, and the tide was finally out so they would have enough space to set up the equipment.

"This is perfect," she said, but as they closed in her heart sunk. Someone had beaten them to the spot. A couple was sunbathing exactly where the models would have to pose. The yacht surged closer and Velvet froze.

"Oh, my God, I think they're dead!"

She was answered by the sound of waves slapping against the

hull of the boat. It seemed everyone else was stunned into silence and unsure how to respond.

Marion slid up and put an arm around her. "Velvet, honey, I think you might be jumping to conclusions." She tried to steer Velvet away from the railing.

"No!" Velvet yanked free of her grasp. "There are bodies on that beach."

She looked around at her staff and friends and was disappointed to find them all staring at her like the stress of the shoot had gotten to her and she'd lost it. There was nothing like crisis situations to reveal what people really thought of you. Let the others think it was driftwood or a dead seal or her own terrible imagination, but she had long since learned to trust her instincts. She was seldom wrong when it came to recognizing a story. Even in that first instant, she was certain this would turn out to be a big one.

She directed the captain to bring the boat as close to the rocky shore as she dared and cast an anchor. Velvet did not wait for the others to confirm what she'd already recognized. She snatched the camera out of the photographer's hands and jumped overboard. The cold water was chin deep and took her breath away. When it hit her breasts, Velvet almost regretted the damnable curiosity that had driven her overboard. Praying that she wouldn't drop the professional, thousand dollar camera in the drink, she held it above her head and struggled toward the rocky beach.

The two bodies lay crumpled together, face down at the base of a sea cliff. Matted hair entwined between them, binding them like lovers, morbid corpse brides bound together forever in the afterlife. Velvet wondered if they'd been lovers in life and how they got here. Had they jumped from the cliff above?

Their bloated, waterlogged bodies brought images of Jeff Conant's distended corpse to her mind. She did not need to feel for a pulse to know they were both dead and had been so for some time. Velvet forced her emotions aside and tuned out the shouts and shrieks of her employees. There was a job to be done. She needed to document the scene. Operating almost entirely on autopilot, she began methodically photographing the area, starting with wide shots and narrowing in until she was photographing only quadrants of the individual bodies. When she was satisfied that she'd documented the initial scene in photographic evidence, she slowly rolled each of the bodies over.

They were both women, no…girls. Children. Crabs had been at them. The eyes were gone, leaving ghoulish sockets staring from their dead faces. Velvet sprinted to the water and threw up. She couldn't stop thinking of Jeff, the way his body had suffered a similar fate. She crouched over and began to sob. She had only just begun to recover from his death and now this. How long would these faces haunt her dreams? What had drawn her here? She felt like the woman from *Medium*, like the dead had brought her here for a reason, like they thought only she could bring them justice. Maybe that was what it meant to be an investigative reporter, to have a duty to uncover the truth and restore justice.

Minutes passed slowly. Velvet focused on the two girls, the vast rocky cliff above them, and the hollow echo of the nearby surf. By the time Marion joined her on the beach, Velvet was no longer an investigative reporter. She was a magazine editor, and more importantly, she was the boss, responsible for the safety and well-being of her employees. She glanced back toward the yacht, taking in the shocked faces streaked with tears. While the sight of two lifeless bodies instilled in her a concoction of dread, grief, and the not long dormant investigative spirit, she knew what she needed to do.

"Okay everyone," she shouted. "Don't worry, it's going to be fine. We need to call the Coast Guard and give them our location. Tell them that we've found the bodies of two young women. We'll stay here until they arrive, and then we'll go back to San Francisco."

She allowed Marion to help her back to the boat. The models were huddled in towels or had gone below to change out of their bikinis. Velvet joined them, stripping from her wet clothes and taking advantage of the shower, which despite being the size of a shoe closet managed to warm the blood in her veins and stave off hypothermia, thus keeping her from ending up naked in bed with Dani and the burlesque girls pressing their bodies against hers for warmth.

You win some, you lose some.

❖

Yoshi was patiently awaiting Aneko's arrival when the phone rang. Perhaps Aneko was calling to apologize for being tardy, though the clock had not yet struck upon the hour. Yoshi preferred clients to be overly polite in regards to their tardiness, rather than arriving at the Blind Eye office without apology or explanation.

"Yoshi?"

The tone in the other woman's voice immediately put Yoshi on edge. "What is it, Aneko? What is wrong?"

"Can we meet somewhere else? Somewhere public and well lit?"

Yoshi felt as though she had just lowered her bare hand into liquid nitrogen. Aneko had been threatened. She was sure of it. She suggested a nearby coffee shop.

"Too crowded." Aneko said. "Plus, nowhere near food."

They agreed on the main branch of the San Francisco public library. When Yoshi walked in she moved instinctually toward a far corner where Aneko's lyrical voice guided her to a rough-edged reading table. The location was a wise choice. From her vantage point, Aneko would see anyone who entered and no one could sneak up behind her. Being a house of silence, any confrontation would be noticed. She heard Aneko rummaging through her handbag. She placed something quite light between the two of them.

"What is it?" If time were not of the essence, Yoshi would appreciate the challenge of identifying an unknown object through sound, sense, and smell. But she wanted to know why Aneko seemed so panicked.

"It's a box. It's made to look like a coffin."

Yoshi could hear fear in her client's voice. "What is inside?" she asked, cringing at one possible answer. *Please don't be the head of Aneko's beloved cat.*

"A dead mouse."

Yoshi felt the repulsion rearranging her features. The repugnant image of the dead animal caused anger to rise and burn her throat like acid. It could be worse, she reminded herself, it could be much worse. She reached across the table and touched Aneko's hand, trying to show her sympathy. Aneko's fingers curled around hers and held them for mere seconds before releasing them.

"There's a note."

Of course. There was always a note. "What does it say?" Yoshi kept her voice stable.

"It says, 'Drop the search or you'll be next.'"

Yoshi swallowed the chestnut-sized lump in her throat. "This is serious, Aneko. I think we should alert the police now."

"No." Aneko was adamant. "No police. We can't prove anything and it could make things worse."

"You believe Barnabas is behind these threats." Yoshi made it a statement, not a question. Her mind worked quickly. She felt strongly about following clients' wishes but threats like this usually escalated, sometimes into violence against the target. She did not want any harm to come to Aneko.

"Barnabas Gage is capable of anything," Aneko said bitterly.

Yoshi nodded. That was her impression also. "Do you want to continue the investigation?"

"Of course." Aneko replied without hesitation.

Yoshi fixed her unseeing eyes in the woman's direction, imitating a stare. "This is serious. Your life is in danger here. I want you to think about what you are risking."

Aneko paused long enough to satisfy Yoshi. "Nothing will keep me from finding Saya. But I'll understand if the risk is too much for you and your staff."

"No, we are committed. You can count on that. I would like to take the box and its contents to one of my colleagues at San Francisco State University. She can perform a necropsy and see if there is any trace evidence we can use to establish who is threatening you. If we can connect this to Dr. Barnabas, our position will be strengthened."

"Do whatever you want with it. I never want to see it again."

"I think there might be a silver lining." Yoshi tried to lighten the mood. "It sure seems as though we are on the right track or someone would not go to such lengths to derail our investigation." She couldn't tell whether her words had encouraged a smile. "There is something that you may be able to help me with. Another matter."

"Anything," Aneko said.

"I wondered if I could requisition your translation skills." As she spoke, Yoshi pulled out the letters Tucker had uncovered when she broke the Lucky Cat. She pushed them across the table. "Tucker was able to determine they represented a period between 1976 through 1980 and were written every three months. That is the extent of what I know."

"All right." Aneko shuffled through the weathered, diaphanous paper. "Well I can see right away that the writer was a native-speaker. As you know the structure of Japanese writing differs dramatically from English and can be very difficult for non-natives to master. One of the traditional elements present is that each letter begins with reference to the season. 'The cold days of autumn continue…the summer has warmed my soul…or what have you.'"

"Who are they from?" Yoshi asked. "Who are they to?"

"They are all personal letters. Most of them are addressed to Hiroki, although a few are addressed to *watashi no koishii*."

Yoshi repeated the phrase slowly. "My darling?"

"Yes. The letters are really lovely, the script is beautiful, too. I assume they're from a woman but the signature line in every single letter is *saiai*."

Yoshi was stunned.

"It means beloved," Aneko said, confusing Yoshi's silence with ignorance.

"Yes, I know," Yoshi, said softly. The vibration of her mute cell phone distracted her. Someone had been calling her for the past few minutes. She was almost relieved to pick up. It was Velvet.

"Yoshi, you won't believe what happened."

Chapter Seven

As Bud followed Highway 101, winding along the base of rolling green hills, Tucker recalled what Saya's friend Lawrence had said before the dramatic events of the past week. *I'm Lisbeth.* Tucker hadn't told Bud or Yoshi and she was starting to feel worse and worse about it as time wore on. At first she'd been able to assuage her conscience by rationalizing that not telling wasn't the same as lying. But Bud was her mentor and her partner at Blind Eye and Tucker knew he'd be hurt to discover she'd been keeping something from him. Evasions had a way of coming back and biting her on the ass, and this one was already starting to do so.

Not knowing meant that Bud had run down a half dozen Elizabeths and hadn't even tried to locate Lawrence's guardian. He was going to be *pissed* when she told him he'd been wasting his time. Yoshi wouldn't like it either. She'd probably accuse Tucker of misplacing her loyalties, and she had a point. Tucker was supposed to be training as a PI. Her employer was investigating a case. How was she going to justify withholding the information?

Tucker sighed. She was going to have to share Lawrence's secret sooner or later. She flipped open her phone and bounced through her menu options until she got to messaging. Tucker quickly typed. Instead of arriving on Yoshi's phone, her message would be forwarded to her email to be accessed via the PowerBraille keyboard Yoshi had recently acquired. When texting Velvet, Tucker used a simple form of shorthand, substituting "4" in place of the word "for" and using commonly understood acronyms like bff in place of "best friend forever." But for

Yoshi, she carefully spelled out her message longhand, making sure there couldn't be any misunderstandings.

First, she confessed that she hadn't shared all the information she'd learned about Lawrence, and that "Lisbeth" was Saya's nickname for him, that Lawrence might be transgender, although they hadn't discussed that before Lawrence hurried away. She added that if Lisbeth was a trans girl Blind Eye should use the appropriate pronouns and call her Lisbeth or she instead of Lawrence or he. But Lawrence was not out to his friends, which meant it wasn't really Blind Eye's place to out him, was it?

Slipping into shorthand Tucker added, "Can u help me tell Bud w/ out outing L/L? Thnx ☺"

"We're here." Bud's voice made Tucker jump, as though she'd been caught doing something wrong. "You done playing games on that thing?"

"Yeah." Tucker hit the send button with her thumb and snapped the phone closed.

Bud parked in the shadow of an exotic building that seemed plucked from a sci-fi film and jammed into the earth.

"Wow, What's this?" Tucker asked.

"Marin County Civic Center. They used it in the movie, *Gattaca*."

"Oh, right." Tucker had seen the film with Velvet.

As Bud executed the acrobatics involved in getting his wheelchair from the backseat without touching the ground, Tucker gawked at the elongated building, noticing how it seemed to mirror the landscape it emerged from. Its golden arches mimicked the blond grasses that draped Marin County's rolling hills, while the blue roof was a clear reflection of the sky.

When Bud was ready, they walked under the upper floors that stretched across the road like a pedestrian bridge. Through the glass and bronze doors doublewide marble stairs led from a small lobby to the main floor. On the right was an information booth that housed a woman in a glass cube. Across the entryway, there was a small elevator. To enter, Tucker pushed aside an accordion gate. She and Bud could barely cram inside and once the contraption began jerking upward with grinding starts and bumping stops, it became clear that it was original to the 1959 building.

Attracted by a historical display, Tucker insisted on getting off on the first floor to read plaques and examine photographs while Bud waited half in and half out of the elevator. The Civic Center had been built by renowned architect, Frank Lloyd Wright. According to the blurbs on the wall, it was the only public building ever designed by the man, and everything, down to the long table and chairs in the county commissioner's boardroom, had been designed by Wright himself.

When Tucker returned, they continued to the second floor and down the long hallway. The whole time she marveled at all the windows, the atrium-like hallways, the balconies that allowed visitors to lean over banisters and look down at the floors below, the trees that grew inside the building, and the way the natural light dispersed from the roof to the lower levels.

"Can you imagine working here everyday?" she asked, in awe.

"No." Bud said. He looked unimpressed. They found the Sheriff's Department at the very end of the long hallway, back where the building disappeared into a hill that held the county jail. To Bud's dissatisfaction, once they opened the door the kid had to take the lead. Wood paneling the color of Scotch whisky greeted him at eye level. From Bud's wheelchair, the counter and information window were over his head. He would have liked to be there when old Frank Lloyd was designing the place. He would've put the bastard in a wheelchair. He was so fucking sick of architecture that penalized the disabled, like they didn't have a right to be in spaces everyone else could wander through.

Tucker apparently sized up the situation too. "Sorry," she said even though she had nothing to do with the Civic Center's unfriendly design. She apologized all the time, like she was to blame for whatever annoyed him. At first Bud had thought it was sign of an overblown ego, like she imagined she was so important the whole world revolved around her and she was responsible for everything that happened. But he'd learned that Tucker was no egotist. She needed more confidence, not less.

The receptionist, a middle-aged woman with a broad ass and full rack restrained under her business suit, led them past closed doors that ringed an open bullpen where Bud imagined deputies filed paperwork when they came in from the field. The receptionist held a door for them, and as Bud rolled past, his arm brushed hers, reminding him that it had been far too long since he'd bagged a babe. If he'd had the ability, he'd probably have gotten a hard on just being this close to this attractive woman, who was neither his boss nor a client.

In what appeared to be an interrogation room, Tucker took a seat at an oblong wood table. In the center lay a single manila file folder with "Closed" stamped in red ink across the front. The receptionist moved aside some chairs so Bud could access the table.

When he thanked her, she blushed and asked, "Can I get you anything else?"

"Nope." Tucker answered without glancing up. She pulled open the file folder and began spreading papers around the table. As soon as the door clicked shut, she waved the now empty folder and asked, "Do you think this is it?"

"Probably. They closed the case awfully quick. Let's see if there's anything worthwhile."

"Well here's the ME report," Tucker handed the stapled papers across the table to him.

Bud scanned the medical examiner's autopsy notes for Sarah Worthington. She'd sustained head trauma and broken bones consistent with a fall from eighty feet. The tox screen was clean, with no indication of alcohol or drugs in her system at time of death, which the doctor put at between midnight and 5:00 a.m. on the night the two girls went missing. From the physical examination the ME had determined there was nothing suspicious to counter a finding of accidental death.

"Where's the other one?" Bud asked, scanning the documents on the table for a similar report.

"There isn't another one."

"What do you mean, there isn't another one? There were two girls, there should be two separate autopsy reports."

"Well, there's not. There's just this," Tucker held up another document. "It's an injunction preventing the county from performing an autopsy on Erica Bingham. Says the practice violated the Bingham family's religious beliefs. It's signed by a judge and everything. I guess since they had another body they could let the family have what they wanted and still figure out the cause of death."

"That's bullshit," Bud grunted. "Guess the Binghams didn't want to know how their kid died. You find the witness statements yet?"

"Sort of. There's one from two brothers, Bubba and Buck Mudd, who were in the camp that night. Another one from Carl Lee James, a counselor at Pioneer. He said there was some commotion involving the Mudd brothers, and then the next morning the female counselor found the two girls missing. Then there's the one from Velvet, you know, describing how she found the bodies."

"That's it?" Bud perused the statements. Each was typed on the one-page form law enforcement agencies across the country used to document witness statements in a standardized manner, producing three copies at once. He was surprised that there weren't statements for each of the students who'd been camping with the girls when they went missing.

Tucker held up another page. "This is from some lawyer called Carrington saying he represents Pioneer and he spoke to the students and staff members there that evening, He says no one witnessed anything relevant to the investigation." She dropped the letter onto the thin stack of paperwork. "Wouldn't you think the cops would have interviewed those kids before a lawyer got involved?"

"Maybe they were worried about them being minors," Bud said. "There's more stringent rules and extra paperwork involved when you question minors, especially without their parents' consent." He thumbed through a few of the other papers, then snorted. "Cheeky bastards. Says here that after they found the girls missing, the counselors loaded up all the kids and hauled them back to Pioneer. They only reported the girls missing *after* they'd conferred with their blood-sucking lawyer. This Michael Carrington individual met with the Marin County Sheriff's Office and he and Carl Lee James led them out to the site."

"I wonder why they didn't find their bodies on the search," Tucker said. "I guess the tide was in and so the little beach where Velvet found them was under water at the time."

"Makes sense. You mind handing me that incident report?"

Bud scanned the brief encapsulation of the actions the sheriff's department had taken during the investigation and the descriptions of the area's geography. An addendum, made after the ME examined the deceased, concluded the incident had been a tragic accident. He mulled over what was there and what was missing.

Pioneer students were on their last night of the so-called Spring Survival Camp, a five-day character building outing during which the kids hiked along the Pacific Coast through the Point Reyes National Seashore. They set up camp near Bolinas on Marin County Parks and

Open Space property, the two adult counselors positioning their tents in between the separate boys' and girls' campsites a few hundred yards apart.

According to Carl Lee James, he was woken by noises sometime after midnight and found two men in the girls' camp supplying beer and cigarettes to the minors. While some students of both sexes partook in the prohibited contraband, others retreated to the boys' camp. After Carl Lee chased off the intruders, whom investigators later determined to be Bolinas locals Bubba and Buck Mudd, the campers went to sleep. When they woke in the morning, the two females had gone missing and a cursory search found no sign of them.

Attached to the report was a hand drawn map of the Pioneer campsite and a notation indicating that the area where the Pioneer students had camped was notorious for sharp cliffs that can crumble without notice. Two signs, Keep on Trails and Dangerous Cliffs were posted nearby.

The Mudd brothers admitted they'd gone to the campsite hoping to score and acknowledged that they'd supplied alcohol to minors, but they insisted the party remained low key and they hadn't had intercourse with any of the underage girls. They claimed they didn't see either of the victims.

"Well," Bud surmised. "I'm guessing two things. First, Pioneer's legal maneuvering succeeded in throwing off the investigation. And second, the cops decided right away that it was an accident and they operated on that assumption."

"So now what?" Tucker fidgeted impatiently.

"We'll get photocopies of these. Then what do *you* think we should do?"

"I don't know."

Bud rolled his eyes and wondered how Tucker could be so unwilling to think for herself. A PI had to use some initiative. Refusing to accept her answer, he prompted, "Ask yourself what a real PI would do."

"Uh, go visit the Mudd brothers?"

"Uh?" he mimicked. "You think?"

Before they left, he asked the receptionist to photocopy the reports. He tried to be suave but couldn't come up with anything subtly flirtatious to say so he asked her where to get a good lunch. She directed them to the local mall for what she said was the best Thai food north of San Francisco. Dubious, Bud drove across the freeway to the Northgate Mall and sent Tucker in to order. She returned with two Styrofoam boxes full of heaven. The clerk knew what she was talking about.

After they dined in the Impala, Tucker directed them to the field office for the Marin County Parks and Open Space. Bud wasn't eager to talk with park rangers, but Yoshi would expect them to cover all bases and he didn't mind sending the kid on a fool's errand. She had to learn sometime. She eagerly bounded into the single story wooden outbuilding while Bud helped himself to a bowl of pipe tobacco. It didn't take long before she was back at the passenger door.

She flopped into her seat. "That was a waste of time."

Bud acted surprised. "Really? No rangers around in the middle of the day?"

"Well, no, there weren't. But I did talk to the chief ranger."

"Really?" Bud was impressed that she'd taken the initiative. Still, supervisors were rarely the great sources of information they could be. They were too political with their responses. "What'd he say?"

"That his rangers don't do law enforcement and they only get out to the Bolinas area on weekends. So they weren't involved in the investigation. The county sent deputies instead. We've already got that report."

"Well, you can't expect every interview to get you ahead in a investigation," Bud said.

Tucker nodded. "I did pick up some maps though." She unfolded one and pored over it as they turned back toward Lucas Valley Road. "It's mostly just trail systems. Won't help us get to Bolinas."

Bud chuckled. "I told you, nothing beats the *Thomas Guide*."

They followed Lucas Valley over the grassy hills and past George Lucas's sprawling Skywalker Ranch, hidden from sight behind a ten-foot concrete wall. After dipping into a thicket of redwood trees they emerged into open fields and approached the tiny hamlet of Nicasio. Bud had driven this way a number of times over the years en route to partying at Stinson Beach and for camping in Point Reyes National Seashore and fishing in Bodega Bay. All things he hadn't done since the accident.

Tucker mused aloud about trout fishing with her father when she was growing up in Idaho, and then marveled about the beauty of Point

Reyes, rambling on about how she couldn't believe such a place existed just hours north of San Francisco. Her yammering made Bud miss the turnoff. At the last minute, he yanked the wheel and the Impala spit gravel from the soft shoulder.

"What the hell?" Tucker demanded.

Bud threw the Impala into reverse. "I just missed our road."

"I didn't see any signs. Are you sure that's the turn for Bolinas?" Tucker sounded dubious.

"There *isn't* a sign. You just have to know where to turn."

Tucker grumbled something under her breath about the California Highway Department.

"It's not the CHD," Bud explained. "It's the weirdos in Bolinas. They don't like outsiders. So every time the department puts up a sign they come out and drag it down."

"How do you think the Pioneer people figured out how to get there?"

It was a fair question. You couldn't just happen upon Bolinas. You had to know your way around or have a damn good map. "They must know the place," he said. "They're out here every year, aren't they?"

Maneuvering through the quiet, narrow streets, Bud noted that Bolinas had not changed in the twenty years since he used to come here on weekends with a friend on the force who had a beach house in town. The town was filled with an odd mix of hippy holdovers, salty characters, roaming dogs, and dirty long-haired kids playing in streets. The women dressed in knee-high wading boots and mismatched clothing while the men could often be found in paint-splattered carpenter pants. If you parked on Cliff Road, next to the public park and tennis courts, you'd see one surfer after another changing from street clothes into wet suits and vice versa. They just stripped butt naked for all to see in the middle of the day. Bolinas was unincorporated and there wasn't a lawman for miles. Instead there were Marin County deputies who wandered in occasionally to respond to a disturbance or take in a change of scenery.

When the occasional vehicle passed them going the other direction, the driver would lift two fingers from the steering wheel in the Bolinas wave. Bud raised his own fingers and tipped his head in acknowledgement. Tucker didn't seem to notice these exchanges. She was too busy discussing how Bolinas looked like the New England of her imagination. Bud couldn't help her there. He'd never seen reason to travel farther east than Nevada.

Bubba and Buck Mudd lived in a single-wide trailer parked just off Jute Road. When Bud pulled onto the dirt driveway, he was relieved to find it was only mildly damp, the result of fog drip, not a recent rain. Otherwise the Impala might have sunk to its axles in mud. From a quick background check, he'd learned that the Mudd boys both had records, mostly two-bit misdemeanors, the worst being a few drunk and disorderlies, possession with intent to distribute, and solicitation of a minor. The last had gotten Bubba added to the sex offender registry. Hopefully this fact would give Bud leverage in their interview. Neither brother had a record of employment and Bud imagined that the possession charge hinted at their main means of support, growing and selling pot to the denizens of Bolinas. He'd bet dollars to donuts that they'd found a remote spot on the nearby federal lands of Point Reyes National Seashore and that was where they had their "garden."

Bud was a little surprised that both brothers came out of the trailer when he and Tucker arrived. They stood side by side on a rickety wooden porch, both dressed in ripped jeans and ratty T-shirts that hadn't seen the inside of a Laundromat in many moons. Their hair was greasy and stuck to their heads. They looked roughly the same age, but Bud thought he saw one of them defer to the other and decided the stronger personality belonged to Bubba, the elder by three years.

"Whatcha want?" Bubba demanded, spitting a long stream of brown chewing tobacco fluid in his wake.

"This is private property," Buck added, smoothing back his classic mullet.

"We're here about the incident ten days ago, you know, when those two girls died."

"We didn't have nothing to do with that," Bubba said.

"Well, we're just following up on a few things and we'd like to ask you a couple of questions."

Bubba stared at them for a long time as though trying to make up his mind. "Why? It was an accident. That's what the sheriff said."

"We ain't the cops," Bud said. "But, if it makes you feel better, we could give the sheriff's office a call and give them some reason to come back out here instead. Being on probation, you know they'll probably want to search your house for any kind of parole violations."

"We don't care what you want to do in your own time, of course," Tucker added. "We just want to ask a few questions." Bubba's eyes popped as though he'd just realized Tucker was a broad and that interested him. Pervert. If that bastard tried anything, Bud would make him regret it.

"Okay, but we ain't going inside," Bubba said. "We'll sit right here and talk."

"That's fine," Bud said, "So long as you don't mind the neighbors knowing about your thing for young girls."

"Did ya hear that, Buck? This guy knows about the *thing* I got. You got me all wrong, dude. I don't have to go after the girls. When they find out who I am, they go after *me*."

"Who are you?" Tucker asked.

"We're the Mudd brothers," Buck announced.

"We're like famous man. Back in the day, Bubba was a world class surf rider and last season he straight up saved CJ Hobgood's life. Snatched him outta the jaws of a great white."

"Wow," Tucker said.

If she was that easily impressed, Bud thought sourly, maybe fifteen and sixteen year olds really did fling themselves at the Mudd brothers. "Who's CJ Hobgood?" he asked.

"He's just one of the top surfers in the country," Tucker said. "Did you really save him from a shark?"

"Sharks don't come this far north," Bud interrupted through gritted teeth. God the child was gullible.

"Global warming's bringing 'em up the coast," Bubba said.

Bud had heard enough. "Tell me about the night the two girls went missing."

"We told all this to the deputies," Buck complained.

"Great. Now tell me."

The brothers told a story that seemed well rehearsed. They saw some Pioneer girls in town buying supplies and followed them long enough to see where they were camping. They snuck into the camp with beer and pot that night. They never saw the girls who fell off the cliff. They were far too busy focusing on two young ladies that joined them by the fire to drink beer and smoke pot. Despite their less-than-noble intentions and the fact that distributing alcohol to minors was a crime, Bubba insisted they did nothing wrong. Before they'd had a chance to take advantage of their easy prey, two of the Jesus-freak counselors chased them off. So, Bubba concluded, they'd probably gone home before those girls even went off that cliff.

"What were they doing wandering around in the dark anyway?" Buck added. "Didn't they know them cliffs drop right off? One wrong step and you're fish food."

❖

Standing on the cliff top where the two girls made that fateful misstep, Tucker gazed down with the wind blowing her hair and the salty fog stinging her eyes. It just didn't make sense. Using a copy of the map they'd found in the sheriff's file, Tucker and Bud had gone over this area for the last hour, plotting the location of the campsites in relation to the deadly cliff. She just couldn't understand why the girls had gone the direction they had. It seemed likely that they'd left the girls' camp after the Mudd brothers arrived. But, regardless of whether they'd been hoping to reach their counselors' camp near the road, go to the boys camp, or simply seek privacy from the rest of the group, it didn't make sense that they'd walk toward the ocean.

According to a report, the counselor with three first names, Carl Lee James, said the students didn't have flashlights or compasses with them, but they'd been through rigorous wilderness training that week. They'd all passed a lesson on using stars to navigate at night. Maybe it was overcast that evening and they couldn't see the stars. Tucker contemplated the idea, closing her eyes to brainstorm. Even with her eyes closed she could hear the waves crashing on the rocky shore eighty feet below. Wouldn't the girls have heard the same warning sounds in the still of the night?

Did they want to go over? Was it some kind of suicide pact where they held hands and leapt blindly into the darkness? Tucker had been doing some reading about organizations like Pioneer. Most articles said that when reparative therapy failed some devout people attempted suicide because they blamed themselves and thought they were weak. Had Erica Bingham and Sarah Worthington been so brainwashed they decided it was better to die than live a life of sin?

The ground near the cliff edge was covered with a layer of native bunch grass, preventing any chance of finding footprints. Tucker would have liked to see the marks of hiking boots in the soil. She'd spent hours with her brother Hunter tracking deer and rabbits by following their prints and observing the way vegetation changed to mark their passing. Depressed grasses, broken twigs, a tiny piece of caught fur. It could all point to the direction the animal was traveling. If she could see the girls' footprints she might be able to tell whether they were walking or running. Did one follow the other? Were they side by side? Was there a sign of slipping or scrambling to regain footing? Which direction had they come from when they fell?

But the bare patches of thin soil between the clumps of native grasses didn't provide much material for footprints. Like San Francisco, Bolinas got its share of fog. If it had been foggy that night, the damp earth might have retained a good print but any that had been there were long gone, obliterated by searchers trampling the area looking for Erica and Sarah after they were reported missing. Some of the grass in the area was still flattened. Tucker pulled a pair of neoprene gloves from her pocket and slid them on before dropping to her hands and knees and spreading bunches of grass. She didn't know what she was searching for, but she carefully parted each clump before crawling to the next one. This site was the last place the girls had been before their deadly fall, but since the sheriff considered it an accident nobody had grid-searched for physical evidence.

Her diligence paid off with a few items that could be evidence or could be nothing more than discarded trash. She took a few snapshots with her digital camera, put each item into a small paper lunch sack she'd brought in her back pocket, and scribbled into a notepad each item's description: two filtered cigarette butts, three strands of hair, one small piece of newsprint, one discarded piece of chewing gum, one book of matches, and a white opaque button.

She leaned forward to peer over the edge of the cliff. Once they'd taken the first step over the brink, the girls never had a chance. The cliff was unforgiving and the vertical rocks were slick with water from fog and ocean spray. She gazed out at the ocean. It was such an amazing sight. So big. Calming and terrifying all at once, especially to a country girl more accustomed to mountains and valleys than wide-open watery vistas.

Tucker stood and turned away from the Pacific. She wondered again why the girls had stepped away from the relative safety of the dirt trail for the unknown dangers of the cliff. She couldn't shake the feeling that they'd only have done so if they were running away from something…or someone. The Mudd brothers were annoying, lecherous drunks. Were they terrifying enough to send the two girls running aimlessly into the dark? If not, what else could have frightened Erica and Sarah so much?

Another thing that had been troubling her was the remote location of the area. If the Pioneer counselors were familiar with the locale, why hadn't they avoided the cliffs? And if they weren't aware of the campsite's dangers, and didn't know the area, how could they have found it in the first place?

Chapter Eight

"I'm enrolling Tucker in the Pioneer Institute," Bud said.

They'd swung by Yoshi's place so Tucker could pack a bag.

"I'm not sure if that is wise," Yoshi said. "But I agree that we need a breakthrough. There seems no doubt that these recent deaths are more suspicious than the police believe."

"If we're going to get a lead on this Saya kid and the other girl, we need to get inside that organization," Bud said. "Tucker can pass for sixteen. Shit, younger than that."

"Great," Tucker said. Even though she was only packing for a week or two, little of her stuff remained in her room at Yoshi's place.

Looking around, she decided Yoshi would probably be relieved to have her dad's room empty again. It seemed as though she felt his ghost still needed the space. Tucker knew how hard it was for people to let go of their dead. After all, her namesake, the older brother who had died from sudden infant death syndrome, still haunted her life. After twenty-three years Tucker thought she would own her own life, but her mother still compared everything she did with what the original Tucker might have done had he lived. Even her intention to become a private investigator was a disappointment. Well, she was on her way to her first big assignment now, and she didn't care what her mother thought.

"Be careful," Yoshi said as Tucker tossed her duffle bag into the hallway. "If you don't know what to say, don't say anything."

"I'll pretend to be shy," Tucker said. That wouldn't be hard.

"The kid'll do fine," Bud said, making Tucker wonder when he'd become so convinced about her aptitude for the job.

On the way to Freemont in the Impala, she read over the material she'd printed off from the Internet about ex-gay groups and programs like those at the Pioneer Institute. Some of the stuff seemed pretty crazy and she wondered what was really true and what was just Web mythology. She looked around as Bud drove into an industrial area. She'd pictured a small but traditional school with lawns and flowers, not a penitentiary huddled amidst warehouses, machine shops, and salvage yards.

Pointing toward a set of spiked metal gates and an expanse of razor-wire, she said, "There it is."

For the first time she wondered if she was making a mistake going undercover.

"You'll do fine," Bud said, as though sensing her concern. "It's a school for rich kids. You'll probably feel like you're vacationing in some hoity-toity resort."

"It's just for a week or two tops, right?"

"At fifteen-hundred a week, you better believe it." Bud paused long enough to roll down the window and press the intercom button.

"They've got surveillance." Tucker didn't point at the camera in case someone was watching, and she kept her voice low. The gate swung open..

"I'm betting Yoshi will probably reconsider the investment in a few days and send me to pull you out of this place," Bud said. "And you'll throw a tantrum and say, 'No, don't make me leave.'"

Tucker smiled at his efforts to lighten her mood. "With all this security, how'd Saya and her friend go missing?"

"Good question. Now get in character before you blow our cover."

"Yes, sir."

They parked and Tucker waited for Bud to get his wheelchair out of the car. From experience she knew better than to attempt to help him. That just pissed him off. She'd learned to wait for twenty minutes while he fought with something she could have done in two. She glanced around. There were only a handful of cars in the small lot, but they each cost more than the combined salaries of the Blind Eye staff. She started to worry that the Impala would stick out. Maybe they should have come in a rental. The building itself was fairly nondescript, just a rectangle of high walls.

Tucker pulled Yoshi's suitcase from the trunk and slung the duffel bag over her shoulder. She patted her pockets, making sure she had the spy gear Blind Eye had sent her with. Remembering her cover, she found some gum and filled her mouth with it.

"You ready, *Jennye*?" Bud had convinced Yoshi that Tucker needed an alias, after all Tucker was a boy's name, probably not the first choice for the kind of parent who'd send their daughter to Pioneer for gender reconditioning.

Tucker matched her pace to Bud's, following behind him like a reluctant daughter as they went down the long hall to an office. Though the outside of the building resembled a juvenile detention center and the interior a mental health facility, Dr. Barnabas's office was like a provincial farmhouse family room, outfitted with shaker wood tables and masculine but functional chairs. For a guy as showy as Barnabas, it seemed odd, not quite as religious as his teachings, not as over-the-top and TV-savvy as she'd expected, based on the brochure. Perhaps this utilitarian but homey look played well with his tony clients. Tucker actually liked the style. It reminded her of home.

"Welcome to Pioneer," Dr. Barnabas shook their hands and pointed at the empty chairs on the other side of the desk from him. "What can we do for you?"

"I'm Bud Williams, I spoke with you over the phone about enrolling my daughter in your short program."

"Of course. Jennye is it?"

"Call me J." Tucker smacked her gum and acted like a belligerent teen.

Dr. Barnabas's smile didn't waver. "Thank you for the offer Jennye, but we stick with birth names. Christian names for a Christian school."

"Whatever." Tucker slouched into her seat.

"Sit up," Bud commanded.

Tucker straightened her back.

"I'm sorry Dr. Barnabas. She's like this all the time."

"Tell me, where is the young lady's mother?"

"My mom's dead. *She* would never send me to a place like this." Tucker glared at Bud.

Barnabas didn't respond to her, he just kept looking at Bud as though waiting for the answer. It made Tucker want to wave her hand in front of his face and ask if anyone was home.

"My wife passed away five years ago, just when I needed her most. Suddenly this one's going through puberty and, well, she isn't my little princess anymore."

"Yes," Barnabas agreed. "I can see that. The absence of a feminine role model within the home is a major cause of pre-homosexuality in girls. But don't you worry, Mr. Williams, you've brought her to the right place. We'll straighten her out." Barnabas winked as though he'd made a joke.

Bud looked relieved. Tucker hoped it was an act.

Barnabas settled back in his executive chair. "As you know, here at Pioneer Institute we encourage change in our clients by affirming their God-given roles and appropriate gender identification. During the program we require clients to pursue integrity in both their actions and appearances. Therefore, all belongings, clothing, verbal expressions, and humor associated with a client's inappropriate past are excluded from the program. We call these hindrances False Images. FI, for short." He made a point of looking Tucker up and down. "In your daughter's case, FI behavior would include her masculine attire, clear lack of attention to her appearance, and her disdain for ladylike behavior. Ladies sit with their legs *crossed*, dear."

Tucker gritted her teeth and wondered if she could make it through two weeks without punching this guy in the mouth.

"So, first things first," Dr. Barnabas said, picking up the phone. "We'll have a counselor come help you pull FIs from your baggage and see that you are properly attired. Girls are prohibited from wearing sweatshirts, T-shirts, pants and any masculine undergarments." Dr. Barnabas spoke into the receiver. "Miss Dix, can you please come to the office and help our latest client with her FIs? Excellent."

Tucker looked at Bud and widened her eyes at him. "F-u-ck" she mouthed. What the hell was she getting into? Two weeks in skirts and dresses.

"I didn't bring anything but pants," she protested. "I don't even *own* a skirt."

"Oh, that's no problem," Dr. Barnabas assured her. "We'll be happy to provide the appropriate attire."

Tucker was starting to feel panicky again. She clutched her iPod. "What about my music?"

"No secular music is allowed during your stay here. You may listen to Christ-centered music, which we find to be the best accompaniment to the program, regardless of a client's faith," Dr. Barnabas addressed Bud. "We do our best to minimize external influences, Mr. Williams. Children cannot be bombarded with the culture's distorted messages if they are to absorb our message. We do all we can to create an environment that will help them contemplate the changes needed in their lives."

"That's wonderful, Dr. Barnabas," Bud gushed.

Bastard. He was enjoying this. Tucker discreetly flipped him her middle finger.

"Now, Jennye," Dr. Barnabas said with a voice that made Tucker fear he'd seen her gesture, "why don't you take your things and wait in the reception area while your father and I go over a few things? Our counselor, Miss Dix, will be right with you."

Tucker was relieved. She glanced at Bud, and caught the wink in his eye.

He added, "You be a good girl, Jennye, and I'll be back before you know it."

As soon as the door closed behind her, Tucker began rifling through her duffel bag. Clearly they were going to go through her things and maybe even strip search her. While her spy gear was camouflaged enough not to raise suspicions, she wasn't sure which devices would pass inspection and which would be considered FI. Her fingers closed around her slimline pen recorder. It seemed less likely to draw attention than the photo frame with the tiny spy camera embedded. She could leave the pen on the receptionist's desk, where it might not cause suspicion. But it wasn't much good on its own; it could only record an hour or two at a time and she probably wouldn't be able to get back to listen to the material. She could pair it with a wireless receiver so recordings could be downloaded remotely. Of course it couldn't be accessed from the Blind Eye office, which was too far away, but Bud could loiter outside Pioneer's gates and activate the feed. Tucker hoped he would find an opportunity to bug Dr. Barnabas's office, since the doctor was the prime target of Blind Eye's investigation.

Miss Dix was a bit of a surprise. Tucker had expected a middle-aged zealot with a beehive hairdo and Tammy Faye Baker makeup.

Aimee Dix was actually sort of attractive with stunning, pale blue eyes, long blond hair pushed back in a green headband, and a slightly upturned nose reminiscent of actor Nicole Kidman's. In fact, save for her height, which was no more than 5'4", Aimee shared Kidman's aura of translucent delicacy, if not her icy demeanor. And, if she wasn't all smiles and sunshine, Tucker would have been tempted to push her over and run down the hall screaming toward the exit.

What the hell was Bud thinking?

Miss Dix asked Tucker to unzip her suitcase and hold up each item for her to evaluate, and everything was sorted into two piles: clothing and items intended to combat boredom in the first; and in the other, a notebook, pens, toiletries, a wash cloth and towel, and a Gideon Bible Bud had stolen from some hotel and given her for the occasion. Miss Dix relegated her Cool Water men's cologne and the Butch Wax she used on her hair to in the prohibited FI pile. She added Tucker's preferred undergarments, men's tank shirts and Calvin Klein briefs.

"You poor thing." Aimee Dix sighed. "This is what happens when one doesn't have female influence in the home."

Tucker ignored the jab at the mother she wasn't supposed to have, and asked, "What do you want me to do? Go commando?"

"What undergarments are you wearing now?"

"Same thing."

"Well, it's too late to do anything about it tonight. Someone will go to a store tomorrow and buy you appropriate bras and panties."

Miss Dix gave her a grocery bag for the keeper items and placed everything else back into the luggage, which they took to a nearby a storage unit. Tucker slid the suitcase onto a shelf and wrote her name on a label taped to the suitcase. Miss Dix held a school uniform style skirt up to Tucker for measurements. When she found appropriate sizes, she handed Tucker the skirt and a tragic, old lady blouse she normally wouldn't be caught dead in.

"If you don't like the blouse, I've got a dress you can wear instead," she said, waving toward a floral atrocity when Tucker groaned. "I'll turn around while you get dressed."

Tucker could have made a break for it while the counselor's back was turned, if she was really a troubled teen her against her will. She wondered if anyone did that, and what the punishment was. She took a deep breath and reminded herself that this was an opportunity of a lifetime. Even though she hadn't yet completed the training to become a full-fledged private investigator, Blind Eye had sent her on an important undercover mission. Bud and Yoshi were counting on her, and she wouldn't let them down. She took off her comfortable Levis and oxford shirt and stepped into the girliest outfit she'd worn since the Easter dress her mom had got her into when she was six. She was glad there was no mirror in the storage room and even more relieved when Miss Dix did not lead her back to Dr. Barnabas's office. If Bud saw her in this getup, he'd never let her live it down.

Instead, Miss Dix walked her out to a courtyard. and they followed a stone path under the shade of Douglas fir trees, which Tucker recognized from the pine cones. In several areas the landscape architect had created small hills covered with the kind of lawn grass that begged to be flopped down on. They had just passed a row of beckoning benches when Tucker stopped abruptly, staring at what was for her the best part of this outdoor sanctuary, an arching wooden bridge over a man-made creek. The sound of tumbling water pulled her gaze downstream, where a miniature waterfall fed into a small pond brimming with brightly colored Koi.

"Wow, it's beautiful," she gushed. The garden felt so out of place in the industrial area where it was situated.

"I'm glad you like it." Miss Dix smiled. "We spend a little time here everyday in quiet reflection, and you can earn more time here with good behavior."

They left the serenity of the pool and arrived at a dormitory decorated in a style Tucker decided was Ikea-meets-prison. She almost felt dizzy staring around a girlish nightmare of blush and bashful pink walls, white cabinets, dressers, and tables, and pink and white gingham bedspreads. *Gingham for chrisssakes.*

All that was missing from this nightmare were Doris Day tunes, nightly pillow fights, and mandatory pedicures. Miss Dix explained the dorm room set up was divided into mini quadrants where each person was assigned to a family-like team. These teams worked together in chores, classes, and group lessons, helping the girls form "healthy" same-sex friendships. As Miss Dix explained it, all that was missing from her life, leading to her unfortunate slide to dykedom, was this ability to see other girls and women simply as friends. That and Christ, of course.

Miss Dix remained perky and undisturbed by Tucker's smothered snickering. "Before we join the others I'd like to go over the material in our orientation packet and see if you have any questions. Okay?"

"Sure." Tucker dropped onto the bed and picked up the packet of materials there. A blank nametag fell into her lap and Miss Dix handed her a pen to write her name in the gap.

"Until everyone has a chance to get to know you, please wear the tag. Remember to use your full *Christian* name. We don't use nicknames here."

Tucker nodded but she wasn't paying attention because she was too busy mentally repeating, "My name is Jennye," so she wouldn't forget and write Tucker out of habit. She wrote slowly and watched herself make each letter, in case her hand started off on some kind of automatic pilot. When she was done she peeled the sticker from its backing and slapped it on her chest.

"The biggest misconception about what we do here at Pioneer is that our program is a cure for homosexuality," Miss Dix told her. "The struggle with homosexuality isn't a disease. That means it can't be *cured*."

Tucker was surprised to hear that. She thought the ex-gay movement was all about "curing" gays and lesbians. If they recognized homosexuality wasn't a sickness, what did they think it was?

"There are many factors that can contribute to a person's developing homosexual leanings," Miss Dix continued. "You'll find a list of triggers in your handouts."

Tucker pulled out a brochure titled *Environmental Elements in Homosexual Development* and followed along as Miss Dix read aloud from a litany of "factors" like absence of the same-sex parent, social isolation, and seeing TV with adult content. The Pioneer Institute cited various impressive-sounding studies

Tucker couldn't help but think about her own childhood. She hadn't been sexually abused or exposed to pornography or anything like that. But she hadn't liked the stuff other girls did, like playing with dolls and she *had* felt really isolated from other kids. No one had wanted to play with her and kids called her names. Her mom had been so busy taking care of Hunter and Anastasia that she didn't have much time for Tucker. But that didn't mean…

Tucker realized Miss Dix had stopped speaking and was staring at her expectantly.

"I'm sorry," Tucker stammered. "What did you ask?"

"Were you thinking about your mother, dear?"

Tucker nodded.

"It must be difficult. When did she pass away?"

"My mom's not–" Tucker caught herself just as she started to correct the counselor. Damn. She was going to blow her cover in the first hour if she wasn't careful. "She hasn't been with us since I was ten."

"You poor thing, and just before puberty when you needed her most. I suppose you didn't have a female relative or anyone to fulfill that role?"

Tucker shook her head.

"So, we know that absence may have played a part. It's only natural you'd become identified with your father—he was your only parent. Did any of these other factors ring true for you?"

"I had a hard time making friends with girls," Tucker said, mining her own experience for inspiration. She hoped this didn't get *too* real. "I didn't like to play their silly games."

"Good." Miss Dix offered an encouraging nod. "We'll be exploring these experiences in our group and individual sessions. It's important to recognize that same-sex sexual attraction is rooted in a *legitimate need* for same-sex affirmation and love. Active homosexuals are merely trying to meet the needs of that wounded child within through adult, sexual means. So our focus here at Pioneer is not about *creating* heterosexual feelings."

Good, Tucker thought. Because that was never going to happen. It didn't matter if what Miss Dix was saying sounded surprisingly rational. Nothing was going to turn Tucker *straight*.

"But rather, we're focused on healing that child." Miss Dix really seemed to believe what she was saying. "We have found that young people need a caring and compassionate same-sex mentor to heal the wounds and confusions of relational brokenness. As your counselor, I hope I can fill that role for you." Apparently sensing Tucker's resistance, she added, "It can take time to develop trust. I understand that, but I just want you to know that I'm here if you need anything. I'd like nothing more than to be your friend."

Tucker didn't say anything to that. Miss Dix seemed nice enough, but Tucker *seriously* doubted they were going to become fast friends.

Miss Dix held a hand out to Tucker. "Why don't we take a break from this and go meet the other students?"

❖

Years of practice had helped Bud appear unconcerned about abandoning his "daughter" at a place that seemed like an overly cheerful mental institution. The bright fluorescent lights illuminated happy Christian murals that seemed innocuous, but there was something forced about the cute little lambs frolicking with friendly lions.

After the pretty counselor led Tucker away Dr. Barnabas immediately got down to the business of the tuition,.. Bud handed over the cashier's check Yoshi had given him and hoped she planned to bill the cost to their client instead of taking it from company coffers. It was her business to run into the ground, but he didn't want her messing with his bottom line.

Check in hand, Dr. Barnabas launched into an unnecessary soliloquy about the Institute's remarkable program. Bud felt like saying *You already sold me. I've given you 1500 dollars and handed over my 'kid,' what more could you want from me?* But he just tuned the guy out. Something about the Institute bothered him. He felt it in his gut, and in the small of his back, the place a quack doctor had once described as his new friend after he'd been paralyzed. The spot on his lower back was supposed to tell him when he was doing something he shouldn't. At this moment there was an ache in that spot, but it was probably caused by the long drive more than anything else.

When Dr. Barnabas was done talking, he handed Bud a brochure, slapped him on the back a couple of times and walked him out the door. Before Bud knew what was happening he was alone in the hallway still thinking about his guy.

It wasn't Pioneer's politics that bothered him or their efforts to turn queer people straight—he could understand that. Hell, he probably had more in common with the Pioneer parents than he did with Yoshi

Yakamota. He could see that from looking at them. He and Tucker had apparently arrived during Pioneer's visiting hours, which were just concluding.

A man and woman about his age loitered in the hallway as though waiting for someone. The man was dressed in business casual, jeans and a sports coat that didn't make him seem like he was Daddy Warbucks, even if Pioneer did cost an arm and a leg.

"Your kid new here?" the guy asked as Bud rolled up.

"Yeah."

"Boy or girl?"

"Some days, I wish I could tell," Bud snorted.

"Damn, isn't that the truth." The man's lips pulled back in a smile, revealing teeth not perfectly aligned, suggesting a childhood bereft of expensive orthodontics. If he had money now he'd earned it the old-fashioned way, not gotten it by virtue of pedigree. "Our boy came home one day with his ears pierced. Next thing we know he's started wearing makeup."

Bud introduced himself and was shaking the man's hand when he caught sight of a hot MILF walking toward them. Her brunette hair was curly and full of volume, in a style women didn't seem to have anymore now that fashion demanded hair that hung in straight, flat sheets. Her body was curvy with the kind of weight and proportions of early pinup girls and her clothing was tight fitting and low cut. A fat cross, hanging around her neck on a chain, drew his eyes to her plentiful cleavage. He had a hard time not staring.

"A few of us parents get together for lunch after our weekly visitations," she paused to breathily inform him. "Would you care to join us?"

Bud hadn't expected the opportunity to meet Pioneer parents and gain their insight into the case, but now that the offer had been made, he certainly couldn't pass it up. Yoshi would tell him to go. Hell, if his dick weren't dead dumb and blind, it would tell him to go. Bud forgot all about the bad feeling he'd had about Pioneer. Without a word he followed the apparition to a restaurant, where she introduced herself as Barbara Parkins. The name couldn't have been more appropriate. She looked a lot like the beauty from the classic *Valley of the Dolls.* Never much of a conversationalist, Bud found it even more difficult forcing words out of his mouth in her company. Rather than coming across as a babbling idiot, he limited his speech, peppering the conversation with questions about Pioneer when it began to wind down. He didn't want the meal to end, because he would never see her again.

Although clearly Christian, the parents at his table did not come across as overtly religious zealots. They simply wanted the best for their children. They felt their children were suffering now, or would suffer in the future, for being different. One of the dads quoted statistics about the high number of gays and lesbians who tried to kill themselves. His wife added that a high percentage lost their faith in God and stopped going to church.

"It's our duty," she said, "To save our children's souls."

Everyone seemed to agree that they shouldn't condemn their children to a miserable life as a second-class citizen when Pioneer could help them back onto a righteous path. Bud could see their point. He went to church every Sunday and he didn't see a lot of gays there.

"But, don't they resent it?" he asked. "I mean I can't see my kid accepting this that easily. Without some kind of brainwashing or something."

"You'll be amazed. Give it a few weeks and then suddenly, you know that sweet kid you thought you lost when she turned twelve, you'll see her again."

"Be glad you got a girl," the man Bud talked to earlier interjected. "It works better on the girls. For some reason the boys are harder to get through to, and if it doesn't work, they go in for more of a debauched lifestyle."

"It's not really all that surprising." Barbara Parkins spoke with a voice as soft as kittens. Bud could swear he hear a purr in every word with the letter R, "If you were to unleash normal men from the civilizing influence of the women in their lives they'd run wild too."

"Can't argue with that." Bud chuckled. "Without women the whole world would be like the Internet—full of porn. Men are dogs. We need women to train us."

"Where is your wife in all of this?" Barbara asked.

"She passed away," Bud lied. He felt a twinge of guilt but told himself he was in character and this character's wife had died respectably. She hadn't run off like Bud's.

"Oh, I'm sorry." Barbara reached across the table and took his hand.

The touch of her fingers on his skin sent little shockwaves of delight rippling through his body. "So it's just you and your daughter?"

Daughter? Oh, right. "Yes, it's just Jennye and me. I'm afraid that's why she's…this way. She didn't have a good female role model."

"You may be right," Barbara said without letting go of his hand. "Having single parents like us can be really tough on our kids." Her eyes searched his as though she wanted to be sure he understood.

Looking into her eyes seemed to make everything else in the room disappear—the kitchen noises, the sound of people eating, the other parents—until it was just the two of them alone in the universe. Then Bud realized that before he came along, she was probably the only single parent at Pioneer. No doubt she believed her son was gay because he hadn't had a father figure, and she was to blame for that. She seemed relieved to have another single parent to share the burden.

"At least you don't get accused of not being man enough," one father said, breaking the spell and bringing the roar of the world back into Bud's consciousness.

"That's our burden, man," another added. "Either we're being told we made our kids sexually confused or people accuse us of being bad parents for sending our kids to a place like this. What are we supposed to do?"

Dessert arrived, Barbara retracted her hand from Bud's, and the conversation trickled off as forks clinked against porcelain. They were headed to their cars twenty minutes later and Bud was working up the courage to ask Barbara for her number when she stopped walking, reached in her purse and handed him a business card.

"It was lovely to meet you, Bud. My personal number is on the back. If you ever want someone to talk to about Pioneer or the perils of single parent households, give me a ring."

Chapter Nine

It was ten o'clock on Tuesday night and Velvet was still at the *Womyn* magazine's humble Castro Street headquarters. She'd been in the cramped upstairs office all weekend for production and was still there. Some of her friends couldn't believe that, as the boss, she would put in these crazy hours, giving up weekends and sometimes not going home for days, catching catnaps on the office couch. But Velvet knew the demands of lesbian publishing. It was a demanding mistress who'd consume all a paramour had to offer, time, money, love.

She'd grown weary of it a decade ago, longing for the stability of the *Chronicle*, but now she was torn. Half of her missed the ability to just pick up her digital recorder and run out the door, chasing down drug dealers in the Tenderloin or rogue parking meter attendants in the Mission, all for the good of the people. Her old editor Stanley had always let her run her own show, popping in and out of the office as she pleased. But now she was the boss at *Womyn*, and there could be no long lunches or afternoons spent jaunting about the city. She loved being back at the magazine, but being the boss was overwhelming sometimes.

A staff full of women was empowering and thrilling but often fraught with drama. The worst girls, who Velvet labeled Drama Mamas, seemed addicted to emotional extremes, experiencing the highs and lows like some kind of roller coaster thrill ride. Try as she might, she couldn't keep them from infecting everyone else with it and spreading it around the office like a contagious disease. Some days—like today—the whole office came down with a bad case of drama-titis and had to be sent home. Which was why Velvet was still at the office, making corrections to the galleys two hours before midnight and just ten hours before she was supposed to meet with Showtime about a collaboration between *Womyn* and the hit lesbian soap opera, *Isle of Lesbos*.

Velvet grabbed a clove cigarette. It was admittedly a filthy habit, something that she hadn't done since she was sixteen years old, sitting with the eyeliner-laden Goth kids at Denny's in Van Nuys after the clubs had closed. In times of stress, especially now that she was monogamous, she often relied on habits from high school regardless of how bad they were for her. Hiding in the open alcove near the emergency exit, she blew smoke out the grated open window, hoping that security did not have a camera in the rarely used cemented stairwell.

She tried deep breathing and meditating, both to no avail. Every time she closed her eyes, she thought of a million little things that had to be done yesterday. So fuck it. She went back to her desk and checked her voicemail. She was initially thrilled to hear Yoshi's voice, then dismayed, then angry. Yoshi had sent Tucker undercover to the Pioneer Institute earlier that day. It filled Velvet with a sense of rage and doom and longing that she couldn't easily explain, even to herself. If anyone should be going undercover in a place like that it should be a reporter like her, not—God love her—Yoshi's administrative assistant turned PI wannabe, Tucker Shade. Sure, at Velvet's age, there was no chance she could go undercover at Pioneer and pass as a wayward teen. And, after her previous encounters with Dr. Barnabas, she would have been recognized anyway. But it was the principle of the matter. *She* was the reporter, after all, *not* Yoshi, and especially not *Tucker*.

Yoshi should have had better sense than to let Tucker do something so damn dangerous. For godssakes, Tucker was still suffering from a posttraumatic stress disorder after being whacked on the head and kidnapped during Blind Eye's last big investigation. How could Yoshi think she was ready for such a stunt? Had she even considered Tucker's well-being? And had either one of them even stopped for a second to consider Velvet's feelings? Come to think of it, why in Gods name was she being *monogamous* with Tucker if the girl didn't even bother to tell her about the assignment before agreeing?

Velvet was steamed. She hit the speed dial and heard Yoshi's voice. Fuck simple greetings. Velvet wanted to get straight to the point. "Did you even *think* about talking with me first?" she demanded.

"Good evening, Velvet. I hear you got my voice mail." Yoshi sounded polite, but Velvet could tell she was annoyed.

"Yes, I did."

"You must understand, Velvet, Tucker is my employee. She is, quite frankly, the only employee capable of fulfilling this assignment."

"Fine, but you have to understand she's *my* girlfriend. So you'd think I'd get some say in this."

"I am aware that she is your girlfriend, but this is exactly why I asked you not to get involved with her in the first place. In matters of business, you can't really expect me to place your feelings before the company's needs, do you?"

"Why the hell not?" Velvet raged. "What if something happens to her? She's still really green. She could get hurt."

Yoshi was silent for a minute before speaking again. "Vel, is this about Tucker, or is this about you?"

Yoshi somehow always knew how to cut to the heart of the problem. Tucker had used her PTSD as a reason not to come home for months on end, at a time when Velvet was overwhelmed by stress and grief and desperately needed not to be alone. She needed Tucker there to talk to or even just to curl up in bed beside her. But Tucker was still staying in Yoshi's guest bedroom.

At the same time, Velvet was watching her old life as a reporter fade away while she dealt with so much work she barely had time to speak to friends or put on makeup in the morning. This was very much about her. Yoshi's assignment would let Tucker do two things Velvet didn't want: she would be doing the kind of tasks Velvet had been so good at, and she would have another reason not to come home. Velvet welled up, but remained silent.

"Sweetie," Yoshi said quietly, "When can you leave the office? Why don't you come over for some tea and we can talk?"

❖

Velvet was still feeling a little peeved when she left Yoshi, but she'd decided to use her anger to fuel her own investigation. She'd show up Yoshi and Tucker, beating them at their own game by solving the mystery of Saya Takahashi's disappearance before them. She could smell a connection between Saya and the two dead Pioneer students whose bodies kept invading her dreams. At first she'd felt relieved when they'd taken Jeff's place, but it wasn't long before she missed seeing her childhood friend, even in nightmares.

Velvet was starting to wonder if there wasn't some kind of conspiracy going on. No one seemed willing to speak with her, on or off the record, and their reluctance was beginning to feel like a deliberate cover-up. Even Aneko hadn't spoken with her that day at the courthouse after the Pioneer hostage debacle, but Velvet put that down to the events of the day and the mob of reporters. The lawyer by Aneko's side had hustled her away before she could say more than a few words. It didn't take much to figure out that Aneko hadn't hired Michael Carrington, but Velvet was surprised to learn who had.

Why would Dr. Barnabas have sent Pioneer's lawyer to represent the woman who'd held him at gunpoint? Of course, Velvet had tried asking him but she'd only managed to provoke threats of a restraining order. Aneko still wouldn't return her phone calls, so Velvet had tried staking out Pioneer's grounds and ambushing anyone who left. After that desperate measure, she contacted the parents of the two dead girls, but they insisted they had nothing to say on the matter, and pressuring them only gained her the displeasure of a phrase repeated ad nauseam until it stuck in her head like the lyrics of a particularly annoying song, "On the advice of my lawyer I decline to answer."

From the brush off, Velvet concluded that the parents were under nondisclosure agreements. She wondered what kind of parents would settle potential wrongful death suits just days after their kids had died in a tragic accident. Was it more than an odd coincidence that both families had settled so quickly? In her experience, any business wanting to throw money at bereaved families had reason to believe they were at fault. Or they were hiding something else, information that might come out if there was an investigation or a wrongful death suit. Velvet was determined to discover what Pioneer had to fear.

❖

It was high school all over again. At least the other kids weren't tormenting Tucker. She was actually making friends, even if they weren't with whom she'd first imagined. When Aimee had taken her to meet the other Pioneer inmates, Tucker had felt an immediate kinship with Isabelle and thought the two of them would become good friends. She hadn't had that feeling a lot in her life but it had always been true before—like when Gita Arun arrived at Marsh Valley Junior High for one semester before her parents broke under community pressures and moved to Oregon.

Tucker had bonded instantly with the dark skinned girl from East India and had been heartbroken when the family moved away again. She could understand why they left. South Eastern Idaho was predominantly Mormon, and ninety-eight percent of the students at Marsh Valley, a higher percentage of the population than in Salt Lake City, were conservative members of the Christian sect and still believed dark skinned individuals bore the mark of Cain.

The Mormon Church so dominated the community that it infiltrated all aspects of family and political life and even the public schools, where kids called the teachers Brother Smith and Sister Miller. The Shade family was not a part of the faith, and Tucker had suffered a certain level of ostracism because of it. Other kids' parents didn't want them hanging out with heathens. They may have not been Mormon, but Tucker's mother had her own out-of-the-ordinary religious convictions. Growing up, Tucker heard so much about Jesus that there was a time, when she was really young, that she'd thought he was an uncle. A little later, the convictions rubbed off and Tucker truly *believed.*

She'd lost that naiveté years ago, and losing her faith had freed her to love who she wanted to love. So when her mother and a few nosy neighbors condemned her to hell for loving women, it hadn't rocked her world.

Tucker was glad some of the girls at Pioneer were being nice to her. But she couldn't figure out why Isabelle was so rude and distant when Tucker had pegged her as a similar soul. If that was what six months in this place could do, Tucker was glad she would only be here a week or two. In the meantime she was trying to make the best of the situation, celebrating not being the school outcast and trying to get to know the students well enough to find an informer among them.

Pioneer tightly regimented the students' time. Their day started at seven o'clock with breakfast followed by a short prayer session. Classes started at eight, with the girls attending indoor courses on hygiene, etiquette, fashion, cooking, and home economics. The boys got to escape the institute for a glorious two hours playing sports at nearby parks with Coach Rawlings. Tucker would much rather be playing football or joining them afterward for auto mechanics, instead of being stuck inside learning which fork to scratch her ass with, but she didn't want to draw attention to herself by complaining.

After lunch the boys joined the girls in Bible study led by Dr. Barnabas, then group therapy with Miss Dix and opposite-sex bonding activities with Miss Dix and Coach Rawlings. Each element was carefully chosen to lure students away from homosexuality. The fundamentalist Christians had gotten craftier with how their insidious brainwashing programs were structured and marketed. What did being able to cook or sew have to do with sexual orientation anyway? Tucker had taken home economics classes in high school, but they hadn't turned her straight. Plus, she knew plenty of crafty dykes who loved to knit or sew their own clothes or throw lavish cocktail parties. Velvet could do all those things when she had time.

It seemed like people were always confusing gender with sexual orientation. They should spend some time in Idaho or Wyoming or really *any* part of the rural Northwest. It was hard to tell the difference between lesbians and straight women because they all sported mullets and wore Polarfleece. That wasn't entirely true, of course. In high school Tucker had been taunted for her butch nature and clothing and though she didn't look much different from anyone else, the other kids somehow knew she was a lesbian.

But Tucker knew now that being butch didn't make her gay and being a lesbian didn't make her butch, especially in the cow towns of Idaho. She wasn't really sure what made someone a lesbian or straight or feminine or masculine, or even why it was all so important to people. Her generation didn't give a flying fuck who slept with who and how people labeled themselves. What did it matter to anyone else why people were the way they were? Compared with some past experiences, Pioneer wasn't so bad. Sure she had to wear a skirt, but so much crap had soaked into her unconscious most of her life, she could *teach* the freaking religious classes at a place like this.

Tucker was relieved. She'd resisted indoctrination long enough that she could step back and focus on her assignment. She was trying to interrogate the other kids without raising suspicions. But asking questions about the runaways and the girls who took a header off the rocky cliffs near Bolinas wasn't easy. There always seemed to be a counselor nearby or she got blank, puzzled stares, or someone put the kybosh on any talk, claiming it violated the rules. During lunch on her third day, she was finally with a group of girls, and out of earshot of the counselors, so she was diving right in.

"I heard about the hostage situation here last month. Did any of you see that shit go down?" Tucker kept her voice low so it would not broadcast beyond the group of girls.

"Hostage?" Isabelle said. "I wondered what the commotion was. I was having therapy then the place was suddenly crawling with SWAT guys."

"Some woman held a gun to Dr. Barnabas's head," Tucker said. "I saw it on TV."

"Oh my gosh. *Really*? Wow," said one of the other students.

"Know why she did it?" Tucker assumed a knowledgeable air. "There was a girl who ran away last year. That was her sister."

"Why would she threaten Dr. Barnabas over her sister running away?"

"No one's found them," Tucker said. "I guess she thought Dr. Barnabas could do more to help."

"You know what's weird?" one of the girls added. "Dr. Barnabas had the staff clean out Saya and Dominique's rooms the day after they ran away."

"Quit talking out of your ass. You weren't even *here* then. None of you were." Isabelle said.

"But you were?" Tucker asked.

"Yeah, I was." Isabelle sounded sad.

"Are you saying that didn't happen?"

"I'm sure Dr. Barnabas didn't ask for things to be thrown away," Isabelle said. "I mean, Carl Lee came and bagged stuff up, but I think he was just moving it to storage."

"Don't you think that's odd?" Tucker asked.

"No. I think it's odd that you just got here and you're asking these weird questions. I think it's odd that you're spreading rumors about Dr. Barnabas. And I bet the counselors wouldn't like that kind of false image behavior either. Maybe I should ask them?"

Tucker was shocked. It sounded like Isabelle had really bought this crap. Maybe she was more brainwashed than the rest because she'd been at Pioneer longer. Maybe the therapy was working. Her remarks had changed the mood and the other students scattered. Tucker was surprised that Isabelle stayed behind. What did she want?

"You haven't accepted Jesus as your personal savior, have you?" Isabelle was channeling Dr. Barnabas. If she didn't sound so serious Tucker might have assumed she was mocking him. "You should really give this program a chance."

"That's great," Tucker said. "But I don't think Jesus cares who I love. And I think reparative therapy fucks people up."

Isabelle responded with a pitying look. "That was what I thought in the beginning. I fought the truth for months until I finally realized what I was missing by not allowing Jesus into my heart. The counselors here are really great. They're not judgmental. They just want to help us break our addiction to sinful behavior, heal our brokenness, and lead us to the path of authentic relationships." She could be a walking billboard for Pioneer Institute.

"If you're cured," Tucker said, "does that mean you'll be leaving soon?"

"At the end of the session." Isabelle snagged Tucker's hand. "I'll pray for you," she said earnestly.

❖

"You've got a call on line one," Velvet's new intern said with a slight lisp.

"Who is it?" Velvet demanded, annoyed that the new intern, whose name she was embarrassed to admit she hadn't remembered yet, still hadn't acquired routine telephone skills. "Never mind, I'll get it." She answered with her signature, "This is Velvet," a greeting both warmly sexy and icily curt all at once.

The caller was silent.

Velvet gave up repeating herself after a few greetings and set the receiver down, pondering whether it was a crossed wire or something related to her investigation.

Velvet felt her BlackBerry vibrate a moment after she'd dropped the phone. God, publicists were such vultures. One of them had her cell phone number and had been hounding her relentlessly via text messages to interview the woman, or girl rather, that he called "the new Britney Spears." Velvet wasn't sure the "old" Britney was down for the count yet. Either way, she hated interviewing subjects with so little real life experience they often gave the dullest answers. But this message wasn't from a publicist or anyone whose number she had previously dialed. The sender info was listed as "blocked" and the five words on her cell phone's tiny screen were cryptic at best: *Help grounding group 6 pioneer.*

What it meant, Velvet hadn't a clue. But this was the kind of mystery she loved to dig into. Right now, however, she had a staff meeting to lead, which in and of itself was a jumping off point for a day full of meetings with reluctant ad sales women, then tired editors, and finally with her board of directors. By this evening she would be exhausted and emotionally spent, all her psychological resources depleted by the demands of the magazine. No wonder they called publishing a cruel mistress.

❖

Tucker woke from a dream and at first she didn't know where she was. She sat up and looked around. It took a moment to get her bearings. She was still at the Pioneer Institute. It was night. Everyone was asleep. She was just about to lay down again when something moved in the darkness. Not everyone was sleeping. Maybe one of the students was sneaking back to bed after a brief rendezvous with a secret lover. Tucker huddled under her comforter and pretended to be asleep. She listened for the sound of rustling sheets and tried to see if any of the girls' beds seemed overly occupied. Nothing. Then the faint light in the room dimmed as someone stepped into the doorway. It had taken Tucker a while to adjust to sleeping with a door open and lights on in the hallway. Apparently it helped the counselors on their nightly rounds. They took shifts staying awake, sitting in the closet-like office between the girls and boys dorm rooms. Every few hours—or when they heard noises—they patrolled the hallway and walked through the dorms doing bed checks with a flashlight.

Expecting one of these routine patrols, Tucker closed her eyes and lay still. She heard feet shuffling but didn't notice the flashlight's bright beam through her eyelids. She opened her eyes. It wasn't a counselor. It was Isabelle. She quickly shoved something under her own mattress then climbed into bed and pulled the covers over her head.

Maybe Tucker's sleepy brain was playing tricks on her, the way it did when she was really tired. Maybe Isabelle hadn't really stuffed something under her mattress. Maybe it was just a dream. She closed her eyes again and slid back into sleep like a boat slipping into water, dreams lapping at her oars. There was a lot of noise. Running. Shouting. Tucker sat bolt upright, swinging her legs over the bed, searching for her shoes. It was always like this when Anastasia, her sister, had one of her late night attacks. Mom would be frantic, running down the hall shouting. Hunter would wail this high pitch sound with no words that bounced like sirens off the close walls. Tucker would feel like a firefighter, slipping into clothes, ready to slide down the pole, knowing at any moment disaster could strike. She was terrified that one day they wouldn't make it to the hospital in time, or the doctors wouldn't come up with a diagnosis or treatment before it was too late.

She was tying her shoes when the overhead fluorescent lights came on. It took a moment for her pupils to adjust to the light. She could hear someone yelling but the words weren't registering. Finally the fuzzy shapes resolved into Carl Lee James standing stiff as a board, his face bright red as he barked orders like a Boot camp instructor.

"Get up ladies. Rise and shine. God damn it, this is not a drill. Get to your feet."

Tucker jumped up and stood at attention. Bud had warned that military-style training was *de rigueur* these days at boot camp style reform schools. What did he call them? Oh, right, character building boot camps for today's incorrigibles. Maybe this was the onset of a whole new tactic, Tucker's unscheduled Femininity Boot Camp. Whatever it was, that prick Carl Lee sure was hamming it up. Tucker flashed Miss Dix a knowing smile and rolled her eyes. Miss Dix did not respond. Her brow was pinched and her face had lost its usual kindness. She looked very serious.

Behind her, Coach Rawlings looked groggy and tweaked about being awake. He leaned against the doorframe for support. Coach Rawlings reminded Tucker of junior high coaches the ones that were washed up athletes with potbellies, whose only muscles were on their cars. She imagined that in his glory days glory days he'd been a local star, high school quarterback or lead scorer on the court. He'd probably been good enough to win a division title, maybe even take state, but his accomplishments had ended there, and twenty years later he was living vicariously through the kids on his team and hitting on girls younger than his daughter. Next to Coach Rawlings, Carl Lee looked like a toned athlete.

All the girls had scrambled out of bed and were standing, waiting.

Carl Lee stalked back and forth in front of them. "I know one of you little brats has them, so why don't we just cut to the chase? Don't think I won't call Dr. Barnabas and have him come down here. You'd better hope it doesn't come to that, you got it?"

One of the girls had raised her hand five minutes ago and her arm was starting to droop from heaviness. "Sir?" She pleaded, "What's this about?"

Carl Lee turned on his heel and rushed at her. He stopped in front of her, towering above her five-foot-two stature. Tucker had always thought the dude a little ferret-like, but right now Carl Lee looked dangerous, like Ed Norton at the end of *Fight Club*. Tucker waited for him to strike the girl for asking questions. He didn't. Instead he looked around the room, his eyes capturing each of the girls in turn.

"One of you," he snarled, "knows damn well what's going on."

"All the same, Carl Lee," Miss Dix interjected, "If I may suggest, maybe you could—"

"Could what?" He swung around to stare at her, looking like he might spring across the room at her jugular. "Coddle these bitches like you would? We've had a serious breach of conduct here. I intend to get to the bottom of it, find the culprit, and make sure it doesn't happen again. Coach Rawlings, let's get on with it!"

Miss Dix lowered her head. Rawlings shuffled into the room.

"Okay, ladies," the coach summoned a scratchy bellow. "We know one of you slipped into the guard room and stole the master keys. I don't know what you think you're going to do with them or how you thought you'd get away with it, but I can assure you, we're going to tear this room apart until we find them, you got it?"

That must have been what Isabelle was up to. What was she thinking? She'd been on her best behavior since Tucker got here, and she'd said a number of times that she would be released at the end of the session, less than a month away. Why would she jeopardize all that now? Stealing the master keys was the kind of offense that could get a girl more time in a place like this. Not to mention the fact that Isabelle had apparently stolen the keys out from under Carl Lee when he was supposed to be awake on guard duty.

Carl Lee struck Tucker as the kind of guy that would feel humiliated by being outwitted. And if Isabelle had used the key to get into a locked room and vandalize it or steal something, or look into Dr. Barnabas' records, there'd be hell to pay. So why had she risked it? Just to put the keys under her bed and go back to sleep?

Another thought rattled Tucker. If anyone should be sneaking around at night, stealing keys and rifling through confidential files, it should be *her*. Why hadn't she attempted something similar? Why hadn't she noticed Isabelle was gone while there was still time to get in on the heist and use it to the benefit of Blind Eye? She was a terrible private eye. Thank God, Yoshi wasn't here to witness her failings.

"We already tossed the boys' room," Coach Rawlings muttered. "Maybe we should just call Dr. Barnabas."

"We're not going to bother Barnabas with this," Carl Lee said menacingly. "We don't need to, because we're going to resolve this right now." He marched Coach Rawlings down to the far end of the dormitory where they stopped in front of the last bed. "Start here," he directed.

The coach shrugged resolutely and began pulling apart the bed sheets. Miss Dix reluctantly joined them and searched the girls' footlockers, burrowing through clothes carefully as though she didn't want to disrupt their folds. Coach Rawlings was far less delicate in stripping the bed down before pulling the mattress off the metal springs. Eventually the tornado reached Tucker's bed. In a minute or two they would toss Isabelle's and find the stolen keys.

While everyone else seemed riveted to the spectacle of destruction, Tucker had been watching Isabelle grow increasingly nervous until she looked like she was ready to panic. She kept eyeing the door like she was planning to bolt. Tucker wondered what kind of trouble Isabelle would get into, and thinking that it really should have been her instead. She'd been sent here to spy on Pioneer and though they could punish her, she was getting out in a week. Her parents hadn't sent her here, which meant they couldn't be disappointed by her behavior and decide she needed to stay longer or undergo shock therapy or something. She was safe.

Before she realized it, Tucker had made a decision. She stepped away from her bed and proclaimed, "I did it."

Isabelle looked at her like she was crazy. The other girl pursed her lips, shook her head and began to pantomime as though she was going into convulsions.

Tucker ignored her. She took another step toward Carl Lee and repeated, "I did it. I stole your keys right off of you."

Carl Lee dropped the mattress. "What did you say?" His eyes dared her.

Tucker had been through puberty. She'd had the requisite power struggles with authority figures. She knew what to say. "I said, I stole your *fucking* keys. So quit harassing everyone else."

"You? You're the new girl." He narrowed his eyes at her. "What'd you want my keys for?"

"Thought I'd go out and pick up a prostitute." Tucker smirked.

He moved toward her and Tucker braced herself for a slap that didn't come. "I *should* wipe that smart ass grin off your face."

Tucker shrugged. "You *should* stay awake on your watch. Is that how those girls escaped? Where you sleeping or did you have company?" She raised her eyebrows and watched the storm brewing in his eyes. She should clam up but she couldn't resist one last jibe: "You like boys? Is that why you work here?"

She flinched as she saw his arm rise. Look what her teenage defiance bought her.

"Carl Lee, don't!" Miss Dix yelled. Then she was by Tucker's side, ready to shield her from blows. "I'll be sure that she receives appropriate punishment. Where are the keys, Tucker?"

Miss Dix's eyes were filled with such disappointment that Tucker almost recanted her confession. Not trusting her voice, she pointed at Isabelle's bed. "They're under her mattress."

Carl Lee rushed to verify her statement and triumphantly held the keys over head as if to prove his prowess.

"Why?" Miss Dix asked. "Why did you hide them there? Were you trying to get Isabelle in trouble?"

Tucker shrugged. "I thought it'd be funny if Miss Perfect was knocked down a peg or two. I'm sick of the self-righteous way she lords it over everyone, like she's better than the rest of the queers."

Tucker hadn't thought it was possible for Miss Dix to look *more* crestfallen. But she did. "Carl Lee," she instructed, "Why don't you orchestrate a clean up while I take care of this." She wrapped a hand around Tucker's forearm, applied undue force and dragged Tucker from the room.

"Where are we going?" Tucker asked.

Instead of answering, Miss Dix said, "I'm *very* disappointed in you, Jennye."

Tucker was relieved by Miss Dix's use of her alias. It took some of the sting out of her words. While her presence here was a facade, Tucker's emotional involvement was real. She'd started to like Miss Dix so her disappointment was a shard to the heart that felt all too familiar.

"I never took you for someone so envious and vindictive," Miss Dix continued as she pulled Tucker down the hall. "Whatever Isabelle may have done to you, I can't imagine that she deserved this...cowardly set up." Miss Dix paused long enough to push open the door and yank Tucker out into the cold and dusky courtyard. Miss Dix had apparently left her flashlight behind, but that did not deter her. She marched through the darkness at a brisk pace, as though her feet remembered the way. "I think it's time that you got a taste of what Isabelle has endured in her quest to be free of her addictions, develop authentic friendships, and re-establish her relationship with Jesus."

Endured? This didn't sound good. What was worse than enforced femininity? What were they going to do? Throw her into solitary confinement? Give her a lobotomy? Make her stand naked and shackled with a hood over her head while they laughed at her genitalia? Her black humor didn't ease the ball of fire that was forming in Tucker's belly. She could hear a voice in her head begging her to give up this silly charade and tell Miss Dix what had really happened and that she was just taking the blame so Isabelle didn't get in trouble. So Isabelle could get out of this place.

But she had no reason to trust Miss Dix with that information. After all, the woman had *chosen* to work at Pioneer, which meant that even if she seemed cool sometimes, she was the enemy. Not to mention a suspect. Sort of. Tucker couldn't seriously imagine Miss Dix had a role in the disappearance of two girls or the deaths of two more. But something fishy was going at Pioneer, and until she knew more Tucker couldn't risk blowing her cover to anyone.

They had reached the other side of the courtyard. Miss Dix unlocked the door, saying, "At Pioneer we take a multi-pronged approach to healing our client's wounded relationship with God. You've already experienced prayer, and our educational unit, but we have other tools in our arsenal."

Maybe Isabelle would be so thankful that Tucker had taken the blame that she would open up and tell her something. Isabelle had been there the longest, after all, and she'd known the girls who ran away. She seemed to have the most potential as an informant. So maybe this would turn out to be the best thing that could have happened. They walked several paces down the hall and Miss Dix used another key from her ring, unlocked a door and pushed Tucker inside. She flicked on the light.

Whatever Tucker had feared, this was not it. At first glance, no room could be less frightening. There were no shackles hooked to a wall. There was nothing medical about the room, which seemed to rule out surgeries and electro-shock therapy. There were no apparent signs of torture at all. There were no religious artifacts, no scripture quoted on the walls, no pictures of Jesus carrying the heavy burden of the world's sins. None of that.

Tucker stared in puzzlement at two rows of public school desks, the kind that were little more than an uncomfortable wooden chair with only one arm, which was stretched out cradling a small pad of wood for writing. The seating didn't look comfortable, and the large screen in front of the room was the kind they had at schools, which was pulled down for an educational film or occasional assembly. Still, films were films and, aside from horror, there was nothing frightening or unnerving about watching one. If this was the punishment, Tucker decided she would have to act out more often.

"I'm going to pop out and get you something to eat from the kitchen," Miss Dix sounded almost cheery. Had she forgotten she was mad at Tucker? Perhaps she knew Tucker was taking the blame for

Isabelle, and now they were going to fake a punishment was and instead eat breakfast and watch movies. "It won't be set up for breakfast yet, but I may be able to find something."

She returned a few minutes later, bearing a banana, a container of yogurt, a glass of orange juice and a plain bagel. Tucker hadn't realized how hungry she was, but she finished off the snack in no time. Miss Dix watched her down the last of the juice before standing and picking up the empty glass.

"I've just given you a nausea-inducing medication," she declared, matter-of-factly.

"What?" Tucker was sure she'd misunderstood.

"It'll take about ten or fifteen minutes before you feel nauseous."

"You've *drugged* me?" Tucker was mortified.

"It doesn't feel very good when someone pulls a trick on you, does it Jennye?"

"So this is some kind of warped *lesson*?"

"No. This is *aversion therapy*. It can be extremely successful. It made quite an impact on Isabelle. Of course she's endured ten sessions over the last few months."

Tucker was starting to feel panicky and a little sick. Were the drugs starting to work or was the fact that Miss Dix could expose her to this sort of barbaric torture making her want to throw up? "You don't have to do this, Aimee," she began to plead, speaking more intimately than she had before.

"Remember, Jennye, that I'm your advisor, not your friend, so you must treat me with respect and call me Miss Dix."

Tucker stared into Miss Dix's eyes, hoping she was conveying the disappointment and loss of faith she'd seen in the counselor's eyes half an hour ago. If she managed to communicate her feelings, they did not dissuade Miss Dix, who turned and walked out the door.

A few minutes later a projector came on in the back of the room and began to roll film. Spliced together were pop culture stills, movie clips, and girl-on-girl pornography. Supermodel Cindy Crawford straddling k.d. lang in a barber chair. Nice. Madonna kissing Britney Spears. That image made Tucker queasy on a good day, let alone with a drug and disappointment making her ill. A closet kiss from *It's in the Water* bled into the love scene from *Desert Hearts*, which faded into Gina Gershon taking Jennifer Tilly, which moved into pornography where obviously straight porn stars did what straight men wanted to see two women doing.

The drug was really taking effect now or Tucker would have laughed. She'd never found mainstream girl-on-girl porn much of a turn on. Did any lesbian? But instead of laughing, she was clutching her stomach and spitting acid into a handy trashcan. The nausea was so bad she thought about sticking her finger down her throat to get it over with. She wondered who put the montage together. Probably Dr. Barnabas. He was obviously a closet pervert.

The longer the film ran the more X-rated its images became. Soon it was splices of Bettie Page and then, surprisingly good snippets of old films, the ones made by lesbians for lesbians, like *Suburban Dykes* and *Dress Up for Daddy*. Just then, Tucker's entire body formed a spasmodic dance of involuntary heaving. She started to form a thought about copyright violations and a serenade of gagging noises and retching began again.

By the time the reel had made it to BDSM, Tucker wasn't able to look up without having another round of dry heaves rack her body. She hung her head over the trashcan, exhausted and desperate for the vomiting to end. Her focus had narrowed until so that she was only aware of shuddering dry heaves and the silent mantra in her head pleading for it all to end. She didn't even notice when the film ran to black.

Chapter Ten

Velvet couldn't imagine fitting anything else into her day. It was already after one in the morning when she got home but that cryptic entry from earlier in the day plucked at the edges of her mind and she knew she couldn't just shower and fall into bed. *Help grounding group 6 pioneer.* What on earth could that mean? Velvet headed for her computer.

Her initial searches were baffling. The Pioneer Institute didn't seem to have a real website, just a placeholder page, and there was nothing on it about groups of any sort. When Velvet searched Google for "group 6 Pioneer," she was equally baffled. There was the *Pioneer*, a newspaper in central Michigan. Another entry detailed Massachusetts-based Pioneer Group's six cents per share loss after some Russian investments. None of the entries seemed applicable and Velvet didn't buy the coincidence that while she was researching events that happened at the Pioneer Institute, she would receive random cell phone spam with "pioneer" in the message. She kept trying word combinations until, bingo: *The Grounding of Group 6* was a Julian F. Thompson book first published in 1983. Velvet's gut tightened as she read the blurb.

> Parents get mad at their teenagers all the time, right? But what if your parents got so mad that they decided to have you killed? That's what happened to the kids in Group 6, but they don't know it yet. They think they've been sent to Coldbrook Country School in order to get straightened out. Sure, all of them admit to having caused their parents a few problems, but they're just normal kids. They have no idea that their

parents hate them enough to kill them. Group 6 is about to find out exactly what's in store for them at Coldbrook. Will they survive?

Was this someone's idea of a joke or was the Pioneer Institute extinguishing the lives of queer kids? Were the disappearances and deaths deliberate? More importantly, where was Tucker in all this? And who sent this note? Was it from Tucker, had she found a way to contact Velvet? If so, why the esoteric message? Velvet was now as worried as she could be, convinced that Tucker was in mortal danger. She wanted to go break her out of that gabby prison but she knew that might not be the best step.

She hesitated to wake Yoshi up based on a far fetched theory. She couldn't contact Tucker and she felt powerless and abandoned. Somehow, taking over the magazine had left her less in touch with what the Blind Eye team was doing. She was out of the loop and losing touch with the people she loved, but Velvet didn't have time to mope. She started phoning everyone she could find and leaving voicemail messages. She had to get hold of a copy of that book and see if more clues lay within its pages.

❖

Damn that broad, Bud thought. Velvet was hot as hell, if you liked thick chicks with big breasts and loud mouths. But damn, she sure was emotional, even for a girl. She'd gotten one garbled text message and now she thought Tucker was going to be killed? She'd seen too many horror movies. Her text message was probably nothing more than a new advertising scheme. After Tucker showed him how to read his text messages so she could send him annoying updates when they were apart, he'd gotten some weird messages himself. He'd even showed them to Tucker and she'd all but laughed him out of the room. She said *everyone* got those messages and it was a marketing technique to create buzz for a new monster movie.

Velvet's Group 6 crap was probably the same kind of shit. The fact that she'd figured out it had to do with a book title was more proof. They were always making movies out of books that were popular twenty years ago. The only way someone like him would know the story was if they filmed it and showed it on cable.

Bud couldn't believe the Pioneer Institute was executing kids. It was so outlandish, he'd chuckled a bit during his breakfast phone call with Velvet. He'd told her nobody would be that brazen, and where was the money in murder? Students at Pioneer brought in fifteen hundred a week. Velvet was overreacting the way chicks always did. She said the way it worked in the book was the parents *paid* the school to solve their teenage problems. But even if the Pioneer parents were in on a dastardly conspiracy like that, it still didn't make sense. Why leave those dead girls where they fell from the cliff? Why bring attention to themselves by reporting kids as runaways if they'd killed them? Who'd be stupid enough to get away with murder and *then* invite the law in? Where was the evidence?

Velvet had no answers to any of these questions except to remind him that Dr. Barnabas had been suspiciously reticent, and Pioneer kept a tight lid on all their clients and employees. After all, that was why Blind Eye had sent Tucker undercover in the first place.

While it was true that Dr. Barnabas was evasive and Bud thought he was probably hiding *something,* that sure didn't equal murder. Velvet had hinted that there was more to the story, but if she wasn't willing to share it with him, that was her problem. He didn't have time to dick around soothing her unwarranted fears. Tucker was a big girl and she could take care of herself for one freaking day while he organized a little bit of fun with his fine new lady friend. This was the first real date he'd been on since he was shot. And the most surprising thing was that he wasn't even nervous. He wasn't sitting in his chair worrying about what would happen when the date ended. What would happen if she invited him back to her place? He wasn't thinking about that or hating his chair or his dead dick. He was totally engrossed in the moment, in imagining that beautiful, sexy woman in front of him.

The only thing he felt bad about was that he had to keep lying to Barbara Parkins. She had a kid at Pioneer after all. He probably should be treating her like a source, interrogating her about the ex-gay school. But he'd promised himself one night where he could put the case aside and just be himself. That was why it sucked that he had to pretend Tucker was his daughter named Jennye. When they'd arranged the date, he had to keep turning the attention back on Barbara so he wouldn't have to keep making stuff up about his life as a single parent. The best lies were always those that were the closest to the truth. If he fabricated too much about his imaginary daughter, at some point, he was bound to forget a detail that might come up later. That was, of course, *if* they had another date after tonight.

Of course, if he had to run off to the men's room to have discreet phone calls with a paranoid lesbo, his date wasn't going to go too well. Tomorrow he'd dedicate time to the case. The sooner it ended the sooner he could come clean with Barbara Parkins. Hopefully she wouldn't hold it against him that he didn't have a kid on his own and had been investigating the institute she had so much faith in.

Bud could feel the stupid smile spreading across his face as he picked up the phone to confirm their date. "Sorry I didn't get back to you sooner," he almost purred. "Work."

"Oh, my, that's not a problem," Barbara sounded truly happy to hear from him. "I'm sure you're a very busy gentleman."

❖

"Why'd you take the blame?" Isabelle asked. "You didn't have to go through that."

Tucker shrugged. She wasn't entirely sure why she'd done it. "Maybe if I'd known what was coming, I wouldn't have," she joked weakly. "I didn't want you to ruin your chance to leave. Why'd you take the keys? You knew what could happen."

"I had to see for sure."

"See what?"

"If Dom's stuff is still in the storage room or if they really got rid of it. Before I made testimony to the Lord, I was in love with her. But she ran off and left me here. They weren't even friends. But when you started talking about Saya's sister… I hated Dom for leaving me here, but what if something bad happened and she didn't leave on her own accord? I just have to know."

"Did you get a chance to find out?"

"No. Right after I snagged the keys I heard someone in the bathroom, so I hid. Then I chickened out."

Tucker wondered if she could tell Isabelle the truth now. Could she trust Isabelle to keep her secret? "I'm sorry. I don't blame you for wanting to find out something more. It really does sound suspicious. And then those other two girls *died.* Were you on that camping trip?"

"Yeah."

"Did you notice anything unusual?" Tucker sensed there was *something*.

"Not really." Isabelle hesitated. "The night before they fell off the cliff something happened. We were at Crystal Lake. I woke up and saw them sneaking away.

"But?"

"I told Miss Dix and she busted them."

"What were they doing?"

Isabelle rolled her eyes. "What do you think?"

"Sex?"

"What else? Matt didn't believe it, but *come on*."

Tucker thought about Isabelle's theory. Of course the two girls could have been sneaking off to have sex, but couldn't there be some other reason? Like they were out smoking or looking at sport magazines or other FI behavior? "Were they a couple? Sarah and Erica?"

"I hadn't thought so before that night. I *thought* they were just friends, but it makes sense now. They were really close. I guess it got them killed though, when they took off together again the next night and fell off that cliff."

Tucker knitted her brows and shook her head. "Except I don't think that's what happened. I mean, I know it got classified as an accident, but there were defensive wounds and we think—"

"What do you mean, *we*?"

"We? No, I meant *I*. Just me."

"You said *we*. And how do you know about their injuries? It's like you know more about what happened than I do and I was there." Isabelle's voice was rising. "Are you a cop?"

Tucker motioned her to be quiet. "I'm not with the police, I swear. Shouldn't you be getting back to class? You're going to lose your bathroom privileges if you're gone too long."

"I don't think so, not after being traumatized last night when you *framed* me."

"But you *know* I didn't."

Isabelle shrugged. "That's not how I'm going to tell it." She stood up and made like she was going to leave.

Damn it. Tucker wished she'd spent more time developing a cover story that would explain her interest in the case. "Okay, okay. Can you keep a secret?"

"Yes."

"Swear. Swear on Dom's life."

Isabelle's face went gray and Tucker worried she'd gone too far. But she needed to know Isabelle would keep her confidence. "I swear."

"I work with a private investigation firm and I'm here to find out what really happened to Dom and Saya, and who killed Sarah and Erica."

"*You*'re a private eye? At your age?"

"I'm twenty-three," Tucker said. "I'm not a PI yet. I've finished the classroom portion but I still have a ton of hours to complete."

"Who hired you?"

"What?" Tucker was surprised by the question. Did Isabelle mean Blind Eye?

"If you're not the police you don't just investigate for no reason. Someone had to hire you. Who's your client?"

Tucker knew she shouldn't reveal the name of the women who'd retained Blind Eye's services. But in this case, it might just help. "Saya's sister, Aneko."

Isabelle looked stunned. She stood, staring for a moment, before she spoke again. "You think someone *murdered* Sarah and Erica?" Her voice dropped as though she didn't want to verbalize the next question aloud. "What about Dom?"

"That's what I'm trying to find out. Do you want to help me?"

"I…I don't know. I should be going." Isabelle ended the conversation abruptly and darted out the door.

❖

Meeting with Aneko Takahashi had become an unexpected pleasure for Yoshi. She always felt that the other woman added an unexpected mixture of sweetness to her day. Even in her grief and anxiety, Aneko was charming, alluring and thoroughly engaging, qualities that Yoshi felt got short shrift in today's almost-pathologically detached, techno-obsessed world. She found herself wanting to spend more time with Aneko than was reasonable, especially when this was a client relationship.

"Should we go, then?"

Aneko's soft-spoken query tore Yoshi from her navel gazing. She spent a lot of time philosophizing around Aneko and, in her presence, was not quite as composed or as orderly as she usually was. She wanted to let her guard down around Aneko. They'd known each other mere weeks and yet Yoshi often found herself daydreaming about the woman. Of course, if Blind Eye did not find her sister, they probably wouldn't ever be able to develop a relationship outside this case. Not that she wanted to. Well, maybe…

"Hello? Yoshi? Where'd you go?"

Damn, she was doing it again. Fantasizing. By now, Aneko must think her a total loon. Or some kind of blind narcoleptic. "Oh yes, of course. Just thinking. I'm heading toward BART myself, so I'll walk with you."

They ambled rather slowly in the direction of the city's underground subway system. After a few minutes Aneko took Yoshi's elbow. She would have found the move patronizing had it come from a different client but, from Aneko, it was a gesture of kindness. Plus, Yoshi couldn't help but feel a sense of electricity between them. She almost willed Aneko to move her hand, to caress her palm and entwine with her fingers. She longed to hold Aneko's hand.

"Aneko, I've been thinking—" Before Yoshi could finish, a cacophony caught her attention. The shriek of tires on warm asphalt sounded too close, and moments before a shot rang out Yoshi threw Aneko to the ground, all the while yelling "Get down!" for anyone in earshot.

Aneko was dead silent and for a split second Yoshi worried she'd been shot. But, as the barrage of bullets whirled past her, Aneko grabbed Yoshi's arms and gathered her whole body close. It was for protection, no doubt, but even in her terror Yoshi recognized that the two women were closer than ever. Screams bounced off concrete, fleeting footsteps pounded the pavement, car horns gave way to emergency sirens, but still she and Aneko huddled together like old lovers, sinewy limbs enmeshed through fear, adrenaline, and perhaps, something even more primal.

"Are you okay? Were you hit?" Yoshi began to pull away. Separating felt like removing an insect from flypaper. It was wrong, she could feel it. There was a charge between them, no doubt, but Yoshi could tell the other woman was still trembling from the attempt on her life. Or on Yoshi's life. Or some stranger walking nearby. Who knew exactly what that attack was about? But Yoshi's instincts were usually reliable and she was certain Pioneer Institute was somehow at the helm.

"I'm okay. Are you?" Aneko's response was tentative and breathless.

Reassured that neither of them needed medical help, Yoshi prodded Aneko for any details she could recall. There was, sadly, very little information to retrieve. Aneko was a mild-mannered translator, a language guru who had probably never seen a gun before the day she held one to Barnabas Gage's temple, much less found herself on this side of the barrel. Yoshi thought about the garbled voicemail messages from Velvet. She was convinced Tucker was in danger, and perhaps she was. But only if her cover was blown. Yoshi had instructed Bud to stay in touch and be ready to get her out, if need be.

After the hours it took to speak to the SFPD officers and go through a quick check-in with paramedics, the two women took a quiet taxi ride back to Yoshi's house so they could deconstruct what had happened. They held hands along the way and Yoshi could feel Aneko trembling.

"I'm sorry, I know it's awful," Aneko said again as they sat down on a couch in Yoshi's living room. "I wish I could remember the car." The police officers had asked her about the color, the make, model or license plate number but she'd been too terrified to notice.

"Aneko, honey, stop apologizing," Yoshi consoled her, wanting so much to pull her close once more. "You were frightened, which is a completely reasonable reaction."

"You just called me honey." Aneko offered that statement with a lilt in her voice. "Do you want me?"

Yoshi was stunned silent. She wasn't sure she understood. "What?"

"Yoshi Yakamota, famous PI, this isn't a time to be coy. Do you want me?"

Clearly sweet little Aneko wasn't as naïve as she had thought. Yes,

Yoshi very much wanted her. She wanted to pull gently on her long hair and lick the contours of her neck, moving down to her breasts and further still.

"Well?" Damn, Aneko really wanted an answer to her rather rhetorical question.

"Aneko, I'm not sure I should really answer that," Yoshi said. "You're a client and we have a professional relationship."

Aneko inched toward her, her face so close that they were sharing the same pool of oxygen. Peppery sweet breath and Aneko's unmistakable scents filled Yoshi with vigor and fear and excitement. "I want you." It was a statement; there was no questioning in Aneko's vernacular now. "And I know you want me."

She pushed Yoshi's shoulders back against the sofa and climbed on top of her like she was gently mounting a steed.

"I do," Yoshi whispered. "I do."

Aneko stopped talking, busying herself kissing Yoshi's face, her neck, her shoulders, everything but her mouth. Yoshi was dying. She wanted that kiss so badly, but Aneko clearly had other plans. Every time Yoshi began to move, to take charge of the encounter, even just to reciprocate, Aneko pushed her back down.

"Not yet," Aneko whispered. She pulled Yoshi's blouse off over her head, unsnapping her bra and unbuttoning her slacks..

Soon Aneko's hand was inside her and around her, one finger rubbing her clit and another two swirling around her G-spot. Between the gentle nibbling on her nipples and the thrusting of Aneko's hand, Yoshi was ready to orgasm almost immediately. Aneko anticipated that, though, and pulled her hand back, slowly.

Softly, she whispered again, "Not yet."

Yoshi could no sooner hold back an orgasm than she could win the Indy 500. She was going to come and it was going to happen now. But when Aneko placed her face between Yoshi's legs, the waiting seemed well worth it. As Aneko swirled and twirled her tongue, using her fingers to dart in and out of Yoshi's wetness and her tongue to spell the alphabet, twice, backward, Yoshi thought she'd reached nirvana. She wasn't usually so moved by sex. She liked it, all right, but not like this. This moment in time felt like no other, it was immeasurable and intense and God, she hated to feel so crazy, but damn it if this moment didn't some how feel life-changing.

By then end of the night, Yoshi found a new sense of her own sexuality and her ability to transcend her normal reserve. Aneko worked on pleasing her for what seemed like hours until, sticky and damp and exhausted, Yoshi rolled on her side, pulling the other woman toward her. "Are you ready for a break?" she panted.

"Yes." Aneko said with a lilt in her voice. "Where are your toys?"

Toys? She couldn't imagine what Aneko had planned next. "Whoa, listen up lady, I'm so over-stimulated I couldn't possibly handle any more."

"It's not for you," Aneko teased. Soon, the younger woman was helping Yoshi fasten a strap on harness, inserting her purple colt dildo that Velvet bought her half a lifetime ago.

Aneko lifted herself up and over Yoshi's pelvis, putting her fingers first in Yoshi's mouth and then in her own wetness. She angled the dildo so it slid easily inside her. Yoshi grabbed Aneko's ass, her hands strong and controlling, guiding the younger woman up and down and rocking along with Aneko's rhythm.. This was the best sexual experience Yoshi had ever had, blind or not. She didn't need to see Aneko to know what was going on. Their lovemaking was primal but soft, tender but explosive, instinctual yet surprising. Soon, Aneko was panting, moaning her name and a litany of prosaic profanities that made Yoshi smile and blush all at once. As her rocking sped up and the throaty refrains gave way to just one quite sincere version of "Oh, God," Yoshi couldn't help but marvel at the woman's beauty and skill. Theirs was a true melding Yoshi had never really ever experienced before, not even with Velvet or AJ, both of whom were quite skilled at lovemaking.

As they lay exhausted in each other's arms, too tired to talk, they simply nodded into a quiet slumber. Two hours later, Yoshi awoke as Aneko was peeling herself off the bed.

"That was really amazing." Aneko spoke first.

"It was for me too."

"What does it mean?" Yoshi wasn't sure what it meant or if it meant anything at all. "I guess it means whatever we want it to mean. We still have a professional relationship, but, that was something entirely different."

She continued to ramble, never fully committing nor backing

down on the real depth of this experience and what was possibly in store for either of them. Before they could transition into awkwardly avoiding the complications their liaison brought, Aneko had clearly become distracted.

"Yoshi?" Her voice had that charming sweetness to it again. "These old letters on the bureau. They're so lovely. I didn't know you had so many."

Clearly Aneko had found the stack of her father's letters, many more than the few Yoshi had shown her initially. Aneko, a savvy translator by trade, was suddenly so eager to decipher them she seemed to have forgotten their awkwardness just seconds ago. She picked up a letter from the pile, leafed through it, and began to read aloud:

December 15, 1981

Dearest Hiroki

The cold winds of winter chill me to my bones. Ikaga osugoshi de irasshaimasu ka? *How have you been? I received your latest letter and though it was, as always, wonderful to hear from you, it saddened me deeply. What you ask of me is almost unbearable. Hearing from you has been the one brightness in my dark days and the thought of no longer corresponding with you is like a dagger to my heart. Knowing this must be painful for you as well; I am in awe of your strength and commitment to Yoshi. I recognize this decision must have been quite difficult to make but I know you make this sacrifice for Yoshi and I cannot fault you for an act of love.*

Just know that you will live in my heart until the last of my days. I know you feel the same. Although I have cherished your letters, I do not require your feelings be committed to paper to know you love me. Still, it will be very difficult not hearing from you. Perhaps one day, when things have changed, we can be together again.

Okarada o taisetsu ni. *Please take care of yourself.*

Your Love

Yoshi was perplexed. "I'm not quite sure I understand these letters. As far as I know, my parents were never apart until my mother died. I can't imagine when she would write these."

"Could they be from someone your father dated?" Aneko asked innocently.

Yoshi snorted. She had never known her father to date. Hiroki Yakamota never once brought a woman home after Yoshi's mother passed away.

"I have an idea," Aneko continued. "Why don't I take them and translate them."

"Really, Aneko, you do not have to go out of your way."

"I'd love to, really."

"Well, if you have the time, I would be delighted. Obviously, I will compensate you, whatever your usual rate is."

Both women were happy to not have to talk about what happened between them. At least until Aneko teased, "We can work out other forms of payment if we have to."

CHAPTER ELEVEN

Tucker slid into the seat next to Isabelle and set down her lunch. There were few moments when they could speak freely, so Tucker didn't waste time with pleasantries. "Hi, Isabelle. I was thinking…do you still want to see if Dom's things are in the storage room?"

"Duh. That's why I stole Carl Lee's keys."

Tucker smiled. "I want to try it again."

"Which part? Stealing the keys? Pissing off Miss Dix?"

"No, I had in mind breaking in." Tucker paused, not sure just how much she should reveal. She thought she could trust Isabelle, but it was better to proceed with caution. Isabelle didn't need to know about the spy gear Tucker had smuggled into the place. "There's something I want from my suitcase," she finished, remaining vague.

"It's impossible," Isabelle said. "Unless you're good at picking locks. There are three or four of them between our dorm room and the storage."

Tucker recalled the day she'd first arrived at Pioneer, when she was sent to wait in reception for Miss Dix. "There's a key for the storage room in the secretary's desk. So I just need to get into the administrative office."

"How are you going to do that? After the thing with Carl Lee's keys, the counselors have increased their rounds. Best case scenario, they'd notice you missing after an hour."

"Maybe, but it's not like they shine flashlights in our faces.

They just count bed bumps. We could make a lump out of clothes and pillows."

Isabelle shook her head. "If you weren't there for hours we'd know. Then everyone would get punished for not reporting you missing."

"I hadn't thought of that."

"One of the others would tell," Isabelle said with conviction.

Tucker tried brainstorming, picturing what Bud or Yoshi do in this circumstance. She had a flash of Bud stuffing his mouth with Thai food and telling her to improvise. Yoshi's approach would be more methodical. She would probably talk her way into the room, or find someone else to do it for her. But Tucker wasn't that persuasive. She'd considered being honest with Aimee Dix, based on a hunch that the counselor wasn't as rigid as she seemed. Aimee obviously cared about the students, so maybe she would listen if she thought criminal acts were being covered up.

"I wish I could get Miss Dix to help," Tucker said. "But since she thinks I tried to frame you it wouldn't matter what I said."

Isabelle glanced around. "What could she do anyway? She's not going to let you into that room."

"I could ask *her* to check. Wouldn't she want to know, too? She cares about us, doesn't she?"

"Yes, but she thinks Dr. Barnabas is a saint. Even if Dom's stuff was thrown away, she probably wouldn't tell us. She'd try to find a way to make it seem normal."

Tucker thought about a detective movie she'd seen with Velvet. *Velvet*. She hadn't thought of Velvet for days. That just didn't seem right, not when Vel was supposed to be her girlfriend. God, she was a terrible person. Any other lesbian would be thinking about Velvet every minute of the day. But after Tucker was attacked in Velvet's house and suffered a head injury, she'd distanced herself from her lover. It wasn't just about geography, although it certainly didn't help that Tucker was staying across town at Yoshi's place. Their emotional distance had started even before that, maybe when Velvet's friend, Jeff, took a header off the Golden Gate Bridge. Velvet had retreated inside herself then, going someplace Tucker wasn't invited. Now Tucker was doing the same thing. Was she freezing Velvet out in some petty form of retaliation? Was she really that shallow?

"Jennye?" Isabelle's insistent voice summoned Tucker back.

"Sorry, I was just thinking, if the biggest problem is how to get into the office after it's been locked, why don't I get in there earlier in the day? Before they lock everything up?"

"And what? Ask the receptionist let you rummage through the storage room?"

"No, but if you distracted her I could sneak into the storage room and hide there until she went home."

"Brilliant. I'm sure no one will miss you at dinner or evening prayers."

"Right." Tucker sighed. "Never mind. It was a stupid idea."

Isabelle didn't disagree. She changed the subject and they finished their lunch. An hour later, in the short break between subjects, she pulled Tucker aside. "Maybe it wasn't *that* stupid. Didn't you say there were keys in the receptionist's desk even though she wasn't there? She must have a spare set. We could make some kind of diversion and you could steal them. Then we'll stuff the bed that night and you can go check the room and get back before anyone notices."

Tucker nodded, relieved that Isabelle was on her side. She almost told her who she really was but held back. The less Isabelle knew, the safer she was and the less she could leak if she had an attack of conscience. "I hope it works."

"Everyone's watching you after what happened," Isabelle said with a worried grimace. "I wish the counselors weren't so suspicious."

"It's their job."

Isabelle's expression became thoughtful. "Maybe we can get one of them on our side."

Tucker laughed. "Yeah, good luck."

"Is that the truth, Isabelle?" Aimee gently asked the young woman sitting on the edge of her chair.

She'd been surprised when Isabelle came to her private quarters, hanging her head and begging to speak confidentially. Normally she might have refused such a request, but she was attached to Isabelle. After all, the child had been at Pioneer longer than any other student.

Aimee had come to think of her as a younger relative or stepdaughter who had gone a little astray. It was her job to lead wayward teens back to Jesus and she wanted to provide Isabelle with a female role model and a maternal figure.

Aimee believed whole-heartedly in the value of her goal, but lately she was having second thoughts about the means Pioneer used with difficult students like Isabelle. Aversion stimulus treatments like ammonium sulfide, nausea-induction, and electroshock therapy, seemed pretty barbaric. Aimee had begun having doubts the first time Dr. Barnabas administered the electroshock treatment to Isabelle. The machine used sensors to discern arousal and applied mild shocks when the student reacted to same-sex imagery. As the only female on the staff, Aimee had to provide girls with the appropriate sensor, with instructions on how to place it on the skin. Fulfilling that duty with Isabelle felt shameful and Aimee still couldn't bear to think of the angry red burn marks on Isabelle's arm when she came out of the treatment room. The sight had disturbed her so much that Aimee had begun to question her relationship with God. What would Jesus say about such therapy? She could not imagine that, in her shoes, the Son of God would have done as Aimee did. She was here to help these kids, not hurt them, and after all that had transpired for Isabelle, Aimee was thankful that the young woman trusted her at all. So she was quick to assure Isabelle that she would keep her confidence, no matter what. Still, she'd been so shocked by what she'd just heard it sent her spinning into a dilemma. She wondered if Jennye had bullied Isabelle into making a false confession.

"You can be completely truthful with me," she said. "I don't know what Jennye has done, whether she's threatened you or—"

"She hasn't done anything." Isabelle's eyes were tear-drenched. "I'm the one who stole the keys. I don't know why she took the blame for me and I should have spoken up. What I did was wrong and I've prayed about it. That's why I'm telling you now."

Aimee felt sick thinking about punishing the wrong girl. Heaven knew how badly she had set back Jennye's therapy. "Why take the keys in the first place?"

"Because of Dominique," Isabelle mumbled, her eyes on the floor. "We were such good...friends, it hurt when she ran away and I just don't understand why she would have gone without saying a word to me. I wanted to get into the storage room and look through her things in case there was a letter or something. That's where her stuff is, isn't it? And Saya's?"

Aimee had not actually seen the runaway girls' possessions, but she was confident they had not been discarded, as some people had suggested. "I'm sure it is. Didn't you find it there?"

"I didn't end up looking," Isabelle said. "I changed my mind but I couldn't get the keys back without Carl Lee noticing."

"So you panicked?"

Isabelle nodded. "I hid them under my mattress and thought I'd wait till he wasn't there, but then he realized."

"It seems we both misjudged Jennye. You haven't shown her friendship but she was very altruistic toward you. And I misjudged her too." Aimee sighed, filled with remorse. "You have a good friend in her, Isabelle, someone who cared for you without expecting anything in return."

"I know." Isabelle wiped her eyes. "I'm trying to make it up to her."

❖

The plan went off without a hitch. Thanks to Isabelle's distraction, Tucker was exactly where she wanted to be at 12:30 a.m. She headed directly to the items she'd hidden when she arrived. She pulled out one of the tiny spy cameras and a USB key that could secretly copy computer keystrokes. Both devices could be attached to any computer in the office without their users knowing and could relay that info right into Blind Eye's office. With the Blind Eye team monitoring the electronic communication it would be like Tucker had back up and wasn't all alone in this place. Sure, she'd found an ally in Isabelle, but she couldn't risk trusting her entirely.

Her heart racing in excitement, she darted out into the dark hallway, pressing herself against the wall. *I've got you now, Dr. Barnabas, if that's your real name.* She tried the keys in his office door one by one. None of them fit. She fought the urge to kick down the door. This just made her even more certain that the wily Dr. Barnabas had something to hide. *Bastard.*

Disappointed, she stole back to the storage room. Before

methodically searching each shelf front to back, Tucker first looked for the garbage bags the staff had reportedly used to haul away Dominique Marxley and Saya Takahashi's belongings the day after they'd gone missing. There weren't any bags. Once she got past the prohibited clothing haphazardly splayed over other 'False Image' contraband, neat rows of file boxes lined the remaining shelves, their contents listed on the outside in marker. She scanned their titles. Most were fairly self explanatory and pedestrian: camping gear, old financial records, reports. Others listed dates and names: Brian Johnson, March 06. Dominique Marxley, November 07.

She was pulling down Dom's things when she noticed a steel box mounted to the wall. It had a small keyhole on the front that matched a similar key from the ring in the receptionist's desk. Tucker retrieved it and unlocked the box. It was a key closet. Rows of keys hung from numbered hooks. On the inside of the hinged door was a decoder list matching numbers with location. "Dr. B's office" was written in red script. Tucker snatched the key from the corresponding hook and hurried back along the hall.

Once she was inside his office, she went straight to his computer. The presence of a new USB drive would raise too much attention, so she stuck the pinhole spy camera onto the in-box on Dr. Barnabas's desk. She aimed it at his desktop so the Blind Eye team would have a good view of whatever he was working on. With her heart pounding, she locked his door again and returned to the sanctuary of the storage room.

Dominique's box didn't contain much. Surely they couldn't fill a garbage bag. Tucker wondered what had happened to her clothing. Was it just added to the piles that dominated the shelving near the front of the room? She went through the box carefully, making a mental note of the contents. In the end she was left holding two items that took her breathe away: Dominique's California ID and a silver locket.

When she'd asked Isabelle earlier what she should be looking for, Isabelle had said there was one thing Dominique would never have left behind. She'd described this locket and the photograph inside. The black and white image showed a beautiful young girl Isabelle said was Dominique's grandmother. Tucker didn't waste time gazing at the picture. She pried it out and extracted a tiny slip of paper from the secret compartment behind it. On it were the initials DM + IS. She reassembled the locket and tucked it into her bra.

It was a move she'd seen Velvet do this a dozen times. It probably worked better when one's endowment was bigger than Harvard's, as Velvet's was. She took some digital photographs of the other items, including the ID, and returned everything to its place. Saya's belongings came next, and she photographed them carefully. After all, Aneko Takahashi was Blind Eye's client, not Isabelle or her family. Maybe Aneko would find something in the photos that was revealing and could lead them to her missing sister. When Tucker finished snapping photos, she popped out the memory card and put it in the other side of her bra before returning her camera to the pile of her own FI items.

She was just about to call it quits when she spotted a box on the high shelf. It didn't bear a label and was hard to reach, but she climbed the shelves and slid the surprisingly heavy box down to mid-shoulder. She inspected the contents in surprise. The box held a curious assortment of cell phones, all different makes and models. Many looked old. There was something creepy about them. On the back of one, the name Jamie York was scratched into the plastic.

Before she could imagine what it all might mean, the door burst open behind her and a gruff voice demanded, "What do you think you're doing?"

❖

The girl swung around, her mouth gaping and blue eyes wide.

Jennye Williams. Carl Lee should have known.

At the sight of him the color drained from her already pale cheeks. She dropped what had been in her hand and it clattered back into the box. She raised her hands in front of her and stepped back as though he might attack her.

He glowered at her. "What the fuck are *you* doing here? How did you get in without a key?"

He was astonished when her eyes widened even more. It took him a second to figure out what had surprised her. He'd fallen out of character. Pioneer's goody two-shoe counselors didn't swear. Then again, their students didn't generally snoop around, steal from teachers, and break into locked rooms.

"Who put you up to this?" he asked.

She just stood there staring, not bothering to make up an excuse. Carl Lee might have taken her silence as rebelliousness, but he could smell her fear. It crossed his mind that she could be working for Dr. Barnabas, checking up on Carl Lee's extracurricular duties. In prison he'd perfected a don't-fuck-with-me stare. He bared his teeth and tightened his jaw, grinning when she backed away.

"What should I do with you?" he asked in a sing-song voice, advancing on her menacingly.

"Don't," she begged, cowering. She suddenly seemed small and frail, like a shivering puppy. Defenseless. It stopped him cold.

"What's going on here?" Aimee Dix's voice made the hair rise on the back of his neck.

He quickly regained his composure. "I found this one, pilfering through the other student's belongings."

"*Jennye?* I must say I am *very* disappointed to find you here." Aimee Dix sounded irate. "After the trouble over Carl Lee's keys, I thought we had an understanding. Clearly my faith in you was misplaced."

"I'm so sorry Miss Dix. I swear it won't happen again." The girl spoke very fast, a tremor of fear in the tenor of her voice. After the key incident Miss Dix had subjected her to the aversion therapy, and it clearly had made an impact, even if it hadn't quite broken her spirit.

"I thought I'd made it clear what happens to troublemakers. But I see now I was too lenient. Carl Lee?" Her eyes raked his face. "Could you possibly take a break from whatever it is Jennye interrupted?"

"Sure," he answered quickly, hoping to prevent any probing questions about what Jennye might have seen while she was snooping around. "Would you like me to punish her?"

"No, no, I'll handle that myself. I would, however, appreciate it if you could take over watching the other kids. The two of us—" she nodded in Tucker's direction, "have a date with the electroshock machine."

Whoa. Carl Lee never would have guessed the righteous Aimee Dix had a sadistic side. Further proof that everyone wore masks, hiding parts of themselves from the world. He had his own secrets. Secrets that might shock even a cold bitch like Aimee Dix.

"No," Jennye begged. "*Please*. I'll be good, I swear."

"It's too late for that." Aimee's voice was icy. "Now, are you going to come on your own or do I need Carl Lee to carry you?"

The girl dropped her head and shuffled toward them. She stopped in front of Carl Lee and pleaded, "Mr. James, don't let her take me please. I'll do whatever you want."

Carl Lee found himself wondering if she really would do *anything*. He shook images of naked jailbait from his mind. No way he was going down on a sex offender charge. That shit followed you to the grave.

Aimee Dix seemed immune to the girl's pleas. Carl Lee didn't want anything to cast suspicion on him. If he protested her stepping in and taking the kid, Aimee could start wondering what it exactly he was doing here this late at night. He couldn't risk her going to Dr. Barnabas. As much as he'd like to be the one interrogating Jennye and figuring out what she was really up to, he thought it better to back down for now.

"Whatever." He shrugged, hoping he appeared more nonchalant than he really felt.

Aimee grabbed the girl's arm and dragged her from the room.

❖

Aimee did not speak again until she and Tucker had entered the therapy room. As soon as the door closed, she hissed, "What the hell were you thinking, Jennye?"

"Nothing," Tucker stammered, terrified that Aimee was truly going to torture her with electroshock treatment despite their previous interactions and Aimee's supposed guilt over the aversion therapy.

"Did Isabelle put you up to this?"

Even though she thought Aimee might go easier on her if the answer was affirmative, Tucker shook her head.

"You have no idea the danger you've put yourself in." Aimee's cheeks were bright red and she seemed to be fighting the urge to yell. "What did he do before I arrived?"

"Who?" Tucker was confused.

"Carl Lee." There was a sense of urgency in her voice.

"Nothing much" Tucker shook her head. *I was too busy pissing my pants*. "Uh, he asked me how I got in without a key and who put me up to it." She wondered if she should be pissed that no one seemed to think she was capable of forming her own intent. She was beginning to suspect she was missing a major component to the puzzle. "What's going on Aimee? Why are *you* afraid?"

Aimee glanced nervously at the door, as though Carl might storm through it at any minute. "I want you to promise to stay away from him."

Carl Lee? Certainly he was a jerk, but his creepiness was nothing like the demonic aura that oozed from Dr. Barnabas's every pore. And Carl Lee struck Tucker more like someone's henchman, not the mastermind behind a grand scheme. Still, she could see Carl Lee doing Dr. Barnabas's dirty work and she could believe he was involved in the disappearance of Pioneer students and possibly the recent deaths. But not out of some zealous conviction he shared with Dr. Barnabas. No, she'd bet Carl Lee was in it for something else. Thrills maybe. Or he was hiding something and a student had found out. She wondered what Aimee knew that made her paranoid.

Tucker didn't ask. Instead she said, "If you think Carl Lee is dangerous, don't you have a duty to tell someone?"

Aimee avoided her eyes. "I worry about judging the book by the cover, so to speak. I have a suspicious nature. It's not very Christian of me."

It's not very Christian to push a couple of students off a cliff, either. Tucker focused on what Aimee had said about not being sure. "You suspect something. Is it about Erica and Sarah?"

Aimee's nodded almost imperceptibly, but she didn't say anything.

In the silence that followed, Tucker fought the urge to blurt out everything, about her secret mission here, about Blind Eye and Aneko and the dubious behavior of Dr. Barnabas Gage. If she came clean, wouldn't that encourage Aimee to speak her mind in return? And to verbalize her concerns about Carl Lee?

"Does the name Jamie York mean anything to you?" Tucker asked, almost surprising herself with her sudden query.

"Jamie York?" Aimee lifted her head. "Jamie was a client here, two or three years ago. She left abruptly when her parents pulled her from Pioneer and sent her to an elite boarding school in France. I haven't heard from her since. Why?"

Tucker wished for the hundredth time in the last week that she was wearing jeans. Silently swearing to never again take her pockets for granted, she grappled with her blouse, finally shoving her hand down the neckline as though trying to readjust a wayward breast. Aimee inhaled sharply. Tucker felt her cheeks burning. Before Aimee could chastise her for the blatant display of self-loving, Tucker yanked her fingers from her bra and stretched them toward Aimee. The counselor stepped back as though repelled

"It's not a come on," Tucker said nervously. "It's a cell phone." She raised it to eye level and was rewarded with the relief on Aimee's face. "It says Jamie York."

This time Aimee accepted the phone. She ran her fingers over the jagged letters, the way Yoshi did when reading Braille. "Where did you find this?"

"In the storeroom. There was a whole box of used cell phones."

"No." Aimee shook her head, as though disagreeing with Tucker's statement of fact. "She would have taken this with her."

"Maybe it's a donation," Tucker offered a rational explanation. "You know a lot of non-profits collect old cell phones these days, it's some kind of fundraising thing."

Aimee didn't reply at first, she just stared at Jamie York's abandoned property. When the silence between them was becoming uncomfortable she asked, her voice choked with emotion. "There were others?"

And then Aimee started to cry.

If he were here, Bud would've responded to the tears by getting mad and yelling. It was like other people's emotional weaknesses threatened him, like crying was not only incredibly contagious but entirely deadly as well. Yoshi wouldn't lose her cool like that. She'd be tactical: displaying sympathy to develop trust and encourage openness, or suggesting solutions like, "You can make a difference by helping us bring this perpetrator in." That might make Yoshi seem calculated or cold, but she was neither of those.

"Who are you really, Jennye Williams?" Aimee asked.

Tucker realized she'd missed her chance to take control of the situation and use it to solve Blind Eye's case, which was why she was at Pioneer in the first place. She should be the one asking questions and seeing through a person's façade, not the other way around. Glad that neither Bud nor Yoshi had witnessed her blunder, she berated herself as she imagined they would. She'd never been good at lying and it probably doomed her to be terrible at this undercover thing that felt like being deceitful 24/7, the way she felt back when she was in the closet. She hadn't relished the feeling then and she didn't appreciate it now.

"What do you mean? I'm Jennye Williams. Who else would I be? *Madonna*?" She tried making a joke to lighten the mood. She couldn't confide in Aimee. Not yet. It could jeopardize the investigation, disappoint Yoshi, and, more importantly, if Tucker's suspicions were correct, sharing them with the counselor would put Aimee in danger, too.

CHAPTER TWELVE

When she'd escorted Jennye back to the dormitory, in a wheelchair feigning the after-effects of shock therapy, Aimee collapsed on her bed. She was desperately grateful that Isabelle had told her the truth about Jennye, preventing her from making another terrible mistake, but something about the girl bothered her. She seemed strangely self-possessed and the discoveries she'd made unsettled Aimee so deeply she knew she would get very little sleep tonight. How many cell phones were there and which former students did they belong to? She had to know.

She thought about Dominique and Saya. Were their phones in the storage room, too? It had been six months. Why had no one heard from them? Aimee remembered Saya talking about her older sister Aneko during group therapy. She loved and trusted her sister. When she rejected the teachings of Pioneer, why had she not reached out to Aneko, who was living an openly homosexual lifestyle?

Aimee was afraid she knew the answer. She was afraid the answer was Carl Lee James. Worse, she suspected her fellow counselor was also behind the disappearance of Erica Bingham and Sarah Worthington. As she had so many times since she'd discovered them missing, Aimee ran through the events leading up to the accident.

They'd trudged into the Marin County Park at three in the afternoon, delighted to see Pioneer's school bus waiting for them. One of the girls needed feminine protection and Aimee had taken the group into the village for a quick stop at the grocery store. Carl Lee had stayed behind, promising the boys would have the camp set up when the girls returned. In exchange, Aimee was in charge of dinner. It was hardly a negotiation, their roles were pretty much set in stone.

Aimee had been in the fresh vegetable section at the store when she noticed several of her girls conversing with two scraggly looking men. She was immediately conflicted. It was delightful to see the Pioneer girls stretching their wings with the opposite sex, but these two were not the finest specimens. They appeared to be Bolinas residents, rather than residents of the nearby resort of Sea Cliff where the wealthy had summer cottages. The girls continue chatting with the pair as Aimee completed her shopping. Isabelle stayed by her side, carrying the grocery basket and tagging along behind as Aimee chose ingredients for the evening meal.

Aimee was thankful to leave the strangers behind them and later reminded the girls about the dangers of encouraging attention from unknown men. Of course that had to be handled delicately, as one did not want to clip the baby bird's wings just as it was beginning to fly on the right path.

After dinner and evening prayer she saw the students to bed and followed suit, determined to enjoy her last night in the open before returning to Pioneer the next morning. She woke with a start just after 2:00 a.m., unsure what had disturbed her. She lay still for a moment, listening. Had there been some kind of noise? She felt anxious, as though her subconscious was trying to alert her to danger.

Frogs and crickets serenaded each other. She could hear the dew dripping onto the tent and rolling down the side. Unable to shake the feeling that something was wrong, she wriggled out of the sleeping bag and pulled on her boots and jacket before crawling out of the tent.

The moon was veiled behind a gossamer curtain of fog. Although visibility was extremely limited, Aimee had no trouble making out Carl Lee's tent a few years away. Like a lot of men, Carl Lee was a master of nocturnal noises and after four night's camping, Aimee could predict his REM state by decibels of his nostril cacophony. The deeper his sleep, the louder his snoring. As she stood next to his tent, she realized that a change to his pattern had awoken her, an absence of sound. She couldn't hear Carl Lee's snores. The thought raised an uncharitable response. Maybe Carl Lee had died in his sleep. Aimee chastised herself for being un-Christian.

"Carl Lee?" she asked. Her normal speaking voice sounded loud in the still of the night.

She shone the beam of her flashlight at the tent, but couldn't tell from the shadows whether a person lay within. She unzipped the flap, all the while rehearsing what she'd say if he was in there and woke up. She ducked her head in. Carl Lee was not there.

Aimee's stomach rose into her throat the way it did when she went on roller coaster rides. She'd never enjoyed that feeling. And she didn't like it now. Where was he and what was he doing? She didn't trust him. He reminded her of the ex-con's she'd ministered through her church. She'd stuck with the program for eighteen months before she resigned. *But, you're so good with them*, Pastor John had said, *they need you.* She hadn't been able to hide the shiver his words had sent rippling through her, and she couldn't tell him, or anyone, why she could no longer bear to be in the program or even set foot in the rectory where she'd run the weekly prayer sessions. It had taken her a long time to recover her faith after that experience, and she understood why some women feared the opposite sex. That insight helped prepare her for her current role with Pioneer. There was a hardness about Carl Lee that brought back memories she wanted to forget. Dr. Barnabas would never hire someone with a criminal history to work around kids this way, so that meant Carl Lee had likely managed to hide his past. At first she thought maybe he was a petty thief and that he wanted to be around children of the wealthy so he could steal from them. It wouldn't be difficult for Carl Lee to palm electronic devices, mobile phones, jewelry, laptop computers, and even credit cards. But nothing had been reported stolen and Aimee's suspicions had moved in a different direction over the past six months.

Carl Lee had been on duty the night Saya Takahashi and Dominique Marxley ran away. When he insisted he saw nothing his words had sparked the memory of another breakout, a year earlier. Aimee had checked the records and discovered that Carl Lee had been on duty that night, too. It added up to more than a coincidence, yet Aimee needed proof of something sinister before she could make allegations.

Standing outside his tent in the dark, shrouded in fog, Aimee felt all her senses on high alert. When she heard muffled voices coming from the direction of the boys' camp, she started off in that direction, careful not to stray from the trail. She never should have acquiesced when Carl Lee set up the camp here, so close to the dangerous cliffs.

As she drew closer to the voices, she could discern the golden radiance of a campfire through the fog. Some of the kids must have gotten the fire going again. Aimee was disappointed that she'd have to assign more detention. If Erica and Sarah were behind this—after she'd had to discipline them for their shenanigans the night before, she'd be furious.

But Aimee didn't hear Erica and Sarah, or Carl Lee's distinctive tenor. There were two deeper, huskier voices and when the veil of fog finally parted, she was looking at the straggly young men from the grocery store earlier in the day. The glowing embers lit their faces and glinted off the beer cans in their hands, on the ground, and frozen to the lips of Matt Lovelorn. From the number of scattered cans and the dwindling firewood, Aimee could see that the men had been in the camp for several hours. Anything could have happened. One of her girls was sitting far too close to them for Aimee's liking and she was certain she could smell cigarettes.

"Put that beer down!" She raised her voice and called each of their names in turn, using full names and the inflections of a disappointed mother. "I am *very* disappointed in you. I cannot *believe* that you would violate our trust this way. You've disregarded all you've learned about personal responsibility on this outing, turned your back on our Savior, and," Aimee snatched the beer from Matt and dumped it over the fire, "polluted your body. I suggest you all think about what you've done on your way back to your tents."

Even the men scrambled to their feet, though they both stood there with idiotic grins on their face like this was all some kind of joke.

"Are you trying to get arrested?" she yelled at them.

Their smiles slipped, but they weren't looking at *her*. Aimee whipped around to find Carl Lee materializing out of the fog like a specter. She shivered.

"Get the fuck out of our camp," he snarled, "before we call the cops. These girls are fucking underage."

"Carl!" Aimee was about to chastise him for his language but noticed the men backing up as though they'd been struck. The kids crowded around her as if they also sensed Carl Lee's capacity for violence. And such foul language. She did not know *what* Dr. Barnabas was thinking when he hired that vile man. She drew the kids to her like a mother hen hustling her chicks.

"Let's move along, shall we?" she said, trying to keep the tremor from her voice. Men were like dogs. They could smell fear, and Aimee did not want Carl Lee to sense hers.

Ten minutes later Aimee had seen the delinquents to their tents. All insisted they had not invited the men, who called themselves the Mudd brothers, and who had convinced the girls that they were surfing legends and local heroes. Aimee rolled her eyes so many times she feared they'd get stuck in that position. Kids these days. They wouldn't trust their parents, teachers, or religious leaders, but throw a couple of disheveled men into the scenario and all common sense went out the window.

When Aimee pointed out that these men could have been rapists or murderers, her girls had giggled and laughed, telling her she was paranoid. If they thought that was paranoid, it was a good thing she didn't mention her fear that Carl Lee was somehow in cahoots with the Mudd brothers. Why else had he insisted they spend their last night far from their usual pick up point?

Aimee carried out a bed check at the boys' camp and was on her way to the girls' when she ran into Carl Lee coming from that direction.

"What happened with those men?" she asked.

"I chased them off."

She didn't hide her suspicion. "You were at the girls' camp?"

"I was worried. They were getting a little friendly with some of girls." He paused. "I guess that's progress." His tone was mocking, as though he was laughing at her and everything Pioneer stood for.

"I'm headed there now," she said. "To finish my bed check."

His hand on her arm anchored her to the spot. Fear raced through her like a wildfire. *I'll scream*, she thought. But they were standing close to the cliffs, and she doubted anyone would hear her over the surf.

"Don't bother," Carl Lee said. "I already checked."

She didn't believe him. How had he had the time chase the Mudd brothers away and do a bed check?

He let go of her arm. "I can use your help with the fire. I'll get the bucket if you'll grab the shovel from the bus."

Aimee wanted to be helpful but she also wanted to check on the girls. If she insisted he'd know she didn't trust him, and if he was as dangerous as she was beginning to fear, she didn't want to be seen as some kind of threat. In hindsight, Aimee wondered if that was the plan. She wondered if Carl Lee had scripted the entire night. She didn't sleep well and she was awake at the first light of dawn. When Erica and Sarah didn't show up for breakfast she wasn't worried at first. She sent Isabelle to wake them.

A few minutes later, the girl returned sulking. "They're hiding from me. How immature can you be? What babies."

Aimee sighed. Perhaps the two girls had found out it was Isabelle who had ratted them out at Crystal Lake. They probably weren't too happy that Aimee would be doling out an appropriate punishment when they returned to Pioneer. Usually this trip was the highlight of her year, the kids on their best behavior because they were delighted to be outside Pioneer's walls. But this year, it had been one hassle after another. She felt like telling Dr. Barnabas to just cancel the whole thing.

She glanced around, looking for Matt Lovelorn. He was friendly with Erica. Maybe he could find the girls and get them to stop playing around. But Matt wasn't in sight and her eyes met Carl Lee's.

Before she could turn away, he said, "I'll go get them."

Aimee got caught up in the camp tear down. Once the kids had loaded all their things into the back of the bus it was already ten o'clock. She still hadn't seen Carl Lee return with Sarah and Erica. She asked a boy if anyone had seen the trio.

"Yeah. Carl Lee came back a while ago with a pile of stuff. He put it in the van."

"Pile of stuff? What kind of stuff?" Aimee asked.

"Like sleeping bags and junk."

"Where'd he go then?"

He pointed up the paved road. Aimee squinted and could barely make him out. He was standing in the middle of the road at the top of the hill on his cell phone. It hit her then that something was wrong. The sun had burned away most of the fog and she could see out past the edge of the park's land, beyond the sea cliffs, and into the ocean. She started for the cliffs. She was half way across the park when Carl Lee stopped her. He must have sprinted.

"They're gone. I'm sorry, but they're gone."

"What do you mean, gone?"

"They've left."

Aimee turned from the cliffs and pushed him away. "Well they can't have gotten far. Let's go find them."

He stopped her again. "No. Dr. Barnabas wants us to come back."

"What? I'm sure he means *after* we find them."

"No. He's very concerned about the impact this could have on the other students. He wants everyone back, right now, before they get exposed to FI behaviors that might undermine our efforts."

"Dr. Barnabas said that? But, we can't just leave. What if they come back? And who's going to speak with the police? Or start a search?"

"Dr. Barnabas is taking care of all of that." He pulled her along with him.

She dug her heels into the dirt. "No. I don't care what he said, I can't leave without them."

Carl Lee suddenly changed tactics. "I'm going to be here coordinating with the search agencies, so you have to drive everyone back to Pioneer." He said it slow. "Dr. Barnabas wants it this way."

"Well, I'm sure Dr. Barnabas knows best." Aimee couldn't imagine the doctor having any part in something suspicious. Maybe he knew something she didn't, after all she couldn't be sure Carl Lee was being entirely straightforward. If Dr. Barnabas wanted them to come straight back to the Institute, that was what she would do. "You stay here. But I'm stopping at the fire station and telling them to come help you."

She wasn't sure what Carl Lee was up to, but she would feel better with someone official involved. "That's a good idea." He surprised her by agreeing. "Why don't you drop me off there on your way out of town?" In response to a couple of questions from the students, he announced, "I'm afraid Erica and Sarah took advantage of last night's commotion to run off. We've been in contact with the police, and I'm going to stay here to organize a search party. But I've spoken with Dr. Barnabas and he wants all of you back at the Institute as soon as possible. After all, we have a commitment to your parents to keep you safe."

The kids reluctantly filled onto the bus, still asking questions.

On the way back to Pioneer, winding down narrow roads through bucolic and surprisingly rural Marin County, a cacophony of voices pounded in Aimee's head. She went from accusing herself of being incredibly naïve to thinking it was uncharitable to think something was wrong with Carl Lee, to remembering his angry tirade and his threatening demeanor. She was certain he was a man capable of dark thoughts. Most frightening was not that her co-worker could have run two helpless and confused girls into the night, but that he may have actually harmed them..

Now she wondered if Carl Lee killed them, willfully or even unintentionally. What if he'd actually killed the other kids who had run away, too? It was all starting to look so grim, and darn it, Dr. Barnabas, who was trustworthy by nature, may have played into Carl Lee's hands by asking to have the children returned immediately. If those girls were dead, Carl Lee had time to cover it up before anyone even came out to the campground. And if they weren't dead, Aimee feared to think what he planned to do with them.

Dr. Barnabas was such a kind, God-fearing man that he probably couldn't imagine an employee of his could be so *evil*. But, these things happen every day, especially among non-believers. Could this really be happening at Pioneer?

Aimee had planned to talk with Dr. Barnabas as soon as she could that day. But he was nowhere to be found. Later, when Carl Lee returned empty handed, she'd been devastated. She should have remained behind until they found the girls.

Now, weeks later, Aimee *knew* the girls had already been dead before she'd learned they were missing. She was sure that Carl Lee must have done something to them during the time he was missing from his tent. How convenient that he then stayed behind. He'd probably wanted to get rid of her and the kids so he could control the search and prohibit investigators from speaking with any of the students. He probably hadn't wanted anyone really looking for the girls. Could he be so diabolical as to hope no one ever found them? She could bet Carl Lee got involved with the search that was conducted only so he could hamper their efforts and prevent them from finding the girls' bodies. How else could you explain that they were right there all along at the bottom of that cliff?

She'd never forget the day that Dr. Barnabas, his face ashen and worn, called the staff into the conference room for a closed-door meeting.

As soon as he started to speak, that rock in the pit of her abdomen reappeared and Aimee fell in to a sort of hazy emotional state where she could hear what was being said, but it seemed as though the sounds—Dr. Barnabas's news, one woman wailing, a few sudden outbursts—were being filtered through bulletproof glass. She could make the words out but she was detached from their meaning. The two girls had been found dead at the bottom of a cliff, outside the campground. A reporter had found them, not Carl Lee. Dr. Barnabas was solemn but remarkably trusting, not even seeming to think anything malevolent could have happened.

"Our job is not to question the ways of the Lord," he told the staff. "It is now of critical importance for each and every one of you, in the face of this tragedy, to know you are doing God's work and to let the children in your care know that what may seem cruel or irrational has a reason. God's hand works in mysterious ways and we shall not query or demand explanation."

"But Dr. Barnabas," Aimee interjected uncharacteristically.

"Miss Dix," Dr. Barnabas cut her off. "This is not the time. My friends, let us pray. Then I'm afraid we'll need to share this terrible news with our clients."

As the group joined hands and chanted from the Old Testament, Aimee stole a glance at Carl Lee. He seemed completely unmoved. Her hatred for him at that moment knew no bounds.

Too bad Dr. Barnabas was such a moral man. She was sure he wouldn't believe her. He could not imagine anyone he was associated with would be involved in a murder and cover-up. Positive that Carl Lee killed Sarah and Erica, but not sure who to turn to, Aimee had finally sent that journalist Velvet Erickson—the one who'd tried to talk to Aimee last year when Dominique and Saya went missing—a cryptic message about Group Six. Velvet was a smart woman, she would figure out its significance. Aimee had to let someone know about her concerns.

As soon as she could find some evidence of his malfeasance, Aimee was going straight to Dr. Barnabas. She knew he'd pooh-pooh her otherwise. She understood. No one in their right mind would believe one of their employees was running a side business killing kids. But it was the only conclusion Aimee could come to. If it were just a kidnapping scheme, the kids would have made it home by now. If he were somehow—and clearly against his nature—helping kids run away from Pioneer, then surely, by now, Saya would have gone to her sister's house. No, it was a horrible thought, but she was sure now that Carl Lee was making kids disappear forever. She just had to prove it.

❖

The private rooms were small shoeboxes of painted cinderblock topped with asbestos laden ceiling that necessitated a small plaque hung by each Pioneer entrance warning visitors that they might be exposed to something known by the state of California to cause cancer. The rooms reminded Aimee of college dorms or prison cells. Each room had a desk and straight-back chair, a chest of drawers three-high, and a squat bed with wooden frame and a single, threadbare mattress. Aimee had spiced up her room with splashes of color—a bright orange rug, a deep blue comforter, a couple of inspirational posters and two plants starving for light.

Aimee lay on her bed in the dark. She could not see the room's contents, but she was going over the way the furniture was positioned, mapping it out in her head. Each of the four rooms was laid out exactly the same, and she was positive Carl Lee would not have moved his furniture around. Aimee looked at the glowing hands of her watch. By her calculations, Carl Lee was making his rounds. It was time.

Aimee got up from the bed where she had been lying on top of the covers, fully clothed, and took measured steps to the door. She pulled it open and peered outside. Not seeing anything, she felt her confidence grow and reminded herself not to get cocky. Since the stunt Isabelle had pulled with the keys, Carl Lee was on high alert, although his attention seemed fully engaged by the teens. He wouldn't pay attention to her or to his room. She slipped out into the hall and crept past Coach Rawling's door. No light shined through the crack under his door so she figured he must be asleep. She reached Carl Lee's door and turned the knob. It didn't budge. No problem, all the counselor rooms were keyed the same. Pioneer Institute's employees had never had reason to fear their privacy would be threatened by one of their own. Until now.

Sneaking into the room, Aimee held the door handle as she closed the door quietly. Flicking on the small flashlight she carried, Aimee surveyed Carl Lee's room. At first glance there seemed nothing of him in the room. It had no character at all. It looked exactly as her room had when she first arrived, before she'd made it her own. Apparently the monastic living quarters were just as Carl Lee wanted them. The bed was made, the desktop and dresser uncluttered. She set the flashlight down and opened the top drawer, lifting it as she slid it toward her to prevent the wood from squeaking. The drawer was filled with a smattering of rumpled clothing, flannel and denim mostly, along with a pocket knife, a roll of dollar bills, a thin elastic band, a blank vintage postcard from Billings, Montana, and a baggie with tiny smattering of white powder. Good Lord, was Carl Lee a drug addict too?

Below all that ephemera and accessories was what she needed all along: a small silver pendant with "faith" in Sanskrit on a torn sterling silver chain. The necklace that belonged to Erica Bingham was in a Ziploc baggie, in pieces, as though it was ripped from the girl's neck in a struggle. Finally, Aimee had proof that Carl Lee had something to do with the death of those two girls and it instantly put a pall over her. Lord only knew what Carl Lee would do if he found that the jewelry was missing. Hopefully God's grace could protect her until she could show it to Dr. Barnabas first thing in the morning.

CHAPTER THIRTEEN

Carl Lee couldn't afford to have anyone poking around in his, or Pioneer's, business. First there'd been that journalist, Velvet-something last year, then the crazy, gun-slinging Takahashi sister who'd brought the whole fucking police department onto his turf. Then there was the blind private investigator asking Dr. Barnabas a bunch of leading questions that made it clear she was on to something. Then Carl Lee found the PI cozying up with the sister. Then that nosey student, Jennye had snagged his fucking keys and had the balls to insist it was some kind of prank. Like hell. She'd been up to something. He could smell it and he didn't like it. If that weasel Barnabas started feeling the heat or thought an investigation might uncover his dirty secrets, Carl Lee had no doubt whose body would end up in the morgue.

His own.

The thought was making him nervous. To top it all off, when he returned from his rounds he was sure someone had been in his room. It wasn't anything obvious at first, just a feeling. One of the things he'd learned in prison was to trust his instincts. He didn't know what gave people those flashes of insight. Maybe it was a smell or a sound so low you didn't even know you heard it. But whatever was behind that gut feeling, it had saved his life more than once. So when he had that feeling walking into his locked room, he checked every corner and under the bed until he was satisfied the intruder wasn't there. Then he thought of the most important possession he had at Pioneer. He opened the drawer where he'd left it under a pile of clothes. It was gone.

Carl Lee tore the place apart. When he was done, the room looked like it had been hit by a thirty foot wave, the kind that splinters houses.

He pawed through the wreckage one more time and then threw himself on the bed and held his head. The necklace was gone. Someone had been in his room and taken evidence that tied him directly to the deaths in Bolinas.

He thought about running. He could get in his car and just drive. He could be in Mexico in a day, Canada in a couple more. He'd known it was all going to catch up to him one day, so he'd mapped out a few escape routes. But maybe he was jumping the gun. The cops hadn't arrived. Whoever had been in his room hadn't called them yet. Or were they already closing in? Was Barnabas getting ready to make him the fall guy?

Carl Lee decided he'd play it cool and wait a couple of days. Then he'd be gone. He'd make himself disappear. He'd done it before. But not recently. For the past five years he'd been comfortable in one place. He'd been a well-paid magician, helping make Pioneer kids disappear. And he'd been doing a damn good job at it too. He'd been great at covering his tracks. No one suspected him. No one imagined he'd been behind the early withdrawals, transfers, and escapes that seemed to plague the institute.

He was amazed he could get away with it. No one seemed to notice or care if a few dozen queer kids dropped off the map. Until Saya Takahashi. Every chance he had, he'd been following one or other of those Japanese women, trying to figure out what they might suspect. The sister, Aneko, was getting far too close for comfort. That's why he'd sent her that dead mouse as a friendly warning to back the hell off. That's why he'd taken a few shots at them near the BART. They were going to ruin the whole thing.

Aneko Takahashi was the reason he'd volunteered to get out of town on that timely outing to Bolinas. The place was a haunt from his early days, when he'd made a living breaking into ritzy Sea Cliff cottages during the off season, ransacking pantries bursting with fancy French jams, black truffles, and Russian caviar. It was the most expensive crap he'd ever eaten and most of it he'd be happy never to taste again. He'd boosted silverware, jewelry, paintings, and collectibles, slipping out during the night and avoiding the gated community's guard shack by skirting along the beach. Sometimes he'd hide the things he stole in the nearby sea caves that rumrunners once used during the prohibition. Then he'd sell it all to a fence who ran a pawn shop in Ross.

The Spring Survival Camp had been an awesome week, a week without worry but then those stupid, *stupid* girls had ruined the whole thing. He'd had to think on his feet and he'd played it brilliantly. He got Barnabas to call in a lawyer who favored rushing Miss Dix and the kids off, and he'd pretended to inform the local fire department right away, when he'd delayed doing so for hours. He'd even convinced the county sheriff's search and rescue unit to let him search the area he'd knew they'd find the girls in.

He'd expected the surf to lift their bodies from the small rocky beach, and carry them out to open waters where they'd be nibbled on by fish and sink to the ocean floor without a trace. How was he supposed to know the tides were unseasonably low? Or that the bodies would just stay where they fell for weeks, only to be found by the same goddamn Velvet person who'd been harassing Pioneer about last year's runaways. Talk about your fucking coincidences.

It didn't look good, Carl Lee reflected. Once foul play was suspected, there was only one person the cops would be interested in. Carl Lee had once beat a gay man unconscious, and he'd spent twenty-five months behind bars, capping a lifetime in and out of the system. Once he got out on good behavior he'd promised himself he would never do time again, but no one was interested in hiring an ex-con except other criminals.

It had only been a coincidence when he ran into an old friend from the pen and the guy told him about Pioneer and said Dr. Barnabas had been putting out feelers, saying he needed an employee with a particular—wink wink—skill set. The only skills Carl Lee had came from a career of petty crimes that escalated to aggravated assault when he rolled a guy who turned out to be gay, but that had turned out to be the thing Dr. Barnabas fixated on, like it made him perfectly qualified to fulfill this particular role at Pioneer.

At first he was only told he'd be a boot camp style counselor, teaching kids to be self-reliant and take responsibility for themselves. Of course with Carl Lee's lack of social skills and limited educational background he wasn't really fit to be teaching kids anything, and he was sure Dr. Barnabas knew it. It had taken little more than a month before Barnabas came clean with his real intentions. When he did Carl Lee had never been so astonished in his life. For about three seconds. Then he realized the Jesus-freak's agenda only confirmed Carl Lee's suspicions about people, particularly the righteous bastards. Evil wasn't limited to the psychologically damaged or criminally minded. It lurked everywhere. It festered under the skin of those who pretended to be its opposition. Everyone was capable of terrible things, if they were pushed far enough. Or offered enough money.

Carl Lee wasn't sure if Dr. Barnabas had ever been a true believer or if he'd always been a shyster taking advantage of his flock. In the end, he supposed it didn't really matter. Barnabas liked to refer to the students as "our clients" but Pioneer's real clientele were wealthy parents disappointed in their children's abnormal behavior and willing to pay outrageous sums for the problem to be taken from their hands. While most were content to have little Johnny or Suzie back home after they were repaired and could pass for straight, a number of Pioneer's exclusive clientele were looking for something a little extra, and they were willing to pay top dollar to get it. They wanted the kind of peace of mind that came not from a temporarily straight son or daughter who'd undoubtedly turn queer again when the treatments wore off. A certain group of parents wanted to be certain that their children's unconventional lifestyles or behaviors would no longer embarrass them. Seeing an opportunity for a new business niche, Barnabas hoped to offer these parents exclusive packages, a more permanent solution to their parental problem. That was where Carl Lee fit in.

Barnabas had described the work in vague and muddled statements that meant something other than they first appeared to. Carl Lee preferred to cut to the chase.

"You saying these folks will pay to have their own kids whacked?"

"I'd rather think of it as a permanent vacation. *Gone*."

"But they'll be dead."

"Yes."

"I'm not a killer." Carl Lee immediately regretted his rebuttal. He'd learned enough to know that turning down a guy like Dr. Barnabas was a good way to get yourself killed. He corrected himself quickly, "I mean, I've never iced anyone. Doesn't that bother you?"

"Not at all. The only thing that kept you from killing that young man was the police. And what was that over? Fifty dollars?"

"A hundred." It wasn't something Carl Lee was proud of.

"A hundred dollars. You'd have to add three zeroes to that to make it into the ball park I'm playing in."

That kind of money would certainly look good in an off shore bank account.

Carl Lee checked again that he hadn't somehow inadvertently moved the dead girl's necklace. Then he tried to figure out why he'd kept it. If it fell into the wrong hands it could be the lynchpin in a circumstantial murder trial. Carl Lee had no intention of going back to jail. He thought about the newest student, Jennye. Could she have rifled through his room?

It didn't make much sense. She hadn't even been at Pioneer long enough to have known the dead girls and she couldn't have known the significance of the necklace, so why would she have taken it? And how could a student have gotten a copy of his key made without leaving the Pioneer compound? If she was involved, she had to be working with someone else. Was it someone on the inside, like that judgmental Aimee Dix whose hooded stares always seemed so accusing? *She* wouldn't need a key; she already had one of her own.

But Carl Lee knew he was dancing around the most likely possibility. Dr. Barnabas had to be behind the necklace's disappearance. Even the possibility was terrifying. Carl Lee knew firsthand about Barnabas's temperament. Barnabas wasn't the type to explode in anger, he kept his emotions held tightly in check and he confronted issues with a cool façade. Below the surface it was a different matter. There his malfeasance boiled like magma, a controlled fury that made the man quite capable of the worst atrocities. If he suspected Carl Lee was behind the deaths of those girls, he had not verbalized those suspicions so far, and that made Carl Lee very nervous. After all, he would have expected Dr. Barnabas to confront him about the necklace and dangle it in front of him as some kind of insurance plan. If Dr. Barnabas had reason to believe that Carl Lee had kept information from him, or gone so far as to make an end run around him, he wouldn't hesitate to lash out against the perceived threat.

Carl Lee had risked a lot over the past few years, but a man had to draw the line somewhere and Carl Lee had little tolerance for his life being threatened. He needed to know, once and for all, if Dr. Barnabas had taken the necklace from his room. He hadn't owned a set of burglar tools since he was arrested for breaking and entering. But he knew how to pick a lock and Dr. Barnabas's door didn't offer much resistance. He stepped into the office and closed the door. His eyes had adjusted to the dark and he found the desk easily. The drawers also required a little persuasion.

Carl Lee rummaged for a good thirty minutes with little to show for it. Apparently Dr. Barnabas was paranoid enough not to leave incriminating evidence behind. Carl Lee would bet the old man kept the dangerous files in the briefcase he carried with him at all times. Still he examined the papers as he shuffled through, shining his pen light for clarification. Then he heard a noise.

Carl Lee flicked off his flashlight and stood still, listening intently. All was quiet. If he had never been to prison Carl Lee might not have remained frozen long enough. He might have gone back to the task at hand, and the ruffling of papers would have concealed the muffled thump. It seemed to be coming from the storage room adjacent to the receptionist's office. The long closet stretched the entire length of Dr. Barnabas's office. Carl Lee crept to the shared wall and pressed an ear to the sheetrock that separated him from the storage room shelves. He could hear the sound of cardboard sliding across the steel shelving.

Someone said, "Oh, God." The muffled voice was female.

❖

"Lord help me." Aimee crammed the cell phones back into their box and lifted it in her arms.

She locked the storage room behind her and returned the keys to the reception desk then hurried back to her room. She felt sick. Would Carl Lee guess she was the one who had uncovered his secret? She had to report him to the authorities before he found out. Dr. Barnabas would know what to do. In just a few hours she would present him with the facts. The cell phones were probably important evidence. She'd retrieved them before Carl Lee could figure out what had happened and start covering his tracks. She took a small overnight case from her closet and tipped the cell phones into it then listened, filled with fear.

She'd heard Carl Lee return to his room a couple of hours ago and had heard the faint sounds of drawers being opened and shut. He knew the necklace was missing. Perhaps by morning he would no longer be at Pioneer. The police would have a manhunt and he would eventually be caught and brought to justice. Meanwhile, things would return to normal at Pioneer. She could hardly wait.

It was that sense of impatience that drove her to her door once more on an impulse she thought she might regret. But, right now, a debate raged in her mind with one side adamantly insisting it was too dangerous to tell anyone what she knew, and the other insisting that Jennye Williams wasn't who she claimed to be. She was a tad too knowledgeable, too resourceful and too suspicious for a rebellious teen. That was why she'd broken into the storage room and shown Jamie's cell phone to Aimee. That was why she hadn't even blinked an eye when Aimee confessed her fear that Carl Lee was dangerous.

A thought crossed Aimee's mind. At first the idea seemed ridiculous, but then she considered the timing of Jennye's arrival, only a week after the bodies were found at the bottom of that cliff. Was she a police officer sent by the diligent Dakota Manning. If so, Aimee's problems were solved. Why wait for morning when Carl Lee could be dealt with right now?

Aimee stuck her head out the door to make sure no one was around, then scurried to the dormitory and gently woke the girl, gesturing for silence. Once she had her sleepy attention, she signaled for Jennye to follow her. No one saw them enter her room and she sagged back against the door in relief.

"Are you a police officer?" She sounded out of breath.

Jennye stared at her, and Aimee tried to figure out what was going on behind those blue eyes. The girl clearly thought someone at Pioneer was a killer. Of course Aimee did too, but she had her own reasons to reach that conclusion and none was as compelling as the broken necklace she'd just taken from Carl Lee's room.

"What makes you think I'm a cop?" Jennye asked.

Aimee didn't bother dancing around the point. She was sure she was right. "I believe Carl Lee was involved in the deaths of Sarah Worthington and Erica Bingham."

"So do I," Jennye replied. "What led *you* to that conclusion?"

"His behavior. And this." Aimee reached into her skirt pocket and retrieved a small ziplock bag. She handed it to Tucker, who turned it over in her hands, looking at the broken chain "It was Erica's."

"Where did you find this?" Her eyes held Aimee's.

"In Carl Lee's room."

"I guess he collects trophies." Jennye slid a hand into her own bra. Jennye allowed a chain to dangle from fingertips between them. "This locket belonged to Dominique Marxley. Isabelle said Dominique never took it off."

"What are you saying?" Aimee was afraid she knew the answer.

"I think whoever killed Sarah and Erica was behind disappearance of Dominique and Saya. But there's one thing I don't get." Tucker narrowed her eyes. "If you thought Carl Lee was dangerous, why haven't you gone to the police? And why didn't you turn over the necklace? Are you part of a cover-up?"

"Of course not. And if mere suspicions were enough to convince the police, I doubt you would even be here." Aimee looked the new student up and down. "Who are you really?"

"I'm sorry I've had to lie to you." The admission still stung, as though verbalization made the deception real. Aimee tried not to take it personally, but inside, she was yelling, *You could have trusted me.*

"So, what are you then? Police Officer? FBI?"

"Nothing as glamorous as that. I'm with a private investigations firm. We're looking into the disappearance of Dominique Marxley and Saya Takahashi. But there seems to be something bigger going on here."

"Yes, I think there is." Aimee dragged out the suitcase and showed Jennye the cell phones as though making a peace offering. "I stole these from the storage room."

Jennye was silent for several seconds, then she touched Aimee's hand briefly. "I'm sorry, Aimee, I really am. I can't tell you a lot, but my real name is Tucker Shade. The guy in the wheelchair, that's not my dad. He's a detective I work with. I mean we kind of feel like a family, but an odd one."

"So, this probably means you're not really a teenager either."

"I'm twenty-three."

"I feel kind of stupid," Aimee admitted. "I thought I knew you, but now I see it's all been lies. You must hate me for punishing you."

Tucker shook her head. "You didn't know. I was being belligerent. I expected to be punished."

"Still, I feel terrible. I'm very sorry."

"Thank you." Tucker said.

Playing a hunch, and allowing her curiosity to surface, Aimee asked, "Are you the caregiver in your family?"

"Yeah. Not for my Dad or anything, but I have an autistic brother, Hunter. He's thirteen. I take care of him a lot."

Aimee thought so. Tucker had treated Isabelle like a younger sibling, protecting her. It made Aimee think the girl had a similar relationship with someone else. "Autism. That can be a lot of work."

Tucker shrugged. "It's worth it." She sounded defensive.

"Oh, no, you misunderstood me. Of course your brother is worth the trouble. It's just that I used to work with autistic children years ago, when I worked with the California Child Development Center. I've always kept up with the research. I'm sure you know that there have been some real breakthroughs in the last few years that have changed the prognosis for these kids. Hunter is very lucky. What kind of program is he in?"

"He's not in any program." Tucker's voice cracked. "He lives at home in Idaho and they just don't have access to a lot of services. He's had to go through some really tough things, you know, like sometimes they used to strap his arms down so he couldn't bite himself."

"Oh. I'm so sorry to hear that. Can your brother speak?" she asked, hoping to build their rapport.

"Yes, he can speak. Plus, we have our own language. I mean, it's not a language, exactly. But I can understand him."

"Wow, it sounds like you are really dedicated."

Tucker smiled wistfully. She seemed lost in her thoughts for a moment, then her focus returned and she picked up one of the cell phones, absently turning in over in her hands. "So…you think Carl Lee is a killer. What about Dr. Barnabas?"

"Absolutely not. Dr. Barnabas is a devout man. He wouldn't hurt a fly."

Tucker looked dubious.

"I'm certain," Aimee was adamant. "That the very *moment* Dr. Barnabas hears our concerns, he'll report Carl Lee to the proper authorities and immediately initiate an internal investigation."

"When will that be?" Tucker asked. "When will you tell Dr. Barnabas what you found?"

"What *we* discovered."

Tucker shook her head. "I think it might be better to keep my name out of it."

"He doesn't know about your true identity and your goal here?"

"No, that would have defeated the purpose. But if he has nothing to hide, he won't need to worry."

"Dr. Barnabas will be horrified." Aimee said, then shared a few more details about Carl Lee's suspicious behaviors.

Although Tucker wanted to call her detective friends right away, Aimee convinced the younger woman to wait. After all, it was 4:00 a.m. and they were getting a little rummy. They needed sleep. First thing in the morning, Aimee was determined to confer with Dr. Barnabas.

Chapter Fourteen

Yoshi was still at her Richmond District home when the phone rang.

"Yoshi?" Tucker's voice was so low, Yoshi had to strain to perceive it, even with her blindness-enhanced senses.

"Tucker, it's good to hear your voice. Are you safe to talk?" In the week Tucker had been behind enemy lines at the Pioneer Institute, she had not called once. That was hardly a surprise, after all Pioneer students were not allowed access to their cell phones or other electronic devices. Even if Tucker had had the good fortune of accessing a landline, Yoshi had prohibited her from calling. It was far too easy for a paranoid individual like Dr. Barnabas Gage to bug his own phone lines.

"I'm calling on my cell. I'll keep it quick. Nothing on primary subject," Tucker referenced Dr. Barnabas Gage.

"Any good news?" Yoshi prodded.

"Yeah. I've got eyes in the office but they are local," Tucker said, indicating that she'd managed to install one of the spy cameras in Dr. Barnabas's office. By 'local' she meant that the digital cameras were recording but were not attached to a receiver. Someone would have to go pick them up in order to download whatever had been captured. It was too bad she hadn't been able to utilize the more complex version, which could relay the images to a nearby receiver in an inconspicuous service van or through an Internet connection, straight to the Blind Eye computer.

"There's growing circumstantial evidence that points to the ex-con." Tucker went on to tell Yoshi that the other counselor suspected him of killing kids and that he'd caught Tucker snooping around in the storage room. "She's covering so I can call you," Tucker added in a hoarse whisper. "She's going to talk to the doc this morning."

"Does she know your identity?"

"Yeah, and she thinks I'm in danger." Tucker's urgent half-whisper grew more rapid. "Get me out of here, okay?"

"Okay," Yoshi said. "Be careful."

She didn't know if Tucker heard her before ending the call. Yoshi was disappointed. Tucker should never have revealed herself to Aimee, who was, after all, working for their primary person of interest in this investigation. Carl Lee might be the triggerman, but Yoshi was certain he was not the ringleader. Dr. Barnabas was. And she feared Aimee would expose Tucker, mistakenly trusting the doctor. Blind Eye needed to get their young investigator out before Dr. Barnabas learned her true identity and decided to clean up the problem himself.

Yoshi dialed Bud's cell number and cursed when he did not immediately pick up. Sometimes she believed he used his aversion to technology as an excuse to jerk her around. Over the years she'd developed her own ways to cope with his belligerence. Bud had no idea that a tiny but efficient global positioning satellite unit was attached to the undercarriage of the rickety Impala he so adored, enabling her to track his movements wherever he was. It was Orwellian, but Yoshi thought the measure was prudent. If Bud was ever in real danger, she would be able to find him.

She dialed again and didn't waste her breath on pleasantries when he picked up. "You need to get to Pioneer right away and withdraw Tucker from their program."

"Why? Has she been cured?"

"This isn't fucking funny. Tucker is in danger."

"Geez, what the hell is up?" Bud sounded perturbed and confused, probably in large part because Yoshi's speech was peppered with profanities, a rarity.

"Bud, just get your ass out to Freemont right now." Hanging up, Yoshi was still mired in her own emotions. But she could not allow herself to panic. People were counting in her. She placed another call. "I need to see you immediately."

San Francisco Police Department's Detective, Ari Fleishman replied, "Good morning to you, too. I haven't even had coffee yet."

"Meet me at the coffee shop and I'll buy you a cup."

Yoshi took a cab there. She detected Ari's cologne the moment she stepped into the building. She made her way toward him slowly, using her telescoping cane to avoid stepping on toes or tripping over chair legs. She heard him stand to greet her.

"Hey Yoshi," He shook her hand, and held it for a moment longer. Like a gentleman. "You're looking well. Much better than when we pulled you out of the Bay."

She smiled at him, even though she didn't feel lighthearted. "Speaking of the Devlin case, I am afraid Tucker Shade may be in danger. *Again*."

He sat down hard in his chair. Yoshi imagined him shaking his head. "Why can't you keep that girl out of trouble?"

"Risk seems to be inherent in the business we are in."

"Yeah, isn't that the truth." He sighed. "What can I do to help?"

"As you know, Blind Eye has been investigating the disappearance of a teenager from the Pioneer Institute."

"Right, that ex-gay school over in the East Bay."

"Correct. Tucker is undercover there."

Ari interrupted her with a guffaw.

Yoshi sent him an icy glare. There was nothing humorous about the current situation.

"Sorry," he apologized. "I just imagined them killing her with Bible verses. Please go on." Even though he was trying to be attentive, she felt he was not taking her seriously. Not yet.

Yoshi quickly briefed him on the details of the case—the broken necklace, the suspicious behavior of ex-convict Carl Lee James, the unusual collection of personal belongings in Pioneer's storage room, Dr. Barnabas Gage's efforts to derail their investigation. She could tell the air of amusement had evaporated.

"Damn, you need to get her out of there right away."

"I sent Bud to do so."

"Yoshi, I'm not really sure what you think I can do here," Ari said. "I don't have any jurisdiction with the East Bay. I could put you in touch with Officer Manning or one of the detectives, but…" He may have shrugged or stared at her pointedly as he trailed off. Sometimes even the people who knew her best acted as though she could see.

Yoshi supposed it was an odd compliment, proof that she was using her eyes appropriately or not "acting" blind. She was passing as sighted. "This counselor, Carl Lee, the one we suspect is behind the disappearance of our client's sister, keeps a room at the Pontiac Hotel, right here in San Francisco."

"Ah, it's a rent-by-the-week place full of junkies and hookers down on Minna. Lovely neighborhood."

"Yes, well, Tucker has not yet located evidence directly linking him to these crimes." Yoshi immediately regretted her use of the term "crimes" to describe what were at best suspected activities. She rushed on, hoping to preempt Ari from launching into a linguistics lecture about habeas corpus and circumstantial evidence.

"I understand, of course, that the deaths of the girls in Marin were ruled an accident and there is nothing to indicate foul play in the disappearance of Saya Takahashi. Still, I feel compelled to implore you to do anything in your power to obtain more evidence. Is there any way to procure a search warrant in a situation like this?"

From his silence, Yoshi determined that Ari was weighing the information she had given him. "We really don't have grounds."

Not one to focus on her own danger, Yoshi realized she had forgotten to mention the attack on herself and Aneko Takahashi. Wanting to add additional weight to her plea, she added, "Also, someone opened fire on me and Aneko Takahashi recently. I believe we were being warned off this investigation."

She felt Ari's temperament change. He was agitated. "Yoshi. Why the hell am I just hearing this now? Did you report it to the police? Damn it, Yoshi." His voice had gone husky, the way she remembered it from that day at the pier, after she had been pulled half dead from the water. He turned away, as though embarrassed by his emotional response. Clearing his throat, he asked, "Do you have anything that ties this Carl Lee James character to the shooting?"

She shook her head.

He sighed. "I just don't know. It's a lot of circumstantial evidence that might not add up. But here's what I'll do, I'll write up the paperwork for a search warrant and put a rush on it, hand it to the DA, and if she let's me, I'll personally walk it to a friendly judge. But I can't promise anything."

"I take that to mean you think it is a long shot."

"Yes, I won't lie to you. Like you said, the ME ruled the girls' deaths an accident." Ari drummed his fingers on the table, something he did when he was problem solving. "Wait. You said Carl Lee was an ex-con? Is he still on parole?"

"No such luck," Yoshi replied.

That would have been convenient. Parolees did not enjoy the rights and privileges of other citizens. They had to refrain from a veritable host of activities such as using drugs and owning firearms. If they violated the conditions of their parole they would be tossed back in prison. Likewise, they did not have the same expectation of privacy. Law enforcement officers could perform random checks of their residences at any moment. Alas, Carl Lee's last parole date had long passed. He was a free man.

❖

"Velvet, it is Yoshi."

The urgency in Yoshi's voice sent a chill down Velvet's back and caused an involuntary straightening of her spine. The movement lifted her ample bosoms. It was as though they had risen on their own accord the way oxygen masks automatically dropped on airplanes during a crisis.

"Is she okay?"

"For now."

Yoshi's answer did little to quell Velvet's rising panic. She imagined Tucker the way she'd looked in that hospital bed, so frail and delicate, black bruising under her closed eyelids. Velvet had been in such turmoil then, blaming herself for Tucker's kidnapping, she had barely heard the doctor telling her about the head injury and the subsequent CAT scan that showed nothing more than an unusual thickness in Tucker's skull. The abnormality had saved her life.

Velvet had sworn that day at the hospital that she would never let Tucker be in that position again. It had been her secret promise to a higher deity: *If you let her live, I'll make sure she is never endangered again.* Velvet's shrink, Artemis Jones, had dismissed the oath as ordinary bargaining, nothing more than a step in the grief process, taken when Velvet thought Tucker would die. Furthermore, Artemis contended, Velvet was in no position to make such a promise. Like it or not, some things in life were out of her control and keeping loved ones safe was one of those things.

Velvet hadn't wanted to accept such helplessness philosophically. She'd enlisted Yoshi and Bud's help to keep Tucker out of harm's way, making them promise to talk to her before they involved Tucker in risky situations. Yet, six months later, here they were again. If anyone had bothered to seek her advice before Tucker went undercover at Pioneer, Velvet would have told them it was too dangerous. That place was as good at making people disappear as Argentina during Operation Condor, when political dissidents were drugged and thrown from airplanes far above the Atlantic Ocean.

"Just tell me what's happening," Velvet demanded.

She couldn't keep putting herself through this. The loneliness she'd endured while granting Tucker the space she wanted was unbearable. Then there was her guilt at not being there when Tucker was attacked—in Velvet's own home! She was constantly fearful and angry that her lover kept putting herself in dangerous situations. *No more*. It was time to put her foot down. When this was over and Tucker was no longer at risk, Velvet would issue an ultimatum. Tucker would have to choose, once and for all, between Velvet and Blind Eye. She couldn't have both. Either she had to abandon her fantasy about becoming a PI or she'd have to give up being with Velvet.

Once Yoshi told her Bud had gone to rescue Tucker, Velvet managed to gain some emotional distance. She wasn't surprised to hear that Tucker had found evidence linking Carl Lee James to the disappearances of Pioneer students. After all she couldn't imagine Dr. Barnabas Gage getting his hands dirty. Carl Lee must be the muscle, the hired gun. It fit with the information Velvet had gathered, and Carl Lee certainly had the kind of access to the teens that gave him plenty of opportunity. The only thing missing was motive. Was he sleeping with the students, or coercing sex in exchange for contraband? Or did he just hate queers and imagine he could kill a few with impunity. With parents paying a fortune to have their kids reprogrammed in a place like Pioneer, that didn't seem likely.

And what was Carl Lee getting for his part in all of this? In Yoshi's review of Pioneer staff's financials, nothing had raised suspicions. If money was changing hands, it certainly wasn't doing so in the open and if Carl Lee was getting a boost in his income, he wasn't reporting it to the IRS. Not that criminals usually did so.

"Ari is trying to get a warrant to search Carl Lee's room at the Pontiac," Yoshi said. "But we don't have probable cause so I expect the DA will throw out his petition."

"Typical," Velvet said.

"I think we must take the initiative."

Velvet understood what Yoshi was suggesting. With the police stymied by the bounds of a legal system that sometimes favored the criminals, it would be up to Velvet and Yoshi to uncover the truth and reveal Dr. Barnabas's dirty secrets. Velvet wouldn't want it any other way.

"I'll take care of it," she told Yoshi. "You take care of Tucker."

The location of the Pontiac Hotel looked like it was ripped from an episode of Law & Order. As her cab drove down the alley-like Minna Street, Velvet couldn't help but notice the local denizens got grittier each block. First the daytime sex workers, some once-beautiful but now ravaged by years of trading crack for pussy. Then the junkies and dealers, then the gangbangers. All those groups seemed to coalesce on one block around the Pontiac in an almost poetic indictment of the war on drugs. Plus, two guys standing on the corner were completely naked from the waist down.

Velvet didn't have time to wonder if the men were mentally ill or simply playing an advanced game of mine-is-bigger. She had bigger fish to fry and that meant blending in with the locals to get into Carl Lee's room. First she had to make it through the metal gates that shielded the hotel clerk from the crazies who wandered in.

Velvet screwed up her blouse a bit, tearing a button from the top. Smearing her lipstick and mascara and ruffling her hair, she braced herself. Though she could only pull off a poor imitation of street vernacular, it wasn't that long ago that she rode the rails with homeless vets and went undercover with a Latino street gang. Pretending to be Carl Lee's girlfriend was a cinch compared to that.

"Hey, my fuckin' boyfriend forgot to leave me the fuckin' key and I got all my shit up there. Can you let me in?"

"No key, no entry," the clerk said without even looking at her.

With mousy blond hair that had been slicked back from all directions and a paunch that proclaimed too many nights spent with a beer and a TV dinner, he didn't seem the type to make an effort.

"Man, I gotta get my shit before he comes back." Velvet started to tear up. "You don't know what he's capable of, man. Look what he done to me last night."

She pulled her blouse almost completely open so the clerk got a shot not just of her see-through leopard print bra but also of the enormous magenta bruise on her chest, the result of a particularly tough round of capoeira at the gym last week. She hoped the clerk would buy it because her next option was a lot less palatable. She was sobbing now, shirt open, clerk staring at her enormous bosoms. *Please God, don't let him ask her for more.* Velvet had already circled the building and inspected every other possible entrance. The only way in was through this guy, and if he asked for a hand job, she just might have to do it.

"Okay girlie, stop crying. It's okay."

Velvet wiped her sniffles onto the sleeve of her blouse. It wasn't haute couture or anything, but she hated the damage she was doing. Still...

"Listen, I'm going to give you ten minutes up there just to get your shit and get away from the bastard. But if he comes while you're there, I can't be responsible, all right? If you ain't back in ten minutes I'm coming up to get you."

Velvet snatched the key he shoved at her and practically ran to the diminutive lift that took her to the fifth floor. Once in Carl Lee's room, she quickly surveyed the sparse furnishings, a small twin bed, a television propped on an old pressboard bureau, and an aluminum table with a couple of piles of books and papers. There was no bathroom and the only window was a tiny portal overlooking another concrete building. Velvet was dubious about finding anything, and even if there was evidence here it would not be admissible in a courtroom. She worried about that as she searched systematically. In the bottom drawer of the bureau a large russet-colored vinyl photo album was buried beneath a few items of clothing. The album was the kind rarely seen in this age of digital photography and contained formal school photos and candid snapshots of at least a dozen kids, maybe more. In the mix was a photo of a little baby dyke smiling broadly and looking winsome and beautiful. It was Dominique Marxley.

Why would Carl Lee have a photo album of the kids at Pioneer? From all she'd heard about him from Yoshi, he wasn't one of those uber-caring counselors. Velvet put the album on the bed and continued to rifle through the drawers. Jeans and T-shirts, a metal bracelet, a box of cornstarch, a blue ribbon, and a box of postcards from Portland, Oregon. On each post card was the word "here," written differently, in different colors and penmanship, some with adornments like hearts and smiley faces. Did Carl Lee have a lover in Oregon, or was he involved in something even more dangerous like gunrunning or drug trafficking? Maybe he got a card every time a shipment arrived. Perhaps Pioneer Institute was just a front and these poor queer kids were being used as mules.

Velvet's mind was racing and she only had three minutes left in the room. She started flipping through the piles on the desktop. Nothing. Then she remembered to check the mattress. Could Carl Lee be so cliché as to hide his money, or actual evidence, under the mattress or would she just find herself with a sticky pile of fetish porn?

Within seconds of reaching between the box springs and mattress, she realized his proclivities were much worse. A handful of Polaroid photos fell to the floor, each one an image of one of the kids from the photo album. Except they weren't smiling and sunny in these grim shots, they were whitened and ghostly, some covered in blood, others face up in dirt. They were all dead. Every single one of them. Carl Lee was a serial killer and she was holding his trophies. She stopped counting at fifteen but there were more, and some of the queer and trans kids seemed aghast with the agony of death. Velvet dropped the photos and turned away, unable to breathe. Then she did something she'd never done before. She threw up at a crime scene.

Hearing voices in the hall, she wiped her mouth and rushed to pull together the photos and the album and a pile of newspaper clips about the ex-gay ministries. Stuffing them into her messenger bag, she peered out then bolted toward the bathroom at the end of the hall. She secured the lock and crouched on the floor between the toilet and door. She didn't want to be caught but there was no way she could leave this building without telling someone what she had found.

She hit speed dial and told Yoshi, "Tell Ari to get down here. You have to see what I've found."

CHAPTER FIFTEEN

The girl Aimee had known as Jennye Williams, a sexually confused teenager forcibly enrolled in Pioneer's program, was actually a twenty-three-year-old private investigator named Tucker Shade. Aimee was having a hard time accepting the truth. An elaborate undercover investigation had been launched before she thought anyone else shared her suspicions about Carl Lee. She'd had no idea that Pioneer's track record had already drawn external scrutiny, back when there'd been nothing but a kernel of suspicion in her brain, a small itch that wouldn't go away. But she hadn't even really *suspected* back then, she'd just had the vaguest sense that something was wrong. She was having that feeling again, only now it was much stronger, more insistent. It was a vice grip around her intestines, a burning in her throat, a heavy weight on her chest. Something was very wrong.

Twenty minutes ago she'd distracted the other counselors and allowed Tucker to sneak off to the bathroom with a cell phone. She was supposed to call her boss and then come back to rejoin the group. She still hadn't returned, and if she didn't get back soon, Aimee would have to go to her meeting with Dr. Barnabas without knowing whether Tucker had been successful.

Aimee watched Carl Lee's eyes scan the room. She could see his mind ticking, counting the students, verifying Tucker had not returned. He had been in Aimee's sights the entire time Tucker was absent. Only Matt Lovelorn had gone and returned in the interim. Aimee checked the time again. She simply couldn't keep the doctor waiting any longer. She darted from the room, not looking back when Carl Lee called her name. She loped down the hallway and through the doors that opened out to the courtyard. A quick glance told her Tucker was not sitting on one of the benches or cowering behind a bush, so she scurried across and entered the building. It did not take her long to reach Dr. Barnabas's office.

She hustled inside and found the doctor sitting at his desk. There was something about his presence that had always had a calming effect on Aimee. As soon as he casually but genteelly offered her a seat, she felt her tension slipping away.

"Miss Dix, always a pleasure. What seems to be troubling you today?" He leaned forward attentively. He was such a good listener.

There was so much to tell. The words poured out of her in a rush. It was as though there'd been a cork keeping her fears all bottled up and suddenly it was gone and she was free to share. She forced herself to say the words, "I think Carl Lee may be killing our clients."

Dr. Barnabas laughed and Aimee realized just how ridiculous the accusation sounded, like the ravings of a conspiracy-theory fanatic or those men who stood on street corners proclaiming the end of the world.

"I know. It sounds crazy, but I swear, I couldn't be more serious."

He nodded and obviously tried to look serious for her sake, but his efforts just seemed to distort his features into a strange parody of good humor. Knowing the deaths of several students and her allegations of murder would be no laughing matter to the Dr. Barnabas she knew, Aimee was certain the look on his face did not accurately reflect his sentiments. She rushed on, telling him how her suspicious had grown until she'd come to the conclusion that Carl Lee was a cold-blooded murderer.

"I have proof," she concluded, nearly out of breath.

"Proof?" The skin between his eyes pinched together in a scowl. "What kind of proof?"

Aimee reached into her pocket and handed him the broken necklace. "This was Erica's. I found it in Carl Lee's room."

A shadow settled over Dr. Barnabas's face. Although she hated to give him this bad news, Aimee was relieved to see that he believed her.

"This is very disturbing." He curled his fingers around the necklace and it disappeared into his fist. "Very disturbing indeed. Miss Dix, I wonder if you might accompany me to the other room. I think there's something you should see."

Dr. Barnabas pushed his chair back, rose, and offered her a hand. They were to the door before she realized he must have dropped the necklace in his jacket pocket to keep it safe until they could call the proper authorities. He wouldn't want her to worry over something like that.

She felt honored that he was about to show her something that required discretion. Perhaps he had other evidence even more conclusive than the necklace. She was immensely relieved to have gotten everything off her chest. All this time she'd been afraid of how he might react to her allegations. But it seemed he not only believed her, he may have come to the same conclusion himself. Dr. Barnabas was an intelligent man. He'd probably been quietly looking into the situation ever since the two girls fell from those ocean cliffs. He was probably working with the police at this very moment. They were heading to the storage room, and it struck her that there might be a team of FBI agents hiding in the cramped space. She smiled at the thought.

"Do you mind?" Dr. Barnabas passed her a set of keys.

Aimee stepped in front of him and unlocked the door. Her head flew around and she was transfixed by the glint in his eyes and the smirk on his lips. Aimee understood in that moment that she'd put her faith in the wrong person. She'd been so blind. Her mouth was just beginning to form the word "no" when she was struck by twin lightn\ing bolts that sent her dancing on air. She fell backward, her mouth agape, her eyes barely registering the dimming light until only a sliver remained. Then the door closed and she was swallowed by darkness.

Fuckin' bigots. Bud was still repeating the refrain like a mantra, only now it was under his breath. He'd finally found a broad he liked, hell, a group of normal fucking people he liked and then this had to happen.

Dinner with the other Pioneer parents had been going just fine. Sure Tucker wasn't really his kid but she was the closest he was ever gonna get and the outings with Barbara Parkins and the rest of the gang felt less like PTA meetings and more like when parents attend their kids' sporting events. He was one day away from affixing his Impala's bumper with a sticker that read, "My kid is on the honor roll at Pioneer Institute."

Then things turned. Barbara was emboldened by a few glasses of wine tonight but that was no excuse. Bud was sitting so close to that he could feel a bit of sexual tension between them, even if she was a nice lady who certainly wasn't going to spread her knees for him without some form of further commitment. They hadn't gotten that far but maybe tonight was the night, Bud had mused.

Some of the guys were joking about how steroids affected Barry Bonds's endowments, the women were clucking about some new Bible-based detox diet that sounded like crap but seemed to make them all glow with excitement, and someone started talking about the kids.

"Tina knows this is her last chance with us," one father said. "We can't have that around our other children. I think she'll turn things around though."

"Well," Barbara said, "I think Tina's a lot more likely to succeed than some of the other kids." The group all nodded swift agreement.

"Yeah, well, no parent is going to admit their kid is the group's lost cause though, Barbara," another mother commented, to more knowing nods.

"Oh, I'm sure Bud knows his kid's a throwback." Barbara said it so blithely that Bud thought he must of misunderstood.

"Sorry, babe, what'd you say?" he asked, with a pit growing in his stomach.

"Well, Bud, honey," Barbara drawled, "I'm sure you love her, but your daughter is a lost cause. Really, even with God's love, she's probably the kind of aberration that can't be saved in this lifetime. Some girls, especially the homely ones, fall into homosexuality because boys don't like them. Their only chance, they think, is to have intimacies with other girls who are also defective. And once they're involved with each other, they're ruined. I know you love her, but it's kind of like when a dog bites you and draws blood, you know it's time to put it down."

Bud felt the blood racing to his face as his heart began to pound and his chest constricted. "Who the fuck do you think you are, lady?"

The women seemed surprised by his response. The men at the

table tried to calm him. One said, "Bud, I'm sure Barbara meant no harm. It's true that even with God's help, some kids have been too corrupted by the homosexual movement by the time we seek help for them."

"That's exactly what I meant, Bud," Barbara backtracked, smiling almost maniacally now. "I just meant that with all of her defects your daughter was a prime target. You yourself said she was clumsy and athletic and wouldn't wear dresses or date boys. Honestly, maybe Dr. Barnabas will work magic with her, but in my opinion, once the perverts get a hold of a kid, it takes hell and high water to release that Satan spell."

Bud couldn't believe what he was hearing. Even in amidst these supposedly God-fearing folks, the bigotry and prejudice was deeper than he could have imagined. What was next? "Negro" jokes?

"Let's change the subject," one mom interjected as Bud's cell phone rang. "Did you all get a chance to see Joyce Meyers sermon last week? One fellow used to weigh three hundred pounds until he started listening to God for nutritional advice."

"I think I've had enough," Bud said, quickly unlatching the locks on his wheelchair and pulling away from the table.

"Bud!" Barbara exclaimed. "Please calm down."

"I don't think so, Barbara. I think we're done here." With that he rolled swiftly out of the restaurant and away from the fucking idiots he'd been spending time with as of late.

It dawned on him then, through his rage and the disappointment, that it wasn't just that these folks were homophobes. The big shock was that he no longer was. Though he'd always been quick with the fag jokes and used to think that every dyke just needed a good dick, he didn't feel that way anymore. As much as he bitched about Yoshi and her lesbian ilk, he'd grown to realize that they weren't all that different from him. In fact, Tucker had become, well…precious, to him. And it didn't matter who she loved, or if she liked to do boy things or what not. He didn't care.

Fuck Barbara and fuck her religious freak friends. Bud couldn't forget the things they said about Tucker. He'd defend that kid to the death. And here he was, on his way to Pioneer to do just that.

❖

The first thing Tucker became aware of was the cold floor. She was lying on her side, her legs bare. Where were her pants? The floor felt rough, like cement. What was she doing on a cement floor? A wave of pain and queasiness washed over her. It was a lot like recovering from the aversion therapy she had experienced. No wonder the United Nations said Tasers were a form of torture. She blinked twice to verify her eyes were open. The room was dark. Tucker struggled to sit up but she couldn't move her arms. *Oh, my God, I'm paralyzed!* What did Dr. Barnabas do to her after he hit her with that Taser? Tucker started to freak out. She could feel her heart thudding. *Calm down*, she told herself. *Calm down*. Then she heard the sound of breathing. It wasn't her own.

Still unable to get her arms to work, she rocked around and faced whatever shared the darkness with her. "Who's there?"

She could hear the terror in her own voice. Whoever was in the room with her could probably hear her fear too. There was no answer. He was probably enjoying her terror, feeding off it. That's what predators did, wasn't it? Tucker struggled again to move and realized her wrists and ankles were bound together with rope. Everything started to come back in a flood of memories. Aimee Dix had given her a phone and she'd called Yoshi. That's when things got fuzzy. Dr. Barnabas's angry face came to mind. He'd discovered her in the bathroom. How? Did Pioneer have surveillance cameras in there, too?

The lump on the floor next to her still hadn't moved. Tucker shuffled over and recognized Aimee. The counselor appeared to be unconscious. Well, maybe now Aimee would accept that the good doctor was up to his neck in this shit. Tucker wasn't sure what was going to happen to them when Dr. Barnabas came back, but she wasn't going to just lie here like some helpless victim. She'd survived a champagne bottle to the head. She'd been knocked out, tied up, and thrown in the trunk of a car just a few months ago and she'd come out of it okay. Besides, Bud was already on the way to Pioneer and Tucker knew he'd keep her from harm. Dr. Barnabas had better not hurt her or he'd discover firsthand that Bud no longer felt constrained by the rules he'd followed as a cop. Even in a wheelchair, he could bring down a world of hurt.

She wasn't going to just sit here waiting to be rescued. Bud would never let her live it down. Yoshi wouldn't be impressed. Now that she'd grown accustomed to the dark, she could make out the shelving that lined the walls. They were in the storage room. She could pound on the walls all she wanted and the only one who'd come would be Dr. Barnabas. She remembered the box of cell phones and cursed. If they'd still been here maybe one of them would have had enough juice to send out an SOS.

Tucker slithered across the floor like a snake and scooted her back against the doorframe. She shimmied up it until she was standing and managed to flip on the light with her shoulder. As the fluorescent bulbs rattled to life, the brightness blinded her as though she'd stared straight at the sun. Blinking, Tucker hopped toward the suitcase Yoshi had given her and began pulling out her clothing. It was tedious work, yanking things aside with her wrists tied together.

She heard muffled voices. Dr. Barnabas was speaking to someone else in his office, behind the storage unit's wall. Tucker leaned in awkwardly. She couldn't make out all the words, but Carl Lee's voice was loud enough to be recognizable.

"I have to advise against taking such actions," he said

"You're hardly in a position to tell me what to do." Dr. Barnabas made the words sound like a threat.

Terrified that the men would be on their way to the storage room at any moment, Tucker tore through the clothing in her luggage and slid the back of her cuffed hands along the suitcase's smooth and flat fabric lining until they hit a small weighty bump, the size of a watch battery. It was there, just like Bud said.

A week ago, on their drive to Pioneer, he'd told her Yoshi had started using GPS devices to track her employees. She didn't realize Bud was wise to her little trick after discovering she'd tacked a locator to his Impala. Rather than confronting her or removing the bug, he was planning some kind of ruse that would leave her with egg on her face. He'd pointed out that there was a reason Yoshi insisted Tucker take the new suitcase into Pioneer. Tucker found the gap in the seam where the locator must have been introduced and slid the device through. She brought her clasped hands to her blouse and dropped the cold metal slug into her bra. Whatever happened now, Blind Eye would know where she was.

❖

"I think that you and I have known each other long enough for you to know that the good Lord enables me to go to great lengths to keep my house in order," Dr. Barnabas said.

Carl Lee's mouth had run dry and sagebrush was blowing across the high desert plains. He understood the threat. It seemed underscored by the spiritual advisor's inappropriate reference to the Lord Jesus Christ. "Yes, I understand. But—"

Dr. Barnabas raised a hand and the words died in Carl Lee's throat. The doctor's fist slowly unfurled to reveal Erica Bingham's broken necklace. Carl Lee was certain that the blood had drained from his face. He watched the necklace swing back and forth like a hypnotherapist's pendulum. He'd waited too long to make his escape. He wondered if his shallow grave would ever be found.

"You sly dog." Dr Barnabas winked but there was no smile in his eyes. "Doing a little freelance work, were you?"

"No, sir. I didn't touch those girls."

"Is that why you were so eager to go on this trip? I should have seen it coming, I suppose. Eliminating the middleman would certainly increase your take." Something dark moved across Dr. Barnabas's face and Carl Lee had to fight the physical urge to take cover. "I don't like liars, Mr. Jones. I thought I'd made that abundantly clear."

"Yes, sir. Of course. I hope you'll let me make it up to you."

Dr. Barnabas opened his fingers and let the necklace drop into a drawer, which he closed and locked. "There is something I'd like you to attend to. A little housecleaning."

"No problem."

"That new girl, Jennye, she's not who she appears to be. I've learned she's in association with that Asian private investigator who's causing us a problem. I want you to take care of her. You'll need to do it right away."

Carl Lee had always had ample forewarning in the past. All this time he hadn't been caught, there'd been one reason—planning. Without planning he couldn't pull off a disappearance on a moment's notice. This was fucking crazy. He tried to reason with Barnabas. "We're not talking about one of these throwaway kids whose parents are covering the bill and wouldn't dare declare them missing or bring in the authorities. This will bring down heat."

"Then it's a good thing I hired you to put out fires."

Carl Lee refrained from saying that's what the lawyers where for.

"I'm willing to consider our account settled if you clean up this little problem," Barnabas said.

"Fine." Carl Lee didn't see any alternative.

"There's one more thing."

Of course there was. "I'm listening."

"Miss Dix."

"Aimee Dix?" The man had gone completely mad.

As if sensing Carl Lee's hesitance, Dr. Barnabas said, "You know, she wanted me to turn you in to the police. I'm afraid she's the one who brought me the necklace. My God, you should have seen her face. Apparently she'd been harboring these feelings for some time, that you're a killer."

"We won't get away with this," Carl Lee said. "Someone will notice Aimee missing and come looking. It's going too far."

Dr. Barnabas snorted. "I'll decide what's too far. You just do your fucking job."

CHAPTER SIXTEEN

Tucker peeked through veiled eyelashes at the two men standing in the doorway. She was thankful she'd remembered to turn out the light, otherwise they would probably see her hunching her shoulders and realize she was awake.

"Jesus, what did you do to them?" Carl Lee asked.

"Taser. We should move them now, before they can struggle."

Next to her, Tucker heard Aimee moan, and feared she might pick this moment to wake up. She worried what the men would do if confronted.

"How are you going to do it?" Dr. Barnabas asked.

"Why don't you leave that to me, sir?" Carl Lee sounded offended. "I've never had a problem before."

"Fine, but you can't do it here."

"No shit. I'll bring my car around front. Can you help me get them outside?"

"You know I can't be involved." Barnabas sounded self-righteous. "What if someone saw me with them?"

Tucker almost choked. God, Barnabas was a putz. As soon as the door closed after the men she shook Aimee hard. "Wake up, come on. I don't know how much more time we have."

Aimee looked around in a daze. "What's going on?" Her voice was groggy. "What are we doing here?"

Before Tucker could fully explain, the door swung open again and Carl Lee turned on the lights. He was alone. If you didn't count his handgun.

"Carl Lee," Aimee hissed. "What do you think you're doing?"

"Oh, you're awake. Good. Get up." He motioned with the gun.

Aimee struggled to comply, flopping around on the floor like a fish out of water.

"You." Carl Lee pointed at Tucker. Clearly her cover had been blown. "Don't try anything."

He bent down on one knee, his back to the wall. Facing Tucker, he glanced down at the bindings around Aimee's ankles that had her hobbled. He fussed with the knot for a while, looking up every few minutes. Wondering if she could take him, Tucker looked around for a weapon. One she could grab and swing with her wrists tied together. Tucker wasn't concentrating on Carl Lee when all of a sudden she saw the glint of steel. Aimee gasped. Carl Lee was brandishing an eight-inch hunting knife. Holy shit. Maybe he was going to kill them here, gut them like a fish, the way Tucker's dad had taught her.

Carl Lee grabbed Aimee's ankles and pinned them down with one hand.

"Please, don't." Aimee begged.

Was he going to cut off toes? Tucker wondered. Were they going to be held for ransom?

"I always liked you," Aimee said to Carl Lee. "Please, don't hurt me."

She started to cry. Carl Lee ignored her and lowered the tip of the knife. Aimee crammed her eyes shut and clenched her teeth against the coming scream. Tucker watched, unable to turn away. Carl Lee started cutting, using the blade like a saw. Aimee did not scream. In fact, relief washed over her face.

"Thank you," she sobbed. Freed from the constraints, she stood up, holding onto the shelves for support.

"Now you do her." Carl Lee directed, jerking his chin in Tucker's direction.

Tucker inappropriately imagined porno music playing. It seemed to rise naturally from the surreal situation. Aimee advanced on her, the knife in her hand. Tucker tried to signal her, rolling her eyes toward Carl Lee and then staring at the shiny blade. Rather than spinning around and plunging the knife in Carl Lee's neck, or slipping the weapon to Tucker, Aimee simply stared at her like a slack jawed yokel. Tucker then saw the gun in Carl Lee's hand, trained on them. If he fired the bullet would scalp Aimee and perform a crude clitorectomy on Tucker. Aimee was crying so hard her hands shook as she hacked at the rope around Tuckers ankles.

When the last cord finally broke, Carl Lee took the knife back and tucked it back in its sheath. For appearances sake, he secreted the gun in his jacket pocket, where its pointy tip distended the fabric. "Get moving," he said, marching them down the long hall with their wrists tied.

"Carl Lee, you don't have to do this," Aimee said as they stepped into the late morning sun.

Tucker found it hard to maintain her fear in the sunlight. The brightness of the day seemed incongruous with their circumstances. Abduction and murder were more at home in the dark. She listened to Aimee talking the way victims did on television, when they still hoped they could convince the predator to change their minds. Tucker didn't plan to waste her breath. She surveyed the scene. *Don't let them get you in the car. The farther away they take you, the more likely you'll end up dead.* She wasn't sure where she'd heard that advice came from, but she would love to heed it. Unfortunately, while they were locked inside this fortress, escape would get them nowhere. They would still be within the compound.

When they reached a gray sedan, Carl Lee clicked his remote key and popped open the trunk. *Not this again.* Why were men always trying to force her into their trunks?

"You're going to have to get in there," Carl Lee said.

"Please, Carl Lee. Don't do this," Aimee begged. "For God's sake, whatever you've done, this is only making it worse."

She still seemed convinced he was working alone. Perhaps just to fight that belief, Tucker asked, "So, has the saintly Dr. Barnabas told you how he wants us killed?"

Carl Lee winked. "He doesn't tell me how to do my job. Dr. Barnabas is only concerned about the results."

How about that, Tucker thought. He came clean. She supposed he had nothing to lose by admitting what he'd done. He wasn't going to leave witnesses.

Still in denial, Aimee retorted, "Dr. Barnabas wouldn't have anything to do with the kind of evil you're contemplating."

"Sorry to disappoint you, Aimee, but your judgment sucks." Carl Lee said. "The bastard insisted you had to go. Now get in the fucking trunk before I have to get physical."

Preferring to enter on her own accord, Tucker clambered into the trunk and helped Aimee climb in after her. They curled around each other in the small space. Carl Lee slammed the trunk plunging them into darkness.

"It'll be okay," Tucker said. She knew Bud would find her.

"He's going to kill us, isn't he?" Aimee whispered in her ear.

"No." Tucker said. "He won't get the chance to. My colleagues are on their way."

❖

Bud rolled down the hall to Dr. Barnabas's office. There was a disorganized feel to the place that seemed at odds with Dr. Barnabas's anal retentiveness. A briefcase lay open on the desk, filled with a mishmash of loose papers and manila folders, and the doctor looked weary. But he was as bombastic as ever.

"Mr. Williams, I'm glad you're here. I think we need to have a talk."

"Excellent." Bud replied. "Why don't you send for my daughter and we can chat while she's packing her things."

"Your daughter, yes." Barnabas paused, looking out the window. Was he searching for words or covering something up? "That's what I was just about to call you about."

"Oh, yeah?" Bud narrowed his eyes. "Why? What's going on?"

"I'm afraid I have some very grave news."

If that bastard had harmed one hair on her head, Bud was going to rip his goddamn intestines out of his ear. "I'm here to take my daughter her home, so send one of your minions to get her. *Now*."

"I'm afraid I can't do that." Dr. Barnabas said, sounding ominous. "Your daughter's no longer here."

"What do you mean she's not here?" Bud wanted to grab the man by the throat and choke him. "Where is she?"

The charlatan doctor launched into a litany of allegations against Tucker. Not only did he have the balls to pretend she'd somehow waltzed out of this fortress, but he claimed she'd kidnapped a Pioneer counselor, Aimee Dix, to execute her brazen escape. If he weren't deeply concerned for Tucker's safety, Bud would have laughed, the story was so fucking preposterous. He could hardly believe Barnabas managed to tell it with a straight face. If Tucker had gotten away, she would have found a way to contact him. And if there really was a counselor with her, it was probably Carl Lee James.

"I assume you've notified the police then?" Bud drawled. "Do you mind giving me the name of the case number and the officer in charge?"

Dr. Barnabas sputtered. "I've only just been made aware of the situation."

Bud swooped up the desk phone and punched in 911. He waited until he heard the dispatch answer, then shoved the receiver in the man's face. "There you go."

Bud watched the sociopath act like he was upset, sharing emotions and details he hadn't the first time he shared the story. Liars added a level of details most witnesses couldn't recall, and their stories often changed each time they told them. Dr. Barnabas was like the kind of criminal who knew how to seem plausible.

"Now that we're done with all the bullshit, let's get down to business," Bud said once the call was over. "Where's Tucker?"

Dr. Barnabas raised his eyebrows. "Tucker?"

Bud couldn't tell if the surprise in his voice was authentic or not. "Never mind what her name is." In one seamless motion, he wheeled around the desk, withdrew his retired service revolver, and aimed it at the man's temple. "Talk."

Dr. Barnabas didn't flinch. "You aren't going to kill me."

Bud shrugged. "Maybe not." He fired. The round whizzed over the man's head and buried into the bookcase.

"Jesus Christ!" Dr. Barnabas bellowed. "You're fucking crazy."

"I don't have a lot to lose, and next time I won't miss." Bud aimed the pistol lower. "The next bullet will go through your kneecap. I understand that's very painful and can be quite debilitating. Which side to you want your limp on? Left or right?"

Beads of sweat formed at Barnabas's hairline and raced over the furrows of his forehead before rolling through his brows. He was finally taking Bud seriously. "It's all Carl Lee," he stammered. "He's gone off his rocker. I swear, I don't know why. He took your girl and Miss Dix away at gun point. He would have shot me if I'd intervened. All this time, I had no idea he wasn't at Pioneer to do God's work. I only just discovered that he's had his own perverse agenda all along."

Bud found him so annoying he wanted to put his hands around the guy's thick neck and squeeze. Maybe his head would pop like a zit. "And what agenda is that?" he asked.

"Isn't it obvious? The missing girls? The deaths in Marin? Your girl must have stumbled onto his secret."

"So you're now saying Carl Lee has Tucker."

"Yes."

"Then stop fucking around and tell me where he'd take her," Bud growled.

"I have no idea."

The cell phone vibrated in Bud's jacket pocket. Keeping his eyes and gun trained on Dr. Barnabas, he read the message. Finally, some good news. The GPS bug Yoshi had affixed to Tucker's luggage was on the move. He should have known Tucker would figure out a way to get in touch. She was a clever one. Coordinates were being downloaded at that very moment. Bud felt the blood drain from his face. *No*. It couldn't be. Carl Lee's vehicle was at the Quarry Lakes Regional Recreation Area. It was the perfect place to dump a body and it wasn't far from the Pioneer Institute.

As Bud rolled away from Barnabas, he yelled, "Anything happens to her and you're a dead man."

❖

Peering from a crack in the therapy room door, Isabelle Sanchez had seen enough of today's drama to know something significant had happened. After Tucker revealed that she was really a PI searching for Saya Takahashi, Isabelle began hoping Dom would also be found. Of course it had disheartened her when Tucker showed her the locket that had belonged to her grandmother. How did it end up in the storage room after Dom supposedly ran away?

Isabelle had been hiding in the therapy room ever since Miss Dix went to tell Dr. Barnabas what was going on and not long afterward, she heard Dr. Barnabas paging Carl Lee over the intercom. When she saw Tucker and Miss Dix shuffle past with Carl Lee pointing a gun at them, she wondered what the hell was going on. Then a guy in a wheelchair went into Dr. Barnabas's office. Bud, she concluded, the detective who'd pretended to be Tucker's father. A few minutes later, Bud flew right past her without even noticing her trying to flag him down. He seemed really intense and Isabelle didn't try to stop him. She was sure Tucker and Miss Dix were in big trouble.

Was this how it had gone down with Dom? Had Carl Lee taken her at gunpoint to his car? What happened then? Was she still locked in a dungeon somewhere? Had Carl Lee been keeping her as a sex slave? Or was she some kind of present for Dr. Barnabas? Isabelle believed Dr. Barnabas knew more than he was willing to share. But to get any answers the right persuasion would be necessary. She knew just the thing.

She'd stumbled on it really, just messing around in the fridge while she was waiting here for Miss Dix to come out of Dr. Barnabas's office. Among the vials Pioneer gave as part of the aversion therapy, was one marked Sodium Pentothal. If Hollywood had it right, that was truth serum.

It was her lucky day.

Isabelle waited, and not long after Bud left the building, Dr. Barnabas set off along the hall, his brief case swinging at his side. Isabelle let him pass by, then fell in behind. He was so intent on getting out of there he didn't even notice her until she jammed the top of the drug vial into his back.

It apparently felt like a cold gun barrel because her raised one arm and asked, "What can I do for you *now*, Mr. Williams?"

Isabelle stood on her tiptoes and whispered in his ear, "Call me Izzy, you son of a bitch."

His body tensed and he leaned against the wall. The drug was quick-acting. Afraid he would pass out, Isabelle steered him into the therapy room and shoved him into the chair they used for restraint. She strapped his arms down and cinched a belt tightly across his midriff, then closed the door.

"Scream all you want," she told him. "I don't think anyone's left in the wing. No one can hear you."

"What do you think you're doing?" he demanded woozily.

"I was hoping we'd have a chance to talk, you know, heart to heart."

Isabelle sat down in a chair behind him where he couldn't see her.

After a few minutes of silence he grumbled, "What is it you want to know?"

"How did you find out about Jennye?"

He shrugged. "Matt Lovelorn ratted her out. He overheard her talking on the phone."

Why would Matt do that? Isabelle wondered. There could be a dozen answers. He wanted to be liked by an older male. Or he could be trying to convince Dr. Barnabas he was cured of his homosocial ways and was ready to be released from this prison.

"I knew right then the bitch was getting help from someone in here," he muttered. "How else could she have gotten access to a phone?"

"Are you having them killed?" Isabelle tried the direct approach.

"I think you have me mixed up with someone else."

"Oh, you mean Carl Lee."

"You're a bright girl."

"Bright enough to know he's your patsy." Picking up a bottle of pills, she said, "You know, if these drugs aren't working, I could always use the electroshock."

He squirmed. "You don't want to do that."

"I think I might.

"That's torture. You'll regret it. You won't be able to shake the thought that you did that to another person."

Dr. Barnabas concerned with her emotional health. How touching. Isabelle smiled. "You don't seem to have a problem with that."

❖

Officer Dakota Manning received the assignment over the radio. Dr. Barnabas, in person, had dialed 911. The report sounded crazy. A kid had supposedly gone postal, kidnapped one of Pioneer's counselors, and escaped. The chief himself was on the radio. He seemed to think they were hearing another bullshit story about a runaway, and since Dakota had a history with Pioneer, he wanted her to get to the bottom of it.

Dakota considered the idea of calling Aneko on her way out there, but that could wait. She wanted to interview Dr. Barnabas before he could get his lawyers there, if possible. He wasn't in his office. In fact she couldn't find him.

She began knocking on doors until she heard sounds coming from inside a therapy room. Her instincts told her something wasn't right, so she pulled her service weapon and pressed herself against the wall. Dakota reached for the door handle, took a deep breath, turned the knob, and swung around the doorframe, yelling, "Police!"

In her line of work, it didn't take long to get the feeling you'd seen everything, but what she saw in front of her ranked right up there. Dr. Barnabas was strapped to a chair facing a big screen where images of a lesbian couple flashed by.

"Thank you, Lord." he proclaimed. "Officer, this girl's gone crazy. Please help me."

Dakota holstered her pistol and smiled at the girl standing over him. She remembered her from the day of the hostage drama.

"Carl Lee has Miss Dix and Tucker Shade and I think he's going to kill them." the girl declared.

"Hello," Dr. Barnabas interjected. "Are you going to let me out of this chair or what? I'm the victim here. Do your fucking job."

"I'm Izzy," the girl said. "Izzy Sanchez. Can we talk?"

"I'd like that," Dakota said. "Why don't we start with the make and model of vehicle Carl Lee is driving?"

Chapter Seventeen

Bud was at the Quarry Lakes Regional Recreation Area when he heard Officer Dakota Manning's BOLA announcement over the police scanner. He turned up the volume.

He wasn't counting on the Freemont police, or any other law enforcement for that matter. He was determined to rescue Tucker and he could do it on his own. But Manning's description gave him details about the suspect's vehicle and once dispatch found the information in the DMV database, they'd come back with the plate number. Bud radioed in to Fremont PD's dispatch and added himself to the detail, giving them his current location. They sent officers heading toward him.

Then, ignoring the groans of the Impala as she bottomed out on speed bumps, Bud roared through the parking lot scanning the area as he went. A dark colored, late model sedan matching Officer Manning's description was parked by the boat ramp. Bud left rubber on the pavement, spinning a cookie and racing toward the car. *Hold on Tucker! I'm almost there kid.* He hit the next speed bump so fast he got air, the Impala lifting a few inches off the ground like a stunt car in a movie chase. It took him thirty seconds to reach the vehicle. As soon as he did, he knew he'd made a mistake.

Bud punched the horn and snatched up the cell phone to check the map. Tucker's little blip was no longer at the Quarry Lakes. It was miles away, heading up Niles Canyon Road into the East Bay Hills. Bud had been so sure, so frightened, that the Quarry Lakes was Carl Lee's destination, he hadn't kept his eye on the prize. He'd let his instincts carry him here when he should have relied on the technology, and now he'd just given Carl Lee another ten minutes head start. He sped off in pursuit, determined to catch up with the son of a bitch before he got away.

Niles Canyon Road, also known as Highway 84, was a winding, treacherous two lane road. On the canyon floor it was flanked by stunted junipers and one of the East Bay's last free flowing creeks. At the end of the canyon the road wound into the coyote-brush-spotted hills. Whipping around corners and passing cars, each time Bud glimpsed another late model sedan, he'd feel his heart rev in anticipation. Then he'd see the color or notice the slight differences that distinguished one maker from another. These wasted moments were like wasted oxygen. They stole his air away. His breath was ragged and his chest hurt. Each failure, each wrong vehicle brought Tucker's death closer and closer to reality. He could not bear it. He imagined her lying in the morgue. *No, way. Not gonna happen.*

When he finally found the right car he didn't believe it at first. Checked the plate twice. Then he remembered. His tricked out Impala had no siren. He'd have to get creative if he hoped to pull the guy over without flashing lights. Bud admitted his location to the dispatch. There weren't a lot of intersections along Niles Canyon, and there was a chance California Highway Patrol officers could form a roadblock at the other end and stop Carl Lee before he had a chance to hop on one of the freeways or try to lose them on the maze-like city streets of Pleasanton or Livermore, if that's where he was headed.

There was another option. He could be planning to ditch the car somewhere between Freemont and Pleasanton and march the women into the massive open spaces of the East Bay Regional Park system. There were some places Bud could not follow and hiking cross-country was one of them. In the meantime, he attached himself to Carl Lee's ass like white on rice, staying close enough that Carl Lee couldn't ignore him, but not so close that he risked slamming into the sedan if it stopped suddenly. Nothing would be worse than him causing an accident that killed Tucker while he was trying to save her.

Carl Lee sped up trying to shake him again. The needle on Bud's speedometer crept up. There were California laws prohibiting police officers and highway patrol from engaging in high speed chases, but Bud wasn't a cop anymore. He laid on the horn and flashed his lights repeatedly, but Carl Lee wasn't going to stop that easily.

Far in the distance Bud thought he heard sirens. Flashing blues and reds dotted his review mirror, climbing the hill behind him. The road ahead was clear of other cars. If he could get in front of the sedan, Carl Lee would have nowhere to go but back down, where he'd run into advancing Freemont PD. Bud pushed the accelerator as far as it would go. The Impala started to shake. She was never meant to do these kinds of speeds. He moved into the oncoming traffic lane, praying for space. He pulled even with Carl Lee, and for a moment their eyes met. The other man's face was ashen. They were neck to neck.

As they came around a sharp curve, Bud blanched. Another car was approaching quickly, in his lane. He willed the Impala forward. It inched ahead of the sedan. The front doors drew even with Carl Lee's front bumper. He was playing chicken on a road where there was nowhere for either car to go. Bud did not flinch. A hundred yards. Fifty. The car ahead had stopped. Bud could see the terror in the guy's face. A pileup was moments away. At the very last moment, it seemed as if Carl Lee slowed down. Bud pulled in from of him, seconds away from the oncoming car. Blaring horns whizzed past.

Bud slammed on the brakes and slid the Impala sideways, grinding to a stop across the highway in blocking Carl Lee's approaching vehicle. Bud pointed his revolver at Carl Lee's head. In another miracle, Carl Lee managed to stop before plowing straight into him. For a moment they just stared at each other. Then Carl Lee slowly raised his arms.

Bud took the man down like the high risk felony stop he was, demanding he get out of the vehicle and lie face down on the pavement. When the man dropped his left arm to open the car door, it took him a moment too long. Bud curled his finger around the revolver's trigger, on high alert for Carl Lee to jump out with a gun. Instead the sedan's trunk popped up. Not sure whether it was some kind of diversion, Bud kept the revolver trained on the ex-con as he slowly exited from the vehicle and dropped to his knees.

Cursing his dead legs, Bud began the tedious procedure of getting his wheelchair out of the back seat, made all the more difficult because he tried to do it all with the revolver in his hand.

Carl Lee peered at him from the pavement. "Don't shoot me man. I swear I wasn't going to do anything."

"Don't make me laugh. If she's hurt, I swear to God…"

"Bud!" The yell came from the back of Carl Lee's vehicle and

Tucker jumped down, then helped a bedraggled blonde out of the trunk.

Tucker ran toward Bud and fell into his arms like she'd forgotten he wasn't her real dad. He hugged her with the revolver still in his hand, then pushed her aside, to make sure the bastard Carl Lee was still on the ground. Standing over him was Aimee Dix. She looked pissed. Pulling up behind them was a squad car. Everything was going to be okay.

❖

Behind the two-way mirror, Yoshi listened to Officer Dakota Manning read Carl Lee James his rights.

"Look, this has all been a misunderstanding," he said. "I just want to come clean and clear everything up."

"So, you're waving your rights."

"Yeah," he sounded pained. Captured criminals often did when it hit home that they were going to pay for their crimes. So, Yoshi was not surprised when Carl Lee agreed to talk without a lawyer. But the interrogation took a stunning turn, with his next comment. "I was saving their lives."

Officer Manning snorted. "Yeah. Right. So why were they in your trunk?"

"I had to make it seem realistic. But I didn't tie them up."

"Who did?"

"Dr. Barnabas Gage."

Yes! Yoshi was thrilled. Although Gage was also being held in the Freemont police station, they'd decided to speak with Carl Lee first. If they could turn him, Gage was a bigger prize.

Carl Lee had just gotten warmed up. He revealed that five years ago, Gage had recruited him to get rid of problem students whose parents didn't want them to come home unless they were cured.

Carl Lee described his first victim, a particularly effeminate boy whose limp-wristed ways were an embarrassment to his fortune five hundred CEO father.

"I was planning to hit him over the head and dump him overboard. You dump a body far enough out to sea, and there's nothing left, if it washes up at all." Carl Lee paused. "I couldn't do it. When it came time to kill him, I couldn't go through with it."

"What changed your mind?"

"For starters, I'm not a killer." He sounded weary, like he didn't expect to be believed. "The kid reminded me of myself when I was his age. You know, not fitting in, not living up to what the folks expected."

Carl Lee continued his story, saying the boat he'd used belonged to a friend in Bolinas. While he was out on the water that day, he came up with a plan. The story became more fantastical, then. He claimed that over the past five years, he used his underworld connections and the money Dr. Barnabas paid him to give the kids entirely new lives far away from the Bay Area. He insisted each of the dozen teens he'd supposedly killed were living happily ever after.

Yoshi was despondent. She'd hoped Carl Lee's testimony might bring down Dr. Barnabas Gage, but that no longer seemed likely. The man was beginning to sound entirely delusional. His story explained one thing, though. Yoshi had wondered how the Pioneer students even ended up where they did, on a remote cliff side at the edge of a town that did not appear on local maps. Carl Lee was familiar with the area. He would have known about the danger of the cliffs. No doubt he had pushed the two girls over the cliff, expecting their bodies to be washed out to sea. Instead they'd lain there until Velvet Erickson stumbled on them. Small world.

"Well, this should all be very easy to verify," Officer Manning said. "Give me the addresses and I'll send someone to talk with these kids."

"I can't. I arranged everything so I wouldn't know where they ended up. It was safer that way. For me and for them."

"That's convenient."

"Hardly." Carl Lee's voice held no note of humor.

Yoshi tapped on the glass. It took a few minutes, but eventually Officer Manning joined her in the viewing room. "Can you believe this crap?" she asked Yoshi.

"It is so outrageous it is almost hard not to."

"Maybe he can explain the Polaroids your team found at the Pontiac Hotel."

Carl Lee had an explanation for these, too. "Dr. Barnabas wanted proof. He had more gruesome trophies in mind, like an ear or a finger. I convinced him it wouldn't be a good idea to keep DNA evidence like that. Some of the kids really got into it, faking their own deaths for the camera."

Carl Lee James continued to talk for several hours. Yoshi had inherited a penchant for logic over emotion from her father. In fact, Velvet used to call her Spock during arguments, many years ago when they were lovers. Despite that, Yoshi had always trusted her gut and something felt very odd about Carl Lee James. He was either a man who occupied a fictional world as a form of denial, or he was telling a truth so far-fetched it would never be believed. Either way, if Yoshi wanted to find Saya Takahashi, dead or alive, she had a lot of work to do.

CHAPTER EIGHTEEN

It looked like Dr. Barnabas Gage was going to walk. They had little evidence tying him to any crimes. Dakota had hoped Carl Lee's testimony might be the lynchpin in the case against Gage, but that was before he revealed the depth of his delusions. Once he'd finished talking it was clear that everything he said would be ridiculed at trial. Things looked up briefly when the DA himself insisted that Dr. Barnabas was a capital witness who had shown his willingness to skip town and must be held until the police had a chance to properly debrief him. The judge agreed.

In another surprising move, the hot assistant DA was so excited about the turn of events that she invited Dakota out for a drink, which turned into dinner and might have turned into something more if their cell phones hadn't gone off in unison, dragging them both to county lockup and the biggest surprise of the day.

"What do you mean, he's dead?" Dakota asked in shock.

"Hanged himself with his jail uniform," the warden said. "Guards cut him down an hour ago and the ME declared him at the scene. There'll be a whole IA investigation."

He sounded peeved. Internal Affairs got involved whenever someone died in custody. There was always some finger-pointing.

Dakota wasn't exactly torn up at the prospect of Dr. Barnabas Gage's untimely death. She had the feeling he deserved everything he got. But it was hard to close a case if the suspect died before being convicted. Was that justice? Even the families who'd lost loved ones didn't want the murderer to die before he'd stood trial, and maybe even come clean during sentencing.

Good thing Carl Lee got himself a lawyer, Dakota thought, because with Gage dead there was no one else to blame and no sweetheart deal to be cut. Juries wanted someone to pay, especially when kids were involved. Even if they were queer.

Dakota remembered the briefcase taken into evidence when she liberated Dr. Barnabas from Isabelle Sanchez. It had been processed along with his other belongings so it was fair game, and she was determined to break into it. When she did, she discovered a paper trail that documented the special services Pioneer offered. It also provided incriminating details on the parents who'd paid for what was euphemistically described as "a set-up fee for permanent relocation." The language seemed to give them plausible deniability and perhaps some genuinely believed their unwanted children were going to be resettled in a far-off city. It was hard to indict parents for a lack of unconditional love, and it seemed that was all the police would be able to prove.

Dr. Barnabas had also left the Pioneer office that day with the Institute's own statistics, showing their therapies were failing and worse, that they could cause long term psychological harm. The data would be enough to permanently shut down Pioneer. When the story eventually exploded onto the pages of the *San Francisco Chronicle*, there would be public outrage. Dakota hoped the outcry would lead to some changes. No one should be permitted to use aversion therapies on children within the state of California.

Tucker could understand why Yoshi didn't want to accept the obvious, that Saya Takahashi had fallen victim to Carl Lee's murderous rampage. Even to Tucker, who'd been shut away in Pioneer for most of the investigation, it was clear that Yoshi had gotten really close to Aneko. Tucker was a little jealous, but she could admit that their connection was probably natural, what with Aneko sharing Yoshi's cultural heritage. Knowing how disappointed Aneko would be, Yoshi wouldn't want to admit that Blind Eye had gone as far as they could.

"I called you all here to reexamine the evidence in the Pioneer case, with fresh eyes," Yoshi said. "There are some items that remain unresolved, that I would like us to address, in case they shed some light on the whereabouts of our missing person, Saya Takahashi, either dead or alive."

Bud shook his head. Tucker was familiar with his two theories about Saya. They both concerned geography. He thought Carl Lee had discarded her corpse either in the remote East Bay, or somewhere near the Farralone Islands.

Tucker shrugged in response, mouthing, *Humor her.* So what if they had to spend another day shifting through the pieces of the case.

"Tucker, did you have something you wanted to share?"

Holy crap, how did she do that? Had Yoshi heard Tucker's lips move? Tucker hung her head and could have sworn Yoshi shot daggers at her with her piercing blue eyes. She mumbled, "No. Sorry."

"Fine. One element of this that continues to bother me involves Erica and Sarah, the two girls who were pushed off the Bolinas cliff. First, our main suspect, Carl Lee James, continues to insist he had no involvement in their deaths—"

"But he *does* admit he was involved in the disappearance of a dozen Pioneer students," Tucker said.

"Exactly," Yoshi continued, giving Tucker a verbal pat on the back. "And, unlike those students, neither Sarah nor Erica was mentioned in the paperwork recovered from Barnabas Gage's briefcase. There's no indication that Gage ordered Carl Lee to take care of the girls, as he did the missing students. Nor is there any sign that funds changed hands in that case."

"Who does that leave?" Bud asked.

The Mudd brothers?" Tucker immediately wished she hadn't pronounced it as a question. She could tell Yoshi thought she was expressing self-doubt by raising the pitch of her voice at the end of the statement. She'd been trying to break that old habit. She wondered if Yoshi would ever see her as an equal. Sure she wasn't a full-fledged PI yet, but Tucker had spent a week undercover and during that time she'd even risked her life. Again. What would it take to earn Yoshi's respect?

"If we were talking about sexual assault, sure." Bud addressed Tucker's suggestion. "But the Mudd boys seemed to have their hands full wooing those girls they were drinking with. When do you think they found time to chase another two off a cliff."

"Maybe they were trying to assault them and the girls ran off,"

Tucker was a little peeved that Bud had dismissed her so quickly, and that Yoshi seemed to be doing the same thing.

"The evidence doesn't support that," Bud said patronizingly. "What about the broken necklace Carl Lee had?"

"It was Erica's," Tucker said.

Yoshi frowned. "And there was nothing on her autopsy to support signs of a struggle?"

Bud was silent for so long Tucker checked to make sure he hadn't fallen asleep. "The Binghams got an injunction, remember?" she answered Yoshi. "On religious grounds. There was no autopsy."

"Wait, are you saying there was only a single autopsy report?" Yoshi directed her annoyance at Bud. "Why am I first learning of this now?"

"We told you when you got back from Marin County, didn't we?" Tucker looked at Bud for confirmation. He seemed to be examining his cuticles. Knowing he hadn't gone metrosexual, Tucker felt herself getting angry. "You didn't tell her, Bud?"

"Apparently you didn't either, Ms. High and Mighty."

"I was trapped in that ex-gay prison without a phone. Where were you? Oh right, you were out on a date with that crazy bigot. No wonder you forgot everything else."

Yoshi interrupted. "It does not matter who dropped the ball. Let's get back on point, shall we? Please tell me about the medical examiner's report."

She seemed particularly excited, immediately making plans to enlist official assistance and get that autopsy decision revisited in light of the Pioneer situation.

"So," Bud said pointing out the irony. "Even though you just explained to us why this case is unlike the others, you're going to pretend it's the same so you can convince a judge that Erica's parents were not motivated by their faith but a desire to cover up their role in her untimely death?"

"I believe I will choose different terminology, but yes. This was not an accident and the person who killed the girls is still out there, which is why the additional autopsy is essential at this point. I'd also like you to reinterview the Mudd brothers."

Bud groaned.

"And now that we have access," Yoshi continued. "I want to

interview all the students on that Bolinas trip. In fact, I've already taken the liberty of inviting each of them, and Aimee Dix, to our office, later today. Since Budd will have his hands full in Bolinas, Tucker, you will be interviewing them with me."

Tucker tried to look enthusiastic. Yoshi's feelings about Aneko must be serious, she decided, if she was about to start their investigation all over again even with Carl Lee James facing death penalty charges.

❖

Isabelle slumped into the puffy Starbucks couch and picked up a copy of *Bay Times*, less for reading material and more as a shield to hide behind. Every few moments she shifted in her seat and thought about just taking off. She'd debated for days about whether to share her growing suspicions with Tucker, telling herself it was nothing, and then waking up in the dead of night, certain she'd realized something of profound importance, something critical to the Blind Eye investigation, even if it was coming a little late. During one of those moments of clarity Isabelle had sent a text to Tucker, saying, "We need to talk."

By the time she'd gotten up the next morning her certainty had passed and when Tucker called to find out what was wrong she insisted it was nothing, just some crazy idea that was probably the byproduct of Pioneer-induced PTSD and insomnia.

Tucker insisted they meet for coffee anyway.

Isabelle reluctantly agreed, not wanting to lose the friendship that had developed or letting it become just another virtual relationship playing out in abbreviated chats and text messages. It was funny how close they'd become. She hadn't liked Tucker when they first met in Pioneer and Tucker was pretending to be someone she wasn't. Isabelle had sensed a fakeness there she hadn't trusted. Now, as Tucker sauntered through the glass doors, she exuded a cocky confidence Isabelle hadn't seen during their time in Pioneer. And she had a level of comfort with her appearance that was absent when she wore skirts.

Isabelle hopped up and stuck out her hand, also thrilled to be free of the enforced femininity. But unlike Tucker, she wasn't confident displaying her leanings toward a more masculine look. Tucker pivoted her into a hug, and being in her arms felt mostly like Isabelle imagined it would if they were sisters. *Mostly*. She was suddenly, excruciatingly aware of the curve of Tucker's breasts pressing against hers through the padding of Tucker's suit jacket and long-sleeved shirt. Isabelle felt her cheeks burn in embarrassment.

It had been so long since Dom left, Isabelle yearned to be touched. The feeling had nothing to do with Tucker, and Isabelle's heart still belonged to Dom, but that didn't keep the physical loneliness at bay. She quickly stepped out of the hug and sat down while Tucker stood in line to get a drink. Even with the shocking photographs Blind Eye had uncovered in that freak, Carl Lee's hotel room, Isabelle refused to believe Dom was really dead. She was certain she would know in her soul if Dom was no longer among the living. Until that day, she would wait for Dom's return.

"Let me ask you something," she said when Tucker sat down. "Shoot," Tucker said, sipping from her tall cup. She'd chosen the chair across from Isabelle instead of sharing the couch, as though she'd felt the electricity between them and wanted to avoid physical contact.

"Did they find photos of Erica and Sarah with the others?"

"No. And Carl Lee still claims he had nothing to do with their deaths."

"Strange, isn't it, the way all the others just *disappeared*, but Sarah and Erica didn't? Doesn't that mean someone else killed them?"

"Yeah," Tucker nodded. "It could. That's obviously bothering Yoshi too. That's why she's still got us on the case."

"Really?" Isabelle thought the case had been closed when Carl Lee was arrested. It was really cool Yoshi might be thinking the same thing she was. Yoshi was a totally amazing woman, running her own private eye company even though she was blind. Isabelle would love to work for a woman like that. Tucker was so lucky. "How does Yoshi plan for you guys to figure it out?"

"Well," Tucker drawled like she was a Texas Ranger instead of PI-in-training from Idaho. "Yoshi's totally making us reinterview all the witnesses. She even forced Bud to go out and talk with the Mudd brothers again. I'm glad I missed out on that."

"Those guys were creeps." Isabelle shuddered.

"We're still waiting for the results of the second autopsy," Tucker continued. "There's still a chance it was just some bizarre accident." She broke off, as though she'd read something on Isabelle's face. "What is it?"

"It's all *my* fault."

"What's all your fault?"

"That Erica and Sarah are dead."

Tucker gave her a condescending look, but was nice enough to ask, "What makes you think something stupid like that?"

"Erica was having an affair."

Tucker nodded. "You told me."

Isabelle studied at the cracks in the wood floor and wondered if it was even worth trying to explain her suspicions. She didn't really know anything for sure. But Tucker seemed sincerely interested in what Isabelle had to say. It made her feel good. "I found something." She pulled a carefully folded piece of lined paper from her jeans pocket and passed it to Tucker.

Tucker read a few lines and looked up, eyebrows raised. "Isn't this Emily Dickinson?"

"No, it's Erica's handwriting. I thought it was for Sarah. You know, like she couldn't wait to get out of the program so they could be together. But what if I'm wrong. At first, I thought she and Sarah were hitting it, but I'm not so sure now. What if the poem was for someone else?"

"Who else was there?" Tucker asked.

Isabelle hesitated. "Matt Lovelorn."

"Really?" Tucker looked doubtful. "But Matt's gay, and so was Erica."

"Everyone at Pioneer was there because our parents *thought* we were all queer. Just because we all looked queer doesn't mean we were, you know? Like, Erica had a dozen piercings, dyed her hair blue, wore ripped jeans, and liked Sleater-Kinney. Maybe her parents just assumed she was a dyke."

Tucker stayed quiet, but she nodded, encouraging Isabelle to go on.

"I know Matt hated being gay. He'd always be the one agreeing with the terrible things the counselors said about homosexuals, you know that they were all filthy chicken hawks or mama's boys. Maybe he and Erica were trying so hard to be straight they ended up fucking each other."

"How does that work?" Tucker grinned. "Is that like when someone accidentally cheats, you know, like they slipped and fell on a penis?"

"I'm serious, Tucker." Isabelle wasn't in the mood for jokes. "You weren't at Pioneer as long as I was. You don't understand how desperate it got. What you'd do to have someone touch you. How much you want to feel like someone cares."

"So, you're saying it's kind of like how straight guys go gay in prison?"

"Yeah, I guess."

"Okay, but what makes you think it was Matt?"

"That night at the lake when Erica and Sarah disappeared and got in trouble with Miss Dix, I didn't tell you everything."

Tucker's expression changed. She was suddenly paying closer attention, staring at Isabelle like she was the only person in the room.

"I talked to Matt that night. He was worried about Erica being out of her tent, but he refused to believe she was with Sarah. He just kept saying she wasn't like that, she wouldn't do that, and he got mad at me for suggesting she was. I think he was jealous." Isabelle hung her head. "I'm the one who told him they were having an affair. What if he...did something?"

❖

Aimee's hand shook slightly as she sipped some tea. Looking around the other women in the Blind Eye office, she said, "I only wanted those kids to have a better life, to know the love of God, and to have healthy relationships."

She never could have imagined how misplaced her faith had been. Not in God, but in man. In that monster Dr. Barnabas Gage and his evil disciple, Carl Lee James. In the days since police raided the Pioneer Institute, Aimee had slept poorly. Each new day seemed to turn up some other grim truth she hadn't known of but should have. Why hadn't she followed up when kids suddenly disappeared, supposedly running away or transferring to other schools? How many lives could she have saved if she'd paid more attention? Her lack of awareness didn't soothe her conscience. She still felt culpable.

"I want to do something to help." She wept softly. "I'm certified to be a foster parent, but the Department of Human Services says I can't take in any of the kids from Pioneer that are going into system."

"I am not sure I understand why not," Yoshi said.

"They say being around me could be a trigger for these kids who've already survived so much. Maybe they're right." Aimee didn't wipe her eyes. She let the tears run down her cheeks. "But I parented developmentally disabled kids before I signed on to work for Pioneer full time. I think I can help." She didn't care how terrible she looked. She felt awful. It took her a moment to catch her breath.

"I'm sorry, Aimee," Tucker said. "I always felt like you cared about us, just that you were maybe misguided about the help we needed."

Aimee nodded. That was how she felt. Misguided. She'd been so wrong, she could see it now. She had sinned. She was the one who needed the Lord's forgiveness. Almighty God had a reason for all of creation, so He must have something special in mind for His lesbian and gay children. Jesus had always favored the outcasts of society. If He walked the earth in these modern days, wouldn't He befriend gays and lesbians?

"Decent, God-fearing people can do terrible things in the name of religion," Yoshi remarked softly. "They will take questionable actions when they believe they are doing so for the right reasons, and the ends justify the means."

"I thought I was keeping my students from going to hell." Aimee wiped her face with a Kleenex. "I didn't realize that for them, Pioneer was a hell on earth. I've had such a spiritual epiphany."

Tucker took Aimee's hand. "You were brave. Once you realized what was happening, you did the right thing."

"I wish there was more I could do." Aimee sighed. "I worry about the kids from Pioneer whose parents wanted them to disappear. They deserve so much more. And Isabelle...she hates the place where she's staying, and I'd like to help, to give her the home she deserves."

"I have friends at DHS," Yoshi said. "Why don't I speak with them on your behalf?"

"Oh, Yoshi, would you really? That would mean the world to me. Thank you so much...for everything."

CHAPTER NINETEEN

Are you busy?" Tucker asked in her familiar staccato.

Yoshi waved at the chair opposite her substantial desk, whose smooth cherry desktop Yoshi kept clear of clutter, leaving only her slim black phone, iMac computer and carefully arranged, low profile brunette platters. She did not like to be overwhelmed by clutter. Leather squeaked under her legs as she shifted forward in her executive chair. "Is it here?"

"One autopsy report on Erica Bingham coming right up," Tucker announced.

Yoshi heard her settle into her seat, open the manila envelope, and remove the report. She was delighted that Tucker did not start reading verbatim, from top to bottom, as she'd done so many times in the past. She was certainly maturing as an employee. Tucker was silent for a few moments, scanning the pages for important information. When she inhaled sharply, Yoshi knew she'd found it.

"OMG!" Tucker exclaimed, immediately calling into question Yoshi's assessment of her maturity. Yoshi found these teen-culture texting abbreviations annoying enough in their natural environment. She was absolutely appalled that they had started to infiltrate mainstream culture, including, for God's sake, television news programs. What was this world coming to?

"No way." Tucker whistled.

"Please, do tell," Yoshi prompted.

"Erica was preggers."

Yoshi was certain her jaw actually dropped. "Excuse me?"

"Knocked up, had a bun in the oven, expecting, pregnant." Tucker ticked off euphemisms as though they could make the astonishing news mundane.

This changed everything, Yoshi thought. Blind Eye would have to completely reevaluate their victimology. "How far along was she?"

"Fetal development puts it around five weeks," Tucker reported.

"So," Yoshi mused, "she might not even have been aware she was pregnant."

"I guess Isabelle was right," Tucker said.

"Isabelle knew she was expecting a child?"

"No, but she told me Erica and Matt had been kicking it. I didn't believe her, but now—"

"What reason did she have to believe the two were involved?" Yoshi asked.

"She talked with Matt Lovelorn. She was telling me about it the other day when we met for coffee." Tucker's inflection rose, but it had been at least three days, maybe more since she'd last ended a sentence inappropriately. She *was* maturing, at least in certain areas.

Pleased, Yoshi, asked, "What was the nature of their conversation?"

"Matt got all pissed when he found out that Sarah and Erica weren't in their tents. Isabelle told him what they were doing, but he kept saying Erica wasn't like that. She wouldn't do that to him."

"It sounds like there was an attachment," Yoshi said. "Does the report indicate if they were able to obtain a DNA sample from the fetus?

"Yeah, it's gone to the lab for comparison. This is turning into a Jerry Springer episode. Can we get DNA samples from a bunch of potential baby daddies and then strap them down to lie detectors?"

Yoshi ignored Tucker's dry wit. "There should be sufficient evidence to compel samples from the male staff and students at Pioneer for comparison."

Erica had been confined in Pioneer far longer than she'd been pregnant, so the child's father must have been at the school with her. Was Isabelle correct in her convictions about Matt? Or was the father one of the other students? Or Carl Lee? Barnabas Gage?

Yoshi had never suspected Erica was with child when she died. But she had also never been convinced that Carl Lee murdered Erica and

Sarah. Their deaths didn't fit his pattern and Erica's pregnancy was just one more element that set the two girls' deaths apart from the string of students whose disappearances Carl Lee had admitted orchestrating.

Yoshi thanked Tucker for her time, and she waited until the young woman closed the door behind her before picking up the phone and dialing Officer Dakota Manning. A brief conversation provided her with the answers she'd hoped for. Manning's department had indeed gathered DNA swabs from all of the Pioneer students, counselors, and staff. Budget cuts and caseloads being what they were, the DNA samples were not considered high priority, especially with Carl Lee in jail.

Yoshi spent the next few hours on the phone attempting to push the samples onto a faster track. These days civilians, nourished on TV crime scene investigations, believed DNA samples took minutes, or merely seconds to run. In reality, the backlog in California crime labs was often months or even years behind.

So, Yoshi was delighted when her hard work elicited responses within days. First Detective Ari Fleishman told her a lab technician had been able to extract DNA from skin cells caught in the clasp of the necklace recovered from Carl Lee's room. The lab had that DNA fingerprint waiting to be compared to a swab from Carl Lee's mouth. Thanks to Yoshi's initiative, that comparison would be made sooner than later.

She wondered if that information would ever make it to the inside of a courtroom. After all, they'd been unable to even establish conclusively that necklace had belonged to Erica in the first place, and it had changed hands many times since Carl Lee supposedly found it on the ocean cliff top. There was no chain of evidence, and they only had Aimee Dix's word that she'd found it in Carl Lee's room.

Soon after her call with Ari, Yoshi heard from Officer Dakota Manning, who'd arranged tests for paternity of Erica's unborn child. That was the good news. The bad news was that they were only willing to run one DNA profile at a time. Contending that the most likely contributor of paternal DNA was Carl Lee, the chief had decided to run his sample first. Only if there failed to be a match would the lab run other profiles against that of the fetus, slowly working down the list of Pioneer's males to locate the father.

Yoshi was disappointed. She had hoped to have the evidence to confirm her suspicions before she talked to Matt Lovelorn. On the other hand, even sworn officers of the law were allowed to lie to a suspect. She could claim to have evidence that was not in her possession. And doing so might just loosen the one tongue that mattered.

❖

Matt Lovelorn looked as preppy as an Abercrombie and Fitch model, in jeans and a button-down shirt. As he sat down, his gaze stayed fixed on Yoshi, as if there were magnets in his irises.

"I'll leave you to it then," Dakota Manning told Yoshi and Tucker. "I'll be right outside if you need anything."

Matt Lovelorn's parents were not among those who'd paid Dr. Barnabas to get rid of their child. They were out of town and had arranged for their son to join them once the police had finished interviewing him. They hadn't sent in a lawyer. As far as they knew, their son was one of many witnesses needed to provide the evidence that would convict Carl Lee James.

After the door closed behind Dakota, Yoshi remained silent. Tucker was struck with the urge to giggle, to break the tension. Knowing full well that Yoshi was building it on purpose, she bit her lip. She was privileged to be there at all, in the room during a suspect interview, and she didn't want to blow it.

"What's going on?" Matt broke the silence. "The cop wouldn't tell me anything."

"We would like to talk about the night Erica and Sarah were killed," Yoshi said.

Tucker studied Matt's face. She saw his eyelids lower like a limbo bar. "I already told the cops, I don't know shit about what happened."

"Before we go any further, I want to make sure you understand your rights." Yoshi said. "You have the right to an attorney—"

"What's going on? Am I under arrest? I thought it was an accident."

Yoshi shook her head. "No, you didn't."

"What?" He sounded perplexed.

Yoshi repeated the Miranda instructions. When she finished she asked, "Did you understand those rights?"

"Yes."

"All right then. You certainly do not need to speak with us, but we wanted to give you the chance to clarify a few things. Would you like to proceed or would you prefer to wait for an attorney?"

"What kind of things? I've told you everything I know."

"Now, Matthew," Yoshi scolded. "That is not entirely true. You forgot to mention some very important details. We know what really happened and we would like to give you this opportunity to tell us your side of the story. If there were extenuating circumstances, a judge might be lenient."

"I don't know what you're talking about." His voice wavered.

"Look dude," Tucker said, "we already *know* about Erica."

"You mean Erica and Sarah?"

"Does this mean you're waiving your rights and will talk with us?" Tucker asked.

"Yeah, sure. I mean, *yes*." Matt was almost patronizing now.

"Matthew, the police already know you had sexual relations with Erica. That is why we are here, speaking with you again. Your earlier statements are inconsistent."

He was quiet for a moment and then said confidently, "You're bluffing. There's no way they could know that."

"You left your DNA inside her," Tucker said.

His eyes narrowed as he considered her statement. He shook his head. "I don't think so."

"I am not certain if you are aware of this," Yoshi said calmly. "A judge recently ordered that Erica's body be exhumed. They were able to perform a complete autopsy."

Matt finally looked a little less confident, perhaps even nauseous.

"I don't think she told him," Tucker lowered her voice, confiding in Yoshi

"I believe you are correct," Yoshi affirmed.

"Maybe they weren't as close as he thought," Tucker said.

"What are you talking about?" Matt demanded.

"Erica was pregnant," Tucker said.

His face fell. "No." He said it repeatedly, slowly and softly, all the while examining their faces for any trace of deceit.

"So, you see, we have proof that you two had intercourse at least once," Yoshi said.

"It was mine?"

Tucker assumed his question was just a way of coming to grips with reality rather than questioning Erica's faithfulness.

"Yes." Yoshi answered confidently, although they didn't have confirmation yet. Matt began to cry. The tears seemed to transform him from coldhearted killer to lost and lonely little boy. "Why didn't she tell me?"

"Maybe she didn't know," Tucker said. "She wasn't that far along."

"I thought she loved me." He moaned, sobbing now. "I loved her."

Tucker put her arm around him and let him cry on her shoulder for a few seconds before holding him at arms length. She noticed then that the middle button on his shirt was slightly different from the others, chalk white instead of eggshell, and the stitching that held it in place didn't match the traditional x-shaped crisscross pattern securing the others.

"If you loved her," Yoshi asked, "why did you kill her?"

Matt flinched, jerking away from Tucker in an almost violent manner. "I told you. I didn't. I could never hurt Erica!"

Yoshi clearly didn't believe him. "So you just left her there at the bottom of the cliff? Do you know what she looked like when her parents had to identify her? Do you know how difficult that was for them?"

"Did you think the ocean would carry her and Sarah away?" Tucker asked.

"Was that what you intended?" Yoshi demanded. "Did you expect the waves to do your dirty work for you? Because, believe me, they did no such thing."

She shook the contents of a manila envelope onto the table, scattering the disturbingly stylish crime scene photos in front of him.

Matt tried not to look. He shifted in his seat, turning his body away, but he couldn't seem to keep his eyes from straying back to images of death.

Yoshi continued. "Their bodies lay there while the flies landed and maggots hatched. Pelicans and crabs haggled over their flesh."

Matt gagged. He rushed toward the garbage can.

"And their bodies started to putrefy…"

"That's enough," Tucker interjected.

"They were rotting from the inside, bloated and swollen from the gasses a decaying body produces."

Matt clutched the side of the garbage can while he covered one ear. His rocking was punctuated by a singsong voice pleading, "Shut up, shut up."

Tucker swept the glossy photos into a pile.

There was a knock on the door and Dakota Manning stuck her head in. "I have something for Yoshi."

Yoshi followed Dakota into the observation room. She could still hear Matt crying through the speakers. This was where Dakota had been, observing and taping the interview session.

"How are we doing?" Yoshi asked.

"Looks like you're doing great. Sorry to pull you out right before he cracks, but I have some info you'll want."

"I meant, procedurally," Yoshi said.

She and Tucker were far from deputized, but a judge could rule that, by using the police facilities, they were acting as agents of the law, which meant they needed to comply with the same rules that constrained peace officers. To illicit a confession, they would have to step very carefully. In addition to Dakota, another detective had been observing the entire time. Dakota introduced Yoshi to Detective Smith. "We got back the DNA results on those skin cells we pulled from the necklace," Dakota said.

"It's Lovelorn."

"Detective Smith is chomping at the bit to take a shot at the kid, but he's agreed to give you another fifteen minutes to see if you can crack him. Fair enough?"

"That is very generous, sir," Yoshi offered her hand, which was engulfed in one twice the size of her own and pumped vigorously. Smith handed her a can of soda for Matt.

Yoshi could hear the boy sniffling in the corner when she returned. Allowing Tucker to offer the soda, she waited for a minute or two before asking, "Matt, have you ever worn a necklace?"

"Nooo," he drew out the word to emphasize the laughable nature of her query.

Yoshi held back her smile. "Did you ever give Erica jewelry, as a gift?"

"How the hell could I? It's not like Pioneer let me go shopping on the weekends."

"Right, of course," Yoshi said as though she had not thought her questions through. "So, just to clarify, there is no reason at all why your skin cells would be caught in the clasp of a girl's necklace?"

"I'm not some kind of drag queen if that's what you mean."

"Really think about it," Tucker insisted, playing the good cop, trying to find an excusable reason why Matt's DNA migrated to the necklace. "You and Erica were having sex, right? Maybe you—"

"Wrapped your hands around her neck?" Yoshi interrupted.

"That's not what I meant," Tucker retorted. "He could have helped her put it on, or gotten her hair untangled from it, or—"

"Listen Tucker," Yoshi gave an exaggerated sigh. "I know you bonded with Matt over your shared experience at Pioneer. But we are talking about a cold-blooded killer who pushed two girls, one of whom he claims he loved, over a cliff and then covered it up."

"I had nothing to do with that!" Matt yelled.

"That's very hard to believe." Yoshi laid everything out for him. "Witnesses saw someone leave the boys camp that night. You were involved with Erica and had fathered a child with her that you probably did not want. Tests prove your DNA was on her necklace. It got there because you yanked it from her neck."

"No, no. I swear, I didn't know about the baby, honest."

"I know you didn't," Tucker said. "That's why you have to come clean about everything, Matt. What happened that night?"

Finally, Matt relented, offering up a version of the night's events that kept him from looking bad. It started with the Mudd brothers coming into the boys' camp with beer and pot. Matt went over to the girls' camp, worried for Erica's safety. She and Sarah weren't there. Matt said he returned to the boys camp just about the time Carl Lee and Miss Dix came and broke up the party. He retired to his tent, but couldn't sleep and finally went out again searching on the outskirts of the camp. That was when he heard Erica calling for help.

It took him forever to find her. Finally he found her flashlight on the ground and, looking over the cliff, discovered Erica had fallen part of the way down, landing on a thin rock outcrop. Lying down he could just reach her. She said she and Sarah had gotten lost and stepped off the cliff. Sarah had fallen all the way down but Erica had fallen onto this ledge.

Matt said he wanted to go for help but Erica begged him not to leave her alone. So he was helping her up, and he'd gotten her pulled up most of the way when he lost his grip and she slipped away from him. He grabbed at anything, caught her necklace, which broke. And she fell all the way to the bottom. She wasn't moving and he knew she was dead. He was so overcome with grief, it was like he just blocked it out, pretended it didn't happen. But, the guilt had been eating away at him all this time and he was relieved to finally get it off his chest.

Tucker had not made a sound during Matt's story. When she spoke now, her voice cracked. "Oh, my God, how awful."

Yoshi, certain Matt's story was a load of rubbish, did not express similar sentiments. She wondered how she was going to bring Tucker to the same conclusion. They probably did not have much longer before Detective Smith took over the interrogation.

"Wait a minute," Tucker said, clearly mulling over Matt's narrative. "If you were at the top of the cliff how did you see all the way down to the bottom well enough to know they'd been killed from the fall?"

"I shined my flashlight down there."

Yoshi was certain the claim would not stand up to scientific inquiry.

"I don't know," Tucker said. "I think I'd have gone down there to see if there was any hope."

"How could I? There wasn't any way down."

"What were they doing out there anyway?" Tucker mused. "I mean, couldn't they hear the surf?"

"I guess they were distracted," Matt said.

"Oh, right. You thought they were sneaking off to do it."

"What? No."

"Sure you did. Isabelle told me. She thought you were jealous." From Tucker's voice, Yoshi thought the budding detective was reaching her own level of skepticism. Perhaps all was not lost.

"Is that why you pushed them over the edge?" Yoshi asked. "Did you catch them *in flagrante*?"

"No. I told you what happened."

"Oh, my God," Tucker gasped. "It didn't happen that way at all, did it? You really *are* a killer." Something had changed in Tucker's voice. She sounded mortified. ""Remember the stuff we collected on the cliff? We found a button."

Dakota Manning entered the room with Detective Smith, who instructed Matt, "Take it off."

Yoshi heard the sound of clothes pulled off, then the distinct click of a handcuff snapping around wrists. She liked that the Freemont folks were so responsive. It all happened very quickly. Dakota disappeared, presumably taking the shirt into custody, while Detective Smith pulled up a seat and joined Yoshi and Tucker around the table.

"What the hell's going on?" Matt demanded.

"Go ahead," Detective Smith encouraged Tucker.

"You went after Erica and Sarah to confront them, because you thought they were having an affair," Tucker elaborated. "There was a struggle, and you tore off Erica's necklace. One of the girls fought back. She grabbed a hold of you and yanked your shirt. Maybe she was just trying to regain her balance but her grip popped one of your buttons right off. You sewed a new button back on differently than the manufacturer. It wasn't overwhelming grief that kept you from going for help, it was the fact that what you'd done was on purpose."

"I loved Erica," Matt threw back at her. "We could have had a normal happy life but she *chose* to sin, she chose to betray me. God punished them."

"Bullshit," Tucker spat. "Take responsibility for your own actions."

Matt insisted he just wanted to confront his girlfriend about the rumors that she and Sarah were having sex. Erica kept lying, she kept saying they were just friends. He got mad and shoved her. She fell and he grabbed for her and accidentally got a hold of the necklace. It broke and she fell backward over the cliff. Sarah dove after her, trying to save her from falling, but instead they both went over. He couldn't do anything, but he'd never meant for it to happen. It was a terrible accident. He tried to throw the necklace over the cliff after them, but it didn't go far enough and got lost in the weeds.

The team was silent a moment, then Yoshi said, "Matthew, Erica was not having a sexual relationship with Sarah. They were just friends. They were not having an affair and Erica was not cheating on you. She really was just out for a smoke."

Matt began to sob, this time sincerely, inconsolably.

CHAPTER TWENTY

With a suspected serial killer in the Fremont detention center, the security was intense. As a high-risk prisoner, Carl Lee was only allowed visitation by members of his legal team. Like most public defenders, Carl Lee's lawyer was young and inexperienced. With all the charges stacked up against his client he'd encouraged him to take a plea bargain. The man refused. Instead, he'd demanded his lawyer reach out to the Blind Eye Detective Agency, somehow, convincing him that, despite appearances to the contrary, the PI firm was critical to his defense.

Yoshi relayed this information to Bud after assigning him to visit Carl Lee at the jail where he was being held pending trial. He hadn't outright refused, but he'd sure raised a stink about it. Why the hell should he meet with some mass-murdering freak who'd kidnapped Tucker and locked her in his trunk? How could Yoshi expect him to act civil to a man he wanted to beat the crap out of?

In lieu of a direct response Yoshi reminded him that they had been hired by Aneko to locate her sister, Saya, which they still had not succeeded in doing. His job was to hear Carl Lee out, figure out what his game was, and do all he could to ascertain where Saya was.

Fremont's jail butted up against the Central Park. From the right angle, visitors could convince themselves that they were somewhere remote, like Montana, instead of in the San Francisco Bay Area. Carl Lee's public defender met Bud in the parking lot. He looked to be about fourteen and told Bud he'd never tried a capital case before. They'd have to pretend Bud was part of the legal defense team to get him in to meet with Carl Lee. Bud almost felt sorry for the suspected killer. Poor bastard didn't have a chance with a putz like this defending him.

"Calm down," Bud said as they headed for security. "It's common for defense attorneys to hire PIs. Haven't you ever seen *Perry Mason* reruns?" The kid's blank face said it all. "Just don't say anything, okay? I'll introduce myself."

As he'd expected, Bud had no problem getting through the security. He had to present his credentials, but no one put two and two together and came up with anything unusual. He and the public defender were led to the only room in the station where eavesdropping devices were not allowed. The lawyer opened his briefcase and laid some file folders on the table while they waited in silence for the guard to bring Carl Lee.

He shuffled in wearing an orange jailhouse jumpsuit and shackles around his ankles. He slumped into a chair and didn't move while the guard secured him to the chair, the table, and the floor.

Carl Lee didn't speak until the guard left and locked the door from the outside. "I was expecting Yoshi Yakamota to be an Asian American woman," he joked. "Not this crazy son of a bitch who nearly killed me."

Bud shrugged. "I'd be happy to leave. I don't want to be here anyway."

"Please stay. I'm happy to see you in different circumstances."

"The circumstances haven't changed for me." Bud wasn't about to forget what this bastard might have done to Tucker if he hadn't saved her when he did.

"Fair enough." Carl Lee waited until Bud had settled at the table before continuing. "I asked you here today because I want to hire the Blind Eye Detective Agency to clear my name."

"What?" Bud burst out laughing. He addressed the defense attorney. "I don't want to tell you how to defend your client, but—"

"*I'm* asking, not him," Carl Lee clarified.

"You do realize that we've played a rather substantial role in gathering the evidence that is being used to prosecute you, right?" Bud asked. "Don't you think this is kind of a conflict of interest, or something?"

"I'm not stupid," Carl Lee insisted, although Bud was beginning to wonder how the guy could have hidden his crimes for so long if this was how he did things. "I realize your company got involved because you were hired to look for someone, right?"

"Right." Bud allowed. "Saya Takahashi. You want to tell me

where she is? I'd love to provide some kind of closure for her loved ones. Maybe if you led investigators to wherever you hid the bodies, you could try for clemency."

"There are so many things wrong with that statement I don't know where to begin," Carl Lee said.

Bud could feel the heat rising from the collar of his business shirt at the arrogance of the man. "Let's begin with Saya Takahashi. Where'd you hide her?"

"I don't know where she is. That's how it works. Each player only knows one other link, so if someone gets compromised we don't take down the whole operation."

"What the hell are you babbling about?"

"The underground railroad."

"Are you shitting me? What the fuck is this?" Bud glared at the defense attorney. "This some kind of joke? You trying to establish groundwork for an insanity plea? Because it ain't gonna happen."

"I didn't kill anyone, I swear," Carl Lee repeated. "I was saving them."

"Saving them? From what?"

"Dr. Barnabas. Their parents. People willing to kill these kids because of their gender or sexuality. Look," Carl Lee sighed. "I can see you don't believe me. But I swear I can help you find Saya. Isn't that worth a few phone calls?"

Bud agreed to take the offer back to Yoshi, but beforehand he wanted to know, "Are you sticking with this underground railroad shit? You do know that's something from like the slave days, right?"

"This is not the same thing. There are active railroads today for battered women. I've given my lawyer two contacts for you. Please don't make up your mind before you talk with them."

Bud made no such promises, but when they were in the parking lot, he allowed the attorney to press a folded scrap of paper into his hand. He read it in the Impala. Brian Yves at Theatre Rhinoceros, and Reverend Lea Brooks, San Francisco MCC. Carl Lee's code name was Rainbow Caboose.

Could there be a gayer code name? There was no way in hell Bud was going to whisper, "Rainbow Caboose," even if it was the secret code to a bank vault. And he didn't want his ass near any of those rainbow flag waving, hopped-up-on-marriage-rights caboose pirates.

❖

The Kanbar Performing Arts Center was home of the San Francisco Girls Chorus, and the location where the Metropolitan Community Church held its services. While questing for an online map, Tucker had learned that the six-story, Hayes Valley building on Page Street was built in 1912 as the New Druid Temple. She had imagined Stonehenge boulders circling church pews, and ivy climbing rock walls. The real building was nothing like the one she'd imagined. There were no spire-topped temples, bell towers, or hypnotic chants.

In one of Kanbar's high-ceilinged ceremonial spaces, Reverend Lea Brooks was booked solid with gay and lesbian wedding ceremonies. Tucker's research had revealed that the woman came from a Baptist background, had served overseas in the military for nearly a decade before going through seminary training, then worked as program director of Marin County's Spectrum Center for Lesbian, Gay, Bisexual, and Transgender Concerns.

Unlike a good wedding crasher, who'd dive right in pretending they knew everyone else and using the opportunity to meet available women, Tucker skulked in the back of the room, trying to hide behind the plants without blocking the processional. It struck her as ironic that just as the CA supreme court overturned the ban on same sex marriages, her first real relationship was breaking up. She wondered whether Velvet would also see the funny side. Probably not.

After the two brides said *I do*, Tucker stalked Reverend Lea Brooks to the bathroom and waited until she came out of the stall, ran her fingers through her short dark hair, and cleaned her glasses on the arm of her white robe. A thick silver men's watch was cinched around her wrist. Tucker hadn't thought about the fact even the MCC church leadership might be gay.

Another woman washed her hands and exited the lavatory, leaving them alone for a moment. Tucker took the opportunity. "Excuse me," she said. "Have you ever heard of a rainbow caboose?"

The Reverend chuckled. "It sounds like the end of a gay train, where the party's held. I've got a few minutes before the next wedding, would you like to come to my office and talk for a minute?"

"Yes, of course." Tucker followed Reverend Brooks to a small office and sat down.

"Now, how can I help you?" Lea Brooks asked.

Tucker introduced herself and told her about Blind Eye's case seeking Saya and how that search led her to Pioneer, exposed the disappearance of dozens of students and the arrest of Carl Lee, who'd been accused of being a serial killer.

"That sounds like a very difficult situation, putting yourself in a place like the Pioneer Institute. You're a very brave young woman."

Tucker blushed.

"I'm still not sure how I can be of assistance."

"I know it's crazy," Tucker said, "But this guy, Carl Lee, hired Blind Eye to find these kids, and he said *you* might know something, and to mention the rainbow caboose."

"Well I think I'll have to give that some thought. Can I get back to you?"

"Of course," Tucker handed her a Blind Eye business card. She wrote her name on the back and the number to the cell phone Yoshi assigned her for work purposes.

Glancing at her watch the Reverend noted that she needed to meet with the next couple. "You know," she said, "here at MCC we've been performing gay marriage ceremonies since 1971, but it's so delightful that we can now do so with legally sanctioned unions." As they walked out, Lea Brooks asked, "What was it that made you lose your faith?"

Tucker gaped at her.

She smiled. "I'm told I have a knack for spotting lapsed Christians. So many of us in the queer community have been victims of religion-based oppression. I find this so tragic because our people are spiritually gifted in their expressions of gender and sexuality. Don't turn your back on God, Tucker Shade. Don't hold Jesus responsible for those who've failed to embrace his teachings."

❖

Later that evening Yoshi and Aneko were back stage at Theatre Rhinoceros, in San Francisco's Mission District. They were waiting to connect with Brian Yves, who Yoshi had learned was a stage makeup designer. Brian was a tall African American with a Frenchman's name and the feminine features and high voice of a woman.

When Yoshi explained who she was and why she wanted to speak with him, he shifted nervously and kept scanning the theater. "I assure you, I don't know anything."

Aneko was afraid that would be it, and this one chance that Saya was alive would die right here. She couldn't stop herself from butting in. "Please," she begged, "I need to know what happened to my little sister."

"I heard Carl Lee James was in jail for killing a bunch of kids." Brian didn't sound as though the information had come as a shock. Aneko felt her stomach clench. Could that all be true after all? Had Carl Lee sent them on a goose chase, just to dick with them?

"Did you assist Mr. James in altering those students' appearances?" Yoshi asked.

He shook his head.

"We are not law enforcement officers," Yoshi assured him. "We have no interest in seeing you prosecuted for anything, but if we cannot uncover what occurred we may have to turn everything over to the police."

"Okay, but not here." He jerked his head toward the emergency exit.

Aneko took Yoshi's hand and tugged to indicate the direction they were walking.

Once outside Brian lit a cigarette, sucked in a deep breath and exhaled smoke. "I should've known it wouldn't end with the photos."

"The photos?" Aneko asked.

"Carl knew a friend of mine from prison. A few years ago, he got in touch with me saying Carl was looking for a make-up artist for this special photography project he was doing. He wanted to know if I could do some horror work, blood and guts stuff. I had access to some great material through Kryolan so I agreed to help him. I had no idea it would become a regular thing, I swear. I thought the models looked a little young, but he had release forms that they all signed, saying they were eighteen."

"Let me guess," Yoshi interjected. "You never asked to see identification."

He shook his head. "Look, I didn't want to know what went on after they left the studio. Now I guess we all know what I was refusing to notice. I have to wonder, if I'd come forward, maybe—"

"Walk us through a typical photo session," Yoshi encouraged.

"Basically he'd show up with one or two of these teenagers, mostly girls at first, and I'd make them up so they looked like they'd been murdered. Shot, beaten to death, you know. We tried different things, but by the end we'd pretty much got into a groove, replicating a nine millimeter to the forehead. Meant we didn't do some of the fun bruising patterns and high velocity splatter we did back in the day, but still it worked."

"Now I understand," Yoshi said. She briefly described a couple of the scenes she recalled from the photographs.

"Yes." Brian nodded. "That sounds about right. Is that some kind of crime? Making people look like they're dead? I mean, is that some kind of snuff porn or something?"

"Not based on what we uncovered. Was there sex involved?"

"No. Absolutely not." Brian was adamant. Then he hedged. "I mean, not while I was around. I don't know what happened when they left here."

"So," Aneko had found her voice but it was cracking, "they left your studio made up that way? Like corpses?"

"Yeah, I know. Sick, huh? You don't think he's some sort of necrophiliac who gets turned on by pretending his playmates are dead, do you?"

Was that possible? Had Carl Lee made Saya and the other kids look like they were dead in order to explore his own perversions? If so, what had he done with them afterward? Killed them for real? A sociopathic serial killer might just get a thrill out of setting up this elaborate farce, blurring the lines of what was real and what was fake. Was that who Carl Lee really was. And was Saya dead after all?

It was not until they had left the theater and were heading back to Aneko's home that Yoshi revealed her fears. "We may have single-handedly destroyed the prosecution's case against Carl Lee. Without bodies or significant bodily fluids, the primary evidence of murder was the photographs we found in his home. Now we've just uncovered testimony that those photographs were faked."

There was reasonable doubt, right there. Doubt that there even were murders, let alone that Carl Lee committed them.

She'd viewed the photographs as a serial killer's trophies. They might have been trophies, all right, but if Carl Lee had photographed his victims looking dead when they were still alive, how would anyone be able to prove which of his images depicted a victim he had killed? With Brian Yves's testimony, no matter how reluctant it was, they would never know and a judge would throw out every photo.

CHAPTER TWENTY-ONE

Tucker couldn't get the Reverend's words out of her head. At odd times during the next few days she'd hear *Don't turn your back on God*, and wonder if that was what she'd done. When she was a child she'd been a true believer. Rev. Brooks asked her what had taken her faith away. It was the suffering her brother and sister went through. She'd started to wonder what kind of god caused such pain and anguish to innocent children. She'd done everything she was supposed to do and prayed every night for an end to Hunter and Anastasia's pain, but her prayers were never answered.

So, yeah, she'd turned her back on this idea of a benevolent Caucasian Godfather who granted favors if you asked him the right way and didn't piss him off by forgetting to cross yourself. But she hadn't really been able to shake her faith in *some* sort of creator. It was just much more anamorphous now. She pulled little elements she liked from different cultures and cobbled them together into a working spirituality that encompassed karma and reincarnation and excluded Heaven and Hell and the devil. Her image of the creator was no longer specific to one religious faith and wasn't male. She believed patriarchal religion probably stemmed from men's insecurities over the size of their penis and the fact that they couldn't bear children and thus held less biological power.

Tucker had no idea why anyone would *want* to be a man. What was her friend AJ Jackson thinking? A full-blown transition to maleness? Ick. Why would anyone *choose* that? Maybe AJ would come back from New Orleans having changed her mind. They would know soon enough.

Tucker's cell phone vibrated in her pocket, making her jump. She wondered who could be calling her and why they hadn't used the Blind Eye landline. Yoshi was in the other room, in her office and Bud hated cell phones, so he preferred to call her on the office phone when he needed to communicate. It wasn't like he'd just call up to chat.

Tucker flipped the lid. There was a new text message. It said: *Re: Rainbow Caboose. Can u meet 2nite?*

"Oh, my God, Yoshi. This is it!" Tucker jumped up from her chair, tripped over the electric cords in her excitement and nose-dived into the file cabinet.

They'd decided it would be best for Bud do the meet, even though it had been Tucker who was initially contacted. Yoshi insisted Tucker send a text to say Bud would be replacing her at the meet. The unknown messenger replied that the switch would be acceptable, but Bud must bring along one Isabelle Sanchez. The text was clear: *If Izzy ever wants to see Dominique Marxley alive, follow the instructions exactly.*

As Bud waited in the Impala with Isabelle, he fingered the butt of his Beretta , feeling the cold alloy and hoping he would not need to draw the weapon. The person orchestrating the meet was smart. They'd chosen a location difficult to get to. There was only one road in and nowhere to hide without being noticed.

Still, it was nice to know that Yoshi and Tucker were keeping an eye on him from afar. They'd rigged the cell phone to transmit a duplicate of any message received, so they got the same directions as Bud did and could follow along through the maze of San Francisco's sprawling Presidio. A cautious man, Bud was apprehensive about the meeting location, pinned in as it was by water on three sides. Fort Point occupied the very last tip of San Francisco ground and lay in the shadow of the Golden Gate Bridge. Passing high above them, evening motorists on their way to and from Marin were unaware of the drama playing out below. Bud thought about the bridge and hoped a jumper wouldn't pick this moment to do a swan dive onto his precious Impala.

The cell phone beeped again, making Isabelle jump and indicating a new message. The girl was handling the pressure of the evening fairly well, considering no one was really sure what to expect and why her presence had been requested. Fortunately for Bud's ears, Isabelle responded to anxiety by growing quieter. She hadn't spoken since they'd arrived in the park.

"It says, 'unlock the back doors,'" She finally told him, reading the latest message. "Creepy. What should we do?"

In response, Bud reached around and pulled the golfing tee-shaped lock up to release it.

"Okay." Isabelle followed suit and messaged their compliance.

Bud sat as still as he could while his right hand swung into action, unclipping his gun case and withdrawing the Berretta. He flicked off the safety, turned the pistol upside down and stuffed it between his thigh and the seatbelt.

As if on cue, the door behind him swung open and a hooded figure slid into the backseat, gruffly demanding, "Don't turn around. Drive."

Bud started the car, then returned his right hand to the gun and steered with the left. His eyes had adjusted to the dark, and he'd already tilted the rearview mirror for a look at their guest. He couldn't make out anything but medium body build and the hooded sweatshirt pulled down over the face.

After they'd driven for a few minutes, the figure in the back ordered, "Pull over." They were facing the golf course, but at this time of night it was a sea of darkness. "Keep staring straight ahead, Pops, and no one gets hurt."

"You asked for the meeting," Bud said. "What do you want?"

"Keep your trap shut unless I say. Besides, it was you all who've been pushing this thing. Turn off the car and hand me the keys."

Bud did as he was told.

"Isabelle, step outside with me."

Isabelle had her hand on the door latch when Bud stopped her. "No. She's not going anywhere alone."

"This isn't about you, Pops."

"We're looking for Saya Takahashi. If you have information about her, we'd love to hear it. But I'm not putting Isabelle at risk."

There was silence. Bud slid his hand back to the pistol. Things could go bad quickly.

"Fine." A light flashed on, illuminating the backseat. Isabelle gasped. The girl in the back was still a teenager, a dark haired girl with a short bob.

"Dom!" Isabelle cried out.

The flashlight turned off. Before Bud could stop her, Isabelle leapt out, bounded around the car, and dragged Dominique into a hug.

Dominique Marxley was alive after all. Isabelle had never felt happier. She held Dom's face in her hands, traced Dom's features with her fingers like a blind woman feeling the face of her child for the first time in years. Her fingers remembered most of the details but there were one or two that seemed different. Hadn't Dom's nose been more prominent? Roman even? It was a fleeting thought.

Isabelle kissed Dom's knuckles, her forehead and cheekbones, and her perfectly pouty lips. Very slowly, it began to dawn on her that Dom was not responding with the same level of enthusiasm. She'd hugged back, but wasn't responding to Isabelle's ardent kisses, wasn't melting into Isabelle's arms. The electricity of flesh mingling with flesh wasn't the way it used to be every time they'd touched.

Isabelle backed away, still holding Dom's hand, afraid she would disappear if she dropped it. It had been a long time, six months apart, and no doubt Dom had been through a great deal during that time. They all had. Isabelle couldn't blame her if she needed a little time to reconnect. Bust she was alive. That was all that mattered.

But, a tiny voice chimed in the back of Isabelle's mind, why hadn't she come back? Why hadn't she contacted Isabelle, just once, to tell her she was okay?

"Tell me everything," she demanded breathlessly.

"Carl Lee saved my life." Dominique said.

She described being awakened and told she needed to leave Pioneer immediately. Carl Lee took her to the treatment room, where Saya was waiting, dressed only in her pajamas. Both girls were terrified when Carl Lee told them that their parents had paid Dr. Barnabas to have them killed and Carl Lee was the executioner.

"We both thought it was a bad joke," Dominique said. "We just wanted to go back to sleep. Then he showed us these contracts with our parents' signatures, but you know that can be faked. Finally, he played me a recording with my dad negotiating how much to pay Barnabas so I'd never come back. That was enough for me. He had the same thing for Saya. He told us the first thing we needed to do get them to believe we were dead."

Dom and Saya had been whisked away to a semi-famous makeup artist who put on tons of makeup with blood and a fake bullet hole.

"When we looked like corpses Carl Lee took us to some woodsy, outdoors place and took photos of us lying on the ground."

Then he took them to someone's small apartment and they washed all the makeup off, changed clothes, and slept on the floor. The next morning they were woken by a nice older woman who made them breakfast and promised everything would be okay, so long as they followed the rules. There were a bunch of rules on a list each girl got a copy of. They never saw Carl Lee again.

Dom looked Isabelle directly in the eyes. "Number one was harsh. It said I could never call, email, visit, or contact anyone from my past or I risked death not just for me but for the other kids who'd been saved from Pioneer."

Dom continued to describe a life where she and Saya were transported from one place to another, then she woke up one morning to find Saya had gone with someone else on the rainbow railroad, which is what everyone jokingly called it, even though it was no laughing matter. Dom hadn't seen her since.

"Her sister's been looking for her the whole time," Isabelle said. She told Dom all the lengths Aneko had gone to trying to find out what happened to Saya. "You sure you can't get word to Saya? Aneko deserves to know she's okay."

"We get different names and change the way we look," she said. "I don't know how to contact her, but I'll try."

"So," Isabelle said, "what about you? Will you be coming back now that it's safe?"

"I'm sorry Izzy, but I don't think so. I'm happy where I am."

"But, but what about *us*? I still love you, Dom. I've never stopped."

"I know it feels like that." Dom's words were like a steel blade to Isabelle's heart. "But one day you'll realize that until you really love and accept yourself, you can't truly love someone else."

"What does that mean?" Izzy couldn't believe this was happening. She'd been fantasizing for months about what it would be like if Dom came back. She never gave up hope, she never accepted Dom was dead. This wasn't how things were supposed to be. They were supposed to run into each other's arms and never be apart again.

"I've met someone else," Dom said, twisting the knife once more. "I'm not coming back."

Isabelle couldn't do anything more than stand there and stare at her. She began to choke back salty betrayers of her steely demeanor.

"I'm sorry, Izzy." Dom pulled her into a hug, but Isabelle pushed her away and swiped angrily at the tears that stung her eyes. "What about Carl Lee? He's in jail because the police think he killed you guys. Aren't you going to set that right?"

Dom nodded her head toward Bud in the Impala with a question. "Is that what you're doing with them? Trying to get Carl Lee off?"

"No. *They* saved *my* life. If it wasn't for *them*, I'd still be in Pioneer, where you left me, going through shock therapy. Or maybe I would've killed myself because everyone else told me you ran away and left me behind, because you didn't love me. Which I guess was sort of true. The people at the detective agency have been really wonderful to me, even though they didn't need to be. I came tonight because I wanted to know where you were and I wanted to help Aneko find Saya. But I also came because they make me feel…wanted. Needed. Useful."

"I'm glad to hear that." Dom pulled her into another hug. Then she stepped into the darkness and disappeared.

❖

"What just happened?" Bud demanded as Isabelle slipped back into the front seat of his Impala.

"She's gone."

"What do you mean she's gone? Where'd she go?"

"I don't know." Isabelle started to cry.

Damn it all to hell. He hated when girls cried, especially when he had no idea why. And particularly when he was at work and had important things to do. "Did you get any new information from her?"

Isabelle pushed a digital recorder toward him. "She says she doesn't know where Saya is but she'll try to get word to her."

Yoshi would be disappointed, but what could you do? They hadn't been sure Isabelle could pull it off anyway.

When Isabelle got back in she said, "Well, I could be wrong, but I thought we were supposed to follow her."

"Did you see which way she went?" Bud shook his head. It was pitch dark outside. Isabelle was a little less bright than he'd been led to believe. He dropped the gear into reverse and turned his head to look behind. He saw the smirk on her face and stopped. "Wait! Holy hell. You did it, didn't you?"

"You sound surprised," she pouted.

"Well, yeah. You pretty much flat out refused to consider it earlier. You said if it turned out to be someone you knew it would be an act of betrayal. You obviously knew her so—"

"She's seeing someone else." Her voice was that mixture of anguish, longing, and anger that women seem to first perfect in their teens. He understood now. Never underestimate a woman scorned. "Way to go kiddo," Bud slapped her heartily on the back. "How'd you do it?"

"Slipped it in her pocket when she hugged me good-bye."

"You're a very cool customer." Bud was impressed. He handed over his cell phone. "We'll track it live online. First can you send Yoshi a note to let her know it's been activated? It's good our subject got a little bit of a jump on us, it needs a sixty second lead time."

A soon as Bud could see from the GPS tracker that Dom had taken off through the Presidio golf course, he drove down Washington Boulevard until he spotted Aimee Dix's car. At Isabelle's pout, he said, "Sorry kiddo, but it's late and Miss Dix insists it's time for you to go home."

Tucker got out and rushed to Bud's Impala, clearly waiting impatiently to get in on the evening's excitement. "So," she asked breathlessly, "how did it go?"

"She's a natural, this kid," Bud boasted. "Did a great job. We've got a live bug, thanks to Izzy."

Tucker gave the girl a knuckle bump and Bud waved as she walked away. The fostering arrangement with Aimee Dix seemed to be working out pretty well.

"Let's call it a night." Bud said, knowing they would be able to remotely check in on Dom's position in the morning. He expected her to leave the San Francisco Bay Area.

CHAPTER TWENTY-TWO

Several days later, when Tucker finally got up the nerve to call her supposed girlfriend and update her on Blind Eye's latest gig, Velvet had news of her own. Saya Takahashi was alive and well, and sitting on her living room sofa.

While the Blind Eye team had been busy tracking Dom and trying to uncover the Rainbow Railroad, Saya had shown up on Velvet's steps with two other missing Pioneer students and a tale so outrageous it had to be true. Over the next few weeks, Saya would be joined by half dozen Pioneer alums, who emerged from the mysterious unknown to reveal they were now happy, healthy gay adults. They'd come out of the woodwork not to condemn Carl Lee but to help free him from serving a long prison sentence or facing the death penalty.

What Velvet had originally thought would be a go-nowhere freelance gig, the last vestiges of her life as an investigative reporter, had turned into a remarkable *San Francisco Times* series and a groundbreaking *Womyn* magazine cover story. For the magazine that had previously relied on lesbian celebrities cover models to sell the publication on newsstands, an investigative report about a reparative therapy program that was meant to end in murder—and the dozens of kids who had escaped it thanks to a strange ex-con—was revolutionary. So was scooping the news magazine the *Advocate*.

Velvet took Saya's story and ran with it, investigating not just the Pioneer Institute but delving deep into the entire ex-gay movement, ripping apart their façade of happy heterosexual conversions and illuminating how often their programs end in disappointment, failure, suicide, and, as with Pioneer, even murder.

She wasn't sure she had the emotional resources to spare for a relationship, with everything else that was going on. She'd made some decisions in the last few days and they may or may not shock her friends. The first was that her relationship with Tucker was all but dead, their fires extinguished by their dueling careers. Besides, Velvet wasn't built for monogamy, not even the flexible form of serial monogamy most of her girlfriends practiced. Perhaps Tucker felt fine living with Yoshi all these weeks, not even making booty calls, but Velvet wasn't happy.

She knew that she couldn't rush the younger woman through her growing up process. It sucked, she could admit it, but Tucker was too fucking young. The moment Tucker told the group she was moving in with Bud so Yoshi could have her room back, Velvet knew it was over. And when it came time to tell Tucker, she had apparently known too.

Velvet hoped for a farewell fuck but alas, even in their good-bye, Tucker was satisfied with the status quo. Both she and Bud had insisted their new living situation was temporary, but Velvet could tell that there was something very permanent about it all. It was funny how Bud had become like the father Tucker never had, while Velvet's romance with the budding PI just seemed to wilt under the pressures of their jobs.

Even if Tucker changed her mind at this very moment, Velvet had Yoshi to think about. With her degeneration, she could no longer see shapes, colors, even ghosted images. Despite her determination, she needed Velvet more than ever. Automatically, Velvet reached out and linked arms with her as they waited for their turn to address the audience.

Without Saya Takahashi having gone missing and her sister Aneka fighting for a reunion, the truth about Pioneer might have remained a mystery. Without her return, Carl Lee might have ended up on death row. Though he insisted on his innocence, Carl Lee had never given up the location of any of the Pioneer escapees, nor did he reveal the rest of the underground Rainbow Railroad, a network of individuals across the country who were dedicated to helping LGBT youth escape abusive or life-threatening situations.

Now, Saya stood on a small stage, next to her sister. She held up a copy of *Womyn* magazine with her face on the cover and beamed. "I can't begin to thank everyone who helped." She spoke into a microphone to a large audience outside the Unitarian Universalist Church. "If it weren't for Velvet Erickson, Yoshi Yakamota, Tucker Shade—the whole Blind

Eye team—and the many individuals that pitched in, I would never have gotten my sister back."

Tonight, Velvet knew, marked a new era at *Womyn* magazine. Proof that what she did meant something to the world, and a reminder that she was exactly where she wanted to be, making change one word at a time.

"I wanted to share something incredibly important with all of you," Velvet began, looking out at the crowd, comprised primarily of lesbian women. "There's a reason we're having this month's issue release party here, and not at some hot nightclub. For years this church, and others like it across the country, have offered a safe haven for parts of our community who don't have the same resources some of us do. Especially, they have provided safe spaces for queer youth, just the kind of at-risk kids that are still imprisoned in other Pioneer-like reparative therapy programs. We need to put an end, once and for all to these kinds of programs."

The crowd applauded. The gravity of the situation was immense and it was obvious these supporters understood that.

"Imagine being in a situation where you're locked away for your sexuality, having to choose between brainwashing or permanent banishment from the only family and spiritual community you've ever known. Adding to that situation the fear of death, it's unthinkable, as unimaginable as the torture our government authorized at Abu Ghraib.

Earlier today I spoke with senator Sheila Kuehl who is proposing legislation that would ban ex-gay school programs from the state of California. If we have our way, this ends here. No more children should be exposed to the hell Saya Takahashi, Isabelle Sanchez, and so many others experienced at Pioneer Institute."

As the crowd applauded, hooting like rowdy school children or hippies in protest, Velvet saw Saya and Aneko Takahashi wipe tears from their eyes.

Chapter Twenty-Three

Yoshi had to admit, Tucker was correct. She'd taken quite a shine to Isabelle, who was proving to be a most competent assistant during her after-school internship with Blind Eye. In fact, the girl was swiftly gaining proficiency in the administrative tasks that Tucker had outgrown. If things continued to develop in this manner, and if her foster parent, Aimee Dix approved, Yoshi was prepared to hire Isabelle to fill the receptionist position full time once she graduated. No doubt Isabelle would have to balance work with college classes come fall, but having something to sink her teeth into seemed to keep Isabelle grounded.

It was remarkable how much the Pioneer case had affected everyone at Blind Eye. Bud and Aimee had been getting rather friendly ever since the case wrapped. Yoshi would not characterize it as a full-blown romance just yet, but there was clearly an electricity underlying the relationship. Moreover, Bud had never been the sort of man to develop idle friendships with women. It was rather endearing the way he joined Aimee and Isabelle on weekend outings to the park and to church. For both Aimee and Bud, the world had turned out to be quite different than they'd ever imagined, so if they could find solace in each other it would be a lovely thing.

As a couple, Tucker and Velvet had the opposite response to the Pioneer debacle. Not every disaster can bring two people closer. The weeks apart seemed to have underscored their differences. Tucker had matured immensely from her experience but also seemed to have turned inward. She was quieter, reflective, reserved, and her time at Pioneer seemed to have sparked a new interest in spirituality and personal growth.

Velvet, well, she remained a woman who never let life prevent her from getting what she wanted. She'd found a way to seamlessly merge her investigative past with her glossy magazine future, recreating *Womyn* as a unique amalgam of in-depth news reporting and entertainment coverage. In the end, she and Tucker's breakup was remarkably amicable. Very lesbian of them, Yoshi thought, to transition from lovers to friends so seamlessly. Even she could not always be so charitable.

Of course, romance had found Yoshi too, at least a nascent one. Despite the fact that her father had lied to her about how and when her mother really died, Yoshi found herself smiling. Aneko lifted her spirits, and was helping her build the resilience she would need for the challenges ahead.

She made herself a cup of tea and sat at her desk. She had a feeling the next few months would prove very interesting.

❖

Tucker stopped a few yards from the Blind Eye Offices and took a call.

"Tucker?" It was her brother, Hunter. He was crying. "Need you. In trouble."

"Hunter? What's going on?" He rarely called. His hearing aid made it hard for him to hear and his Autism meant he was far from articulate, especially over the phone. "Are you okay? Where's Mom?"

"The police are here. Everything's bad. They're taking Sissy away. It's all my fault. It's all my fault."

Tucker heard the sound of his padded helmet banging against the wall, in the rhythmic way he used to soothe himself when he was upset.

"What's going on, Hunter? Can you get Mom?"

"You!" A gruff voice yelled in the background. "Get off the phone."

The line with dead.

With the dial tone ringing in her ear Tucker was suddenly certain that whatever had just happened in Idaho wouldn't simply have her breaking her promise to herself and send her rushing home. It would change her life forever.

About the Author

Diane Anderson-Minshall is the executive editor of *Curve* magazine, the world's best-selling lesbian magazine, and an award-winning pop culture pundit. Jacob Anderson-Minshall is the syndicated columnist behind TransNation, a contributor to GayWired.com and *Bitch* magazine, and co-host of the radio show Gender Blender. Between them, the Anderson-Minshalls have appeared in at least three dozen magazines and newspapers and are frequent radio and TV guests. They're also the co-founders of Portland's famed LGBT literary salon, QLiterati! This is the third book in the Blind Eye mystery series. The duo divides their time between San Francisco and Portland, where they're raising two foster sons and two spoiled Chihuahuas.

Books Available From Bold Strokes Books

Green Eyed Monster by Gill McKnight. Mickey Rapowski believes her former boss has cheated her out of a small fortune, so she kidnaps the girlfriend and demands compensation—just a straightforward abduction that goes so wrong when Mickey falls for her captive. (978-1-60282-042-5)

Blind Faith by Diane and Jacob Anderson-Minshall. When private investigator Yoshi Yakamota and the Blind Eye Detective Agency are hired to find a woman's missing sister, the assignment seems fairly mundane—but in the detective business, the ordinary can quickly become deadly. (978-1-60282-041-8)

A Pirate's Heart by Catherine Friend. When rare book librarian Emma Boyd searches for a long-lost treasure map, she learns the hard way that pirates still exist in today's world—some modern pirates steal maps, others steal hearts. (978-1-60282-040-1)

Trails Merge by Rachel Spangler. Parker Riley escapes the high-powered world of politics to Campbell Carson's ski resort—and their mutual attraction produces anything but smooth running. (978-1-60282-039-5)

Dreams of Bali by C.J. Harte. Madison Barnes worships work, power, and success, and she's never allowed anyone to interfere—that is, until she runs into Karlie Henderson Stockard. Eclipse EBook (978-1-60282-070-8)

The Limits of Justice by John Morgan Wilson. Benjamin Justice and reporter Alexandra Templeton search for a killer in a mysterious compound in the remote California desert. (978-1-60282-060-9)

Designed for Love by Erin Dutton. Jillian Sealy and Wil Johnson don't much like each other, but they do have to work together—and what they desire most is not what either of them had planned. (978-1-60282-038-8)

Dark Garden by Jennifer Fulton. Vienna Blake and Mason Cavender are sworn enemies—who can't resist each other. Something has to give. (978-1-60282-036-4)

Calling the Dead by Ali Vali. Six months after Hurricane Katrina, NOLA Detective Sept Savoie is a cop who thinks making a relationship work is harder than catching a serial killer—but her current case may prove her wrong. (978-1-60282-037-1)

Shots Fired by MJ Williamz. Kyla and Echo seem to have the perfect relationship and the perfect life until someone shoots at Kyla—and Echo is the most likely suspect. (978-1-60282-035-7)

truelesbianlove.com by Carsen Taite. Mackenzie Lewis and Dr. Jordan Wagner have very different ideas about love, but they discover that truelesbianlove is closer than a click away. Eclipse EBook (978-1-60282-069-2)

Justice at Risk by John Morgan Wilson. Benjamin Justice's blind date leads to a rare opportunity for legitimate work, but a reckless risk changes his life forever. (978-1-60282-059-3)

Run to Me by Lisa Girolami. Burned by the four-letter word called love, the only thing Beth Standish wants to do is run for—or maybe from—her life. (978-1-60282-034-0)

Split the Aces by Jove Belle. In the neon glare of Sin City, two women ride a wave of passion that threatens to consume them in a world of fast money and fast times. (978-1-60282-033-3)

Uncharted Passage by Julie Cannon. Two women on a vacation that turns deadly face down one of nature's most ruthless killers—and find themselves falling in love. (978-1-60282-032-6)

Night Call by Radclyffe. All medevac helicopter pilot Jett McNally wants to do is fly and forget about the horror and heartbreak she left behind in the Middle East, but anesthesiologist Tristan Holmes has other plans. (978-1-60282-031-9)

I Dare You by Larkin Rose. Stripper by night, corporate raider by day, Kelsey's only looking for sex and power, until she meets a woman who stirs her heart and her body. (978-1-60282-030-2)

Truth Behind the Mask by Lesley Davis. Erith Baylor is drawn to Sentinel Pagan Osborne's quiet strength, but the secrets between them strain duty and family ties. (978-1-60282-029-6)

Lake Effect Snow by C.P. Rowlands. News correspondent Annie T. Booker and FBI Agent Sarah Moore struggle to stay one step ahead of disaster as Annie's life becomes the war zone she once reported on. Eclipse EBook (978-1-60282-068-5)

Revision of Justice by John Morgan Wilson. Murder shifts into high gear, propelling Benjamin Justice into a raging fire that consumes the Hollywood Hills, burning steadily toward the famous Hollywood Sign—and the identity of a cold-blooded killer. (978-1-60282-058-6)

Cooper's Deale by KI Thompson. Two would-be lovers and a decidedly inopportune murder spell trouble for Addy Cooper, no matter which way the cards fall. (978-1-60282-028-9)

Romantic Interludes 1: Discovery ed. by Radclyffe and Stacia Seaman. An anthology of sensual, erotic contemporary love stories from the best-selling Bold Strokes authors. (978-1-60282-027-2)

A Guarded Heart by Jennifer Fulton. The last place FBI Special Agent Pat Roussel expects to find herself is assigned to an illicit private security gig baby-sitting a celebrity. (Ebook) (978-1-60282-067-8)

Saving Grace by Jennifer Fulton. Champion swimmer Dawn Beaumont, injured in a car crash she caused, flees to Moon Island, where scientist Grace Ramsay welcomes her. (Ebook) (978-1-60282-066-1)

The Sacred Shore by Jennifer Fulton. Successful tech industry survivor Merris Randall does not believe in love at first sight until she meets Olivia Pearce. (Ebook) (978-1-60282-065-4)

Passion Bay by Jennifer Fulton. Two women from different ends of the earth meet in paradise. Author's expanded edition. (Ebook) (978-1-60282-064-7)

Simple Justice by John Morgan Wilson. When a pretty-boy cokehead is murdered, former LA reporter Benjamin Justice and his reluctant new partner, Alexandra Templeton, must unveil the real killer. (978-1-60282-057-9)

Remember Tomorrow by Gabrielle Goldsby. Cees Bannigan and Arieanna Simon find that a successful relationship rests in remembering the mistakes of the past. (978-1-60282-026-5)

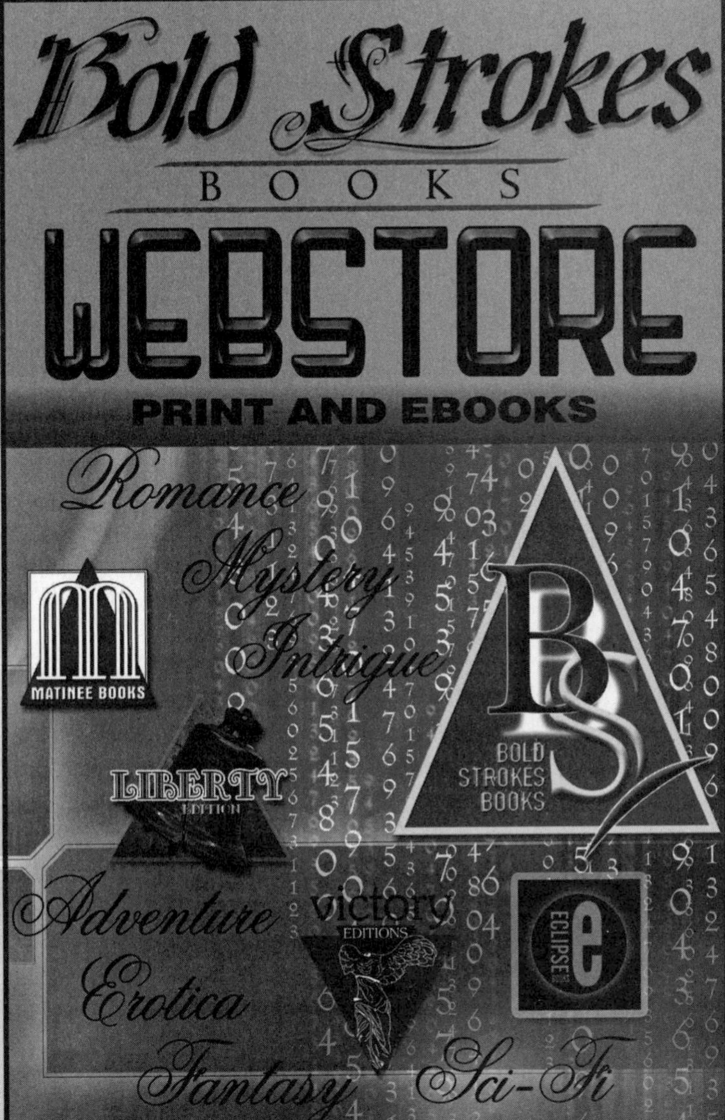

Bold Strokes
BOOKS
WEBSTORE
PRINT AND EBOOKS
Romance
Mystery
Intrigue
MATINEE BOOKS
LIBERTY
EDITION
BOLD
STROKES
BOOKS
Adventure
victory
EDITIONS
ECLIPSE
Erotica
Fantasy
Sci-Fi
http://www.boldstrokesbooks.com